Meth or Myth

by

Ernie Lijoi Sr

Argus Enterprises International
New Jersey***North Carolina

A-Argus Better Book Publishers, LLC

For information:
A-Argus Better Book Publishers, LLC
9001 Ridge Hill Street
Kernersville, North Carolina 27285
www.a-argusbooks.com

ISBN: 978-0-9846439-2-9
ISBN: 0-9846439-2-3

Book Cover designed by Dubya

Printed in the United States of America

Other Works
by
Ernie Lijoi Sr

Street Business

Shoveling the Tide

Chasing Snow

Destructive Obsession

The Cash Mule

The Preyers

Preface

Throughout this great land, in all of our cities and towns, the Police Departments consist of good men and women serving the public. These people are the same as any other person and do the best they can with the tools that they are given. The strongest tool is their mind, giving them the ability to make split second decisions that affect the lives of men and women everywhere and forever.

Amongst these honorable men and women are a separate and special group of investigators that go beyond the normal everyday job of being a Police Officer or a Detective. These men and women are the Deep Cover Investigators or the DCI. Agents of the DCI go out to the streets, bars, clubs, alleys and homes of individuals who are involved in illegal activities, using a deep cover persona. The DCI's investigate the cases that seem impossible to penetrate; they take gun fire, are shot, stabbed and in some cases killed all while under a pseudonym. The public never realizes who these people are or what they have given up in their endeavor to serve the public. They have families and private lives that, at times, have been put on hold and in some cases lost for the good of the public at large.

This book is a glimpse into the true life and experiences of Detective Ernie Lijoi Sr. during his career as a DCI agent.

What if you were witness to a murder? How would you handle it? What if you had to run a narcotics operation? Would you? What if you were involved with the behavior of the criminal underworld? What if during all of this you were a Police Officer doing your job? Would you arrest people or would you play the game?

These are the questions Detective Ernie Lijoi Sr., the DCI under the guise of Eddie Pannoni, will answer and the situations he will face in this novel based on his life experiences, which has been named "Meth or Myth", while he tries to keep his family safe and free of the dreadful undercurrent that springs from a world of illegal and despicable behavior.

One subject in the book is a Mr. Kiefer, who was a man in trouble. He needed help and some work to save himself and his wife from a tough life. He eventually was so deep in problems that he approached a close friend and set up a meeting to inquire about some kind of work. That meeting introduced him to a group that would change his life forever.

Mr. Armando Kiefer worked his way up the Illicit Methamphetamine ladder to the top. He became the major importer of Meth in the United States. After years of distribution he came to know Eddie Pannoni, the street name for Detective Ernie Lijoi Sr. who became the sword that cut the arm off distribution of Meth in New England.

The following story is fictional. However, this story is based upon factual events that occurred in and around New England and Canada in the 1970's and early 1980's.

Some of the events in this book have been enhanced and telescoped to improve dramatic flow. The characters in this book are fictionalized versions of individuals who may or may not have a relationship to a real individual. No one character is based upon a single real individual, with one exception, Det. Ernie Lijoi Sr.

Read "Meth or Myth" and learn how Detective Lijoi demolished the unseen seedy people that roam the underworld, a world that destroys, without conscience, throughout the entire United States.

Ernie Lijoi Sr., Author
November 11, 2009

Meth or Myth

***

MYTH: Meth Increases a person's strength & endurance
TRUTH: Meth may give the user the feeling of energy but it is short lived –it DOES NOT increase one's strength or endurance. This feeling of energy from meth is usually followed by a "crash", where the person is tired & may sleep for a long time.

***

MYTH: Meth is safer & less addictive than 'hard" drugs like crack or cocaine
TRUTH: Partly due to how long meth lasts in the body & the poisonous chemicals used in making it, meth can be more harmful than crack cocaine and users might get addicted quicker.

***

MYTH: Meth only affects you while you are on it
TRUTH: Meth affects brain cells & chemistry & can make you irritable & lessen your ability to feel pleasure for a period of time after stopping meth. Brain chemistry changes can last several months after the last time a person takes meth.

***

MYTH: As long as a meth user showers & brushes their 'Teeth', they won't smell or look bad
TRUTH: Regular meth users can develop sores on their face & body & their 'Teeth' become decayed & worn down from "grinding". People close to meth users will tell you they can develop an unpleasant body odor.

***

MYTH: Using Methamphetamine is a safe way to lose weight
TRUTH: No! Meth is dangerous, addictive & can cause malnutrition leading to anorexia. Meth use causes bone loss, rotten Teeth, sleeplessness, aggressiveness, heart damage & failure, seizures, coma & even death.

***

MYTH: Methamphetamine is less harmful than other drugs
TRUTH: Some users get hooked the first time they use meth. Meth is made from battery acid, drain cleaner, lantern fuel, antifreeze and other toxic ingredients, so there is a greater chance

of suffering a heart attack, stroke or serious brain damage than with other drugs.

***

MYTH: Methamphetamine use does not cause hallucinations
TRUTH: Toxic methamphetamine ingredients combined with sustained sleep deprivation can cause auditory and visual distortions. On binges, users frequently report catching glimpses of "shadow" people or seeing bugs crawling on their skin.

***

MYTH: The meth user is the only one hurt by their use
TRUTH: Meth abuse affects the whole community. Meth labs are environmental hazards. These labs use volatile chemicals and other toxic ingredients that pollute communities. In addition, users' families, friends and communities are often victims of neglect, domestic violence, theft and other violent behaviors.

***Myths and Truths* from www.nothingpretty.org/myth**

Chapter 1

The Knowledge

Monday May 20, 1979 Early Morning Hours

Everyone had gone home after a long day of enjoyment. The sun had set and the sand was still warm from the day's sun, even the water had no chill. The air temperature was still in the high sixties even though it was the middle of the night.

Midnight had come and gone and the only person on the beach was Armando Kiefer who woke from what he thought was a fall and a sleep. He reached down along his body and felt a warm, slimy substance. It was blood oozing from his body. He had been stabbed several times. He was going in and out of consciousness. He wasn't totally aware of where he was or exactly what had happened.

All he remembered was that he was standing up by the wall, finishing a beer; no one was around that he could see when suddenly he felt several stings in his back and side, one right after the other. He fell or was thrown over the wall and he must have hit his head on a rock because his head was bleeding also.

He woke for a short while and heard running steps along the wall. He turned his head to see and he could make out the figure of a man running along the beach walkway, which was a common running area in Quincy, Massachusetts.

Armando yelled out as best he could and the man running heard him.

"Is there someone on the beach?" the runner yelled.

Armando put his arm in the air and was barely speaking, but to him, it was yelling, "Help, help me please."

"I see you, I see someone, I'll be right there."

The runner walked cautiously along the beach wall, making sure he did not slip on the rocks that were damp from the night's dew, trying to make out who was calling for help. He saw a body laying on the sand and approached it. He could tell the man was hurt and knelt down to try and be of some help.

There was nothing that the runner could do to help him except cal the police.

"I'll be right back; I'll go across the street to the telephone booth and call for help."

A few minutes later detectives arrived in an unmarked car and two police cruisers pulled up.

***

While the police were waiting for the ambulance, they could see that Kiefer had almost bled out and they did all they could to keep him alive. They also wanted to get any information he had in case he died, which was referred to as a death bed statement.

One of the detectives that arrived at the scene recognized Armando and mentioned that he was a known speed dealer.

His partner, a young officer, asked what speed was and the older detective explained.

"Speed is a little known narcotic, the official name is Methamphetamine and it is, according to the Office of The National Drug Control Policy, a highly addictive central nervous system stimulant. It can be injected, snorted, smoked or ingested orally. Methamphetamine users feel a short yet intense "rush" when the drug is initially administered. This drug is illicitly smuggled into the United States from Mexico and Canada. Some of the street names of this drug are blue, blue devil, crank, Christy, Chris, Christina (Spanish) as well as many others. This drug is and was one of the most destructive drugs on the street and there are many myths about methamphetamine."

Their attention went back to Armando Kiefer who was laying at their feet dying while they waited for the ambulance.

These men were the youngest and least experienced detectives who pulled the late night shift. Detectives Waldo Franken and John Buffer were on duty when the call came in about a man on the beach with multiple stab wounds.

"Armando, can you tell us who did this to you?"

"I don't know it could have been any number of people." He fell back into unconsciousness.

The ambulance arrived and Det. Franken told Det. Buffer that there was nothing they would be able to do that night. This would go to the day shift. They decided to try and speak with him one more time at the hospital and then do their reports for the day crew.

"He may get his memory back in a few days."

While in the ambulance Armando awakened for a moment. He heard the detective asking him that question, "Can you tell us who did this to you?" His mind slipped into unconsciousness as he tried to answer that question to himself.

***

Armando was later identified as Armando Kiefer, thirty years old, six feet one inch tall, one hundred and eighty pounds, black hair and brown eyes. He had no serious criminal record. He had a lot of experience on the street working the con and setting up different narcotics operations in the minor sales level of marijuana, some cocaine, but mostly his interest was in that newer drug that most people didn't even know about called Methamphetamine, commonly known as speed or crank. He was also suspected of being the head of a car theft ring, but this was very sketchy information.

Speed users were a specialized club of people that enjoyed the enhancement that the crystal meth gave them. This drug was rarely seen in the United States in those days, until Armando Kiefer, who would later become known as "The King of Speed" began his education, learning more and more about the drug Methamphetamine.

While unconscious, Armando began to dream of his past and that question that the detective asked, "Can you tell us who did this to you?" His mind's eye lit up with pictures of his past and how it all began in 1975.

~*~

Monday April 14, 1975, Four Years Earlier

As Armando got out of bed that morning, he saw on television that the air temperature was sixty-eight degrees, very little wind and clear skies. He realized that it must be a beautiful day at the beach.

He had no place to go; he was very upset with himself. He had a wife, a child on the way and bills that had to be paid, no job to speak of and nothing on the horizon. He never expected this to happen to him. His only income was from two meager sources, the small amount of drugs that he could get his hands on than cut to resell and a stolen car now and again.

Armando left the apartment and went down to see his friend Jimmy Orbits who was a druggist in the Mattapan section of Boston.

***

Jimmy Orbits was well known by residents as James Orbits, local druggist and by others as a supplier of methamphetamines. Jimmy was a white male, five feet ten inches tall, thirty-five years of age, one hundred and seventy pounds, balding, with a brown mustache. He was a very good speaker and had a good business supplying the public in his area with legitimate drugs. It was his illegitimate supplies that would one day have him paying the piper.

That day Armando walked into his store and got into a conversation with Jimmy, whom he had known for several years. They discussed Armando's predicament and Armando was hoping that Jimmy could give him a job in the store.

"Armando, I don't have anything right now, maybe in a few weeks when things pick up, its winter and we're very slow."

"Thanks; if you should hear of anything let me know, would you?"

"Yes, I will, I have your phone number."

"I'm outa here, I have to find something," said Armando.

"Armando, wait a minute, come into the back room, maybe I can help you out a little."

"Sure, anything would help at this stage."

"Look, Armando, I have a package that needs to be picked up in northern Maine at the post office. It came in from Canada. A box, you pick it up and bring it back to me. The package is under the name of Walter O'Rielly. I'll pay for your gas, one night at a motel that I tell you to stay in and I'll give you five hundred dollars. What do you think?"

"What's in the box?"

"That's not your concern."

"Then it's illegal."

"You want to make some money or not?"

"I do and I will do it. Just remember, I am no slouch when it comes to illegal activities"

"Yeah, this is not an ounce of grass or those shit quarter grams of cocaine or heroin that you sell."

"It's not. What is it?"

"Just go and get it for me, we'll talk afterwards. Here is fifty dollars for gas, thirty dollars for a room at the Northern Door Inn, 356 West Main Street in Fort Kent and another twenty for some food plus one hundred dollars up front. I'll pay you the rest when you return."

"OK. I'll go home, get some heavier clothes and tell my wife I will be back tomorrow afternoon."

***

Armando left the drugstore and went home happy that he had found a way of bringing in some money for his wife, the medical bills and future baby.

"Hi, Loretta, I have to go somewhere, I won't be home for a while."

"What's a while?"

"I'll be back tomorrow afternoon."

"Where are you going, Armando?"

"I am making a run for my buddy, to save him some time."

"What kind of a run, Armando?"

"That's not important. What's important is that I am getting five hundred dollars to make the run and if I handle it right, who knows what can become of this."

"Armando, this doesn't sound kosher to me."

"It will be OK, don't worry."

"Armando, I am sick and tired of the drugs going through this apartment, the people that come to see you and I know you're only selling small quantities, but it can put you in jail."

"That may be over after this run."

"Sure now you're moving up into larger quantities. I'm telling you, I will not have my baby exposed to this type of shit."

"Don't worry; I won't expose my child to anything bad."

"Remember what I said."

"I'll remember. I have to go."

Armando left the apartment and drove directly to the location. He was given the directions for a small town named St. Francis, Maine, to 161 Main Street, the local post office. Then he drove over to the Northern Door Inn, 356 West Main Street in Fort Kent just down the road from Main Street in St Francis.

***

The next morning, Armando got up, dressed and started out. He had not noticed the air temperature the night before, but that morning he couldn't miss it. He opened the door to exit the apartment and was hit in the face with a blast of cold air that was about twenty-five degrees lower then he was used to. He stepped back into the room and opened the bag of extra clothing that he brought with him. He put on everything he could to protect himself from the vicious weather. He went out to the car and prayed that it started. It did. He left it running and went back into the warmth of the room.

He waited a half-hour before he went back out then drove to St Francis and the post office where he had no trouble getting the package that Jimmy had sent him to pick up.

He headed back to Boston and arrived at the drugstore that afternoon.

***

Jimmy observed Armando pulling into a parking space and went to meet him at the door.

"Do you have the package?" asked Jimmy

"Yes I got it, what's in it?"

"Come out back. Man, now we can get our crank up."

"Crank up? What do you mean?"

"Wait, I'll open it and you will see."

Jimmy opened up the shoebox size package and Armando could see several baggies full of a white crystal substance. That reminded him of cocaine, but cocaine is pure powder no crystals that you can see.

"This, my friend, is blue, crank, Christy, Chris, Christina, it takes many names and forms, but it is always methamphetamine."

"I see I've heard of meth and I know a few people that use it, but it's not very popular."

"You would be surprised; this batch of four pounds will go in a day, once I let the word out that I am holding."

"How do you do that?"

"Did you notice that Coca Cola sign in the front window?"

"Yeah, I did, why?"

"Do me a favor. On your way out, turn it around. It says "Druggist Is In" on the back side. Put that side out for the public to view."

"Oh and that's the designation that you are holding?"

"That's all and as of tomorrow morning they will come and get what they want."

"You need time to cut it down, don't you?"

"Yes, that will give me all night. I only need a couple of hours and then I'm ready for the dealers to pick up."

"And how much do you make on an ounce?"

"I pay fifteen hundred dollars per pound, and it is eighty-five percent pure, from a guy that has a connection to a lab. I cut the original pound five times which is very reasonable, so I get five pounds for the price of one pound. This stuff is so pure it can be cut from ten to fifteen times and still you would have some play in there and it's still the best on the street. I sell the pounds for two thousand dollars each and I make eight to ten thousand per original pound that I start with. And I still have all I need for myself, it cost me nothing. The men I sell the meth to buy it by the pound from me and cut it even more. They make a ton of money. From there it is broken into ounces, which they sell for about four hundred dollars an ounce. Then those people cut it again and they break it down to spoons or grams and sell them for as much as fifty dollars a gram on the street and about ten percent purity.

"So it's handled and sold just like heroin or cocaine?"

"Exactly, but it's easier to cut and faster to work with."

"How come you don't get it directly from the lab?"

"I don't do enough to deal directly with the lab, maybe someday."

"If you need someone to work with, you can count on me, Jimmy. I need the money, I have a kid coming. I need to support that kid, my wife and the apartment."

"Armando, that's why I asked you to make this run, as long as you don't mind doing the runs, I can use you for that alone."

"What if I want to start a little something on my own, would you object?"

"As long as you leave my customers alone, you can build as many of your own customers as you like. I have no objections, just leave my customers alone or we will be on opposite ends of the game."

"It's a deal. When do you want me to make the next run?"

"Next week will be fine."

"Same deal?"

"Sure five hundred plus expenses"

"OK, I'll do it; I'll speak to you in a day or two."

Armando left the drugstore and started to plan for what he considered his big break. To have a business like that would give his family everything they wanted and needed.

~*~

BACK AT THE HOSPITAL 1979

Armando woke up in the emergency room hallway on a stretcher and could hear what was going on, but he didn't really understand until he tried to move. He could not move without serious pain.

"I'll do what I can for him right now, but it looks like he will need to be opened up to sew some of the internal injuries; however, he has lost a lot of blood."

Armando heard a male voice say those words and thought it was his doctor working on him.

"Who said that?"

"I am Doctor Steinberg, Mr. Kiefer; we will take care of you. You have lost a lot of blood, we're getting you a couple of pints so that we can operate and hopefully fix you up."

Armando was in a daze and tried to say thanks, but passed out again.

His dreams took him back to when he had his first confrontation and his first real partner.

~*~

Friday June 20, 1975, His Dreams Continues

Armando had been doing the runs for a while, he was working, making money and before he knew it, the scent of summer was in the air. The winter had melted away as June came into play, a beautiful day, in the low 70's, a clear sky, a day to sit back and enjoy life. The money was coming in fast and furious. Armando was as happy as possible. His wife had a boy who they named Francis, after his father who gave Armando years of joy before he passed on.

Armando's father, Francis Kiefer, was a good plumber, but not a very religious man and Armando resented the religious teachings which his mother Madeline Kiefer drilled into his head.

He always enjoyed being around his dad, especially as his dad got older and wiser in the ways of life. What Armando did not know then was just how much his mother's religious sermons would affect him later in his own life.

Armando's wife, Loretta (Deleon) Kiefer, was a white female, five feet eight inches tall, one hundred and thirty pounds, dark brown hair and brown eyes with a clear complexion, very pretty and very easy to speak with. Loretta was studying writing and art and enjoyed both very much. She was sitting at the kitchen table when Armando entered the room.

"What are you doing today Armando?"

"I think I'll go to the beach."

"OK, I have a few classes and I'll take the baby over to Mrs. Johnson's. She will watch him for us while we're out."

"Sounds good, I'll pick him up this afternoon as long as nothing comes up."

"What would come up?"

"Oh, I am working on a deal to meet the Chemist and buy directly from him."

"I don't like that business. Armando, it's very dangerous for our child and that's my first concern."

"Don't worry; I can handle anything that comes up. Did you see my newest gun?"

"Gun, what gun? I don't want guns around the baby or in the house?"

"Don't worry; I'll keep it at the drugstore so you won't be bothered by it."

"I don't like guns, Armando."

Armando left the house and drove to the beach. He pulled into the parking lot at Wollaston Beach in Quincy. He exited the car; he could see the people that he was supplying with the methamphetamine drug which he acquired through Jimmy's connections in northern Maine.

He walked toward the beach when a car drove down the road towards him and shots began coming from the vehicle aimed at Armando Kiefer.

Armando hit the ground, the shooter missed him. Armando thought that it was strange that he missed at such a close range. He realized that it was a warning of some kind, not a hit.

He got a good look at the vehicle as it passed and he recognized the car as belonging to a Pauli Jameson. Pauli was upset with Armando because Pauli was losing money.

Armando was getting the crank (methamphetamine) and underselling Pauli. This was dangerous. Armando had to figure a way of either taking Pauli into his business as a partner, thereby clearing things with him or he would be forced to eliminate the danger.

Armando was afraid that he may have to kill Pauli the next time they met unless he took the issue in hand. Pauli was hard to talk with. Pauli always went to his guns and figured that settled everything. Armando didn't feel that way. He had a gun, but for self defense. The gun is not for settling every argument.

The men at the beach who knew Armando came over to him and they all knew who did the shooting.

"Armando, that was Pauli's car and I think Pauli was driving."

"Yes, I know it was. I'll talk with him; maybe we can settle our differences."

About twenty minutes later, Armando went into the bar across the street from the beach called the Big Wave and used the phone there to telephone Pauli.

"Hello?"

"Pauli?"

"Yes, who's this?"

"The guy you tried to shoot a few minutes ago."

"I'll get you, you motherfucker, you are costing me my life on top of my business," replied Pauli.

"Wait a minute, what if I could guarantee that you would make more cash than you ever did? The only difference would be that you work for me."

"I'd like to see how that works; I barely get a living out of what I do now."

"You deal at a small level. What I can do is help you to move up, but you must go through me for all your crank."

"What about my current supplier?"

"Where do you think he gets his stuff from?"

"You mean he gets his load from you?"

"Look, Pauli, I'm becoming the major supplier of the crank on the East Coast. You can come with me up the ladder or we part now and whatever happens happens. It's up to you. Make a decision."

"That sounds interesting, but what are you saying, that I'm supposed to forget about what you did? You destroyed my business and my life."

"Yes, Pauli, until we can get together, discuss this, and come to an agreement that is financially beneficial to both of us."

"What is your suggestion?"

"I have limited time. I'll meet you at the beach tomorrow at 1 p.m. I will answer any questions you have, but you have to make a decision before we part tomorrow."

"Agreed, I'll be there at noon tomorrow. We'll talk and settle everything."

"See you then."

***

Armando hung up the phone and went back across the street to the beach. He spent the rest of the day working the crowd on the beach, talking to people, making friends, being the nice guy, making sure people knew him and knew what he was capable of supplying. He was well known for his top shelf methamphetamine rock or crank, as is was called in that area.

~*~

Monday May 21, 1979 At the Quincy Detectives Office

Detective Ernie Lijoi arrived at the office about the same time as Det. Henry Griswold and they were planning their day when Capt. Donald Richards walked over to the two detectives and handed them a report. "This is a report on a man that's in the hospital with multiple stab wounds. He was found on the beach by a runner, bleeding badly. He's believed to be a speed dealer. His wounds are bad, he may not make it; see if you can talk to him ASAP."

"Captain, we have someone down in the cells that we have to speak with."

"I understand, I read your reports. This man may die so he takes priority. You can speak with the other guy when you're done at the hospital with this guy, Armando Kiefer."

Ernie looked down at the report and handed it to Henry. "It says here his name is Armando Kiefer of Quincy and that he is believed to be involved with meth. I never heard of him."

"Well, see what you can do."

"OK, Captain, we'll go to the hospital right now," replied Ernie.

***

The detectives left the office and drove to the hospital to find that Kiefer was unable to speak with them.

"Nurse, who's his doctor?"

"Doctor Steinberg took care of him and will be operating."

"Is the doctor in the hospital?"

"Yes, I'll page him."

A few minutes later the doctor showed up and the detectives spoke with him.

"Doc, what's the chance of speaking with Kiefer, the stabbing patient?"

"Not very good, he has to remain asleep until I can get in, look around and make a determination of how bad he actually is."

"You must have an opinion?"

"Yes I do, he's about the worst I have seen after a knife fight or stabbing."

"OK, here's our card, will you call us as soon as he can speak?"

"Yes, I'll have the nurse call you the moment he is awake and strong enough to talk."

"Thanks, Doc."

The detectives left the hospital and returned to the station while Armando Kiefer went on with his dreaming.

Chapter 2

The Meeting

Sunday June 22, 1975, His Dreams Continues

There was a slight breeze in the air. The weather was cool, but clear, sunny and expected to go into the seventies. Armando arrived on the beach. It was noon. He went down to the sand, put suntan lotion on and lay back on his towel with his head and shoulders propped up. He was watching and waiting for Pauli to arrive, watching his friends for a signal. His friends, who he asked to cover his meeting, were located on the outskirts of the beach area. They would watch him in case Pauli decided to renege on his agreement for a temporary peace.

At one p.m. Pauli arrived. He stood at the top of the stairs that led down to the beach area along the wall that dropped from the street to the rocks. Beyond the rocks was the sandy beach which went on for over fifty feet before it reached the salt water of Quincy Bay. He looked around. He could see that there were other men in the area, men that were known to him as being associated with Armando Kiefer.

Pauli yelled out to Armando.

"Hey, Armando, come over to the steps, I'm alone."

Armando saw Pauli standing on the top platform of the steps to the beach. Pauli Jameson, a white male, five feet nine inches tall, one hundred and eighty pounds, thirty years of age, blond hair and brown eyes. He was a known speed, marijuana and cocaine dealer.

Armando looked around and decided to get up and walk over toward him, even though it may be dangerous.

"Pauli, do you have a bathing suit with you?"

"Yes, I do."

"Let's see how you look in it."

Pauli knew why Armando wanted to see him in his bathing suit. Armando wanted to make sure Pauli was not carrying a gun. Pauli stepped back from the top of the steps, took his clothes off in full view of Armando and laid them on the wall. He then stepped onto the top platform of the steps.

Armando was satisfied that Pauli was not carrying a weapon and approached him.

"Well, what do you think of my proposition?" Armando asked.

"All I heard was that you're planning to be king. I didn't hear anything about me or my place in that plan. You didn't mention how you were going to do this. You didn't mention who your connection was. I could go on."

"I can only tell you so much right now. As we become closer, I will let you know more."

"OK, Armando, what can you tell me right now? I can't make a decision on pure air."

"Pauli, I have a group of people that I m working with. I will have access to the purest meth you have ever seen. You'll get it at my cost for you alone and the purity cannot be matched. I'll place you in charge of distribution in this area. You'll get a percentage of the profits which should amount to hundreds of thousands of dollars per year."

"That all sounds good. But how do I know that you can deliver?"

"That's where our trust will start. You have to have some faith in my abilities just as I am placing my trust in you."

"Armando, something like this could be dangerous. We're going to cross a lot of small guys that are crazy enough to kill us both."

"That's why I picked you, Pauli. You're smart and can handle those people and problems like that for us. You can eliminate them in a safe manner for us and still keep a cool head. You see, I know you very well. I know that those shots yesterday were warnings, not kill shots, or I would be dead right now."

"Yes, that's true. I don't really want to see you dead. I want you out of my way. You present an enticing proposition. I actually like the idea of becoming partners with you rather than us destroying each other."

"Then it's a deal?"

"Let's we say that we're in agreement for the time being. As long as things go the way you say, you can count on me. On the other hand, if I am dissatisfied with the progress, I'll let you know. You agree that you will go your own way. Leave me and my customers alone. We'll part, but part friends."

"That sound fair, I'll agree to that. I believe you will be more than satisfied."

Armando went on to explain that he had a meeting in New Hampshire with some friends. These men are partners in the meth business. He has known them for several years.

Armando stated that he wouldn't be back for a week or more and for Pauli to sit tight and wait until his return. When he returned they would begin their journey into a world of ecstasy and unbelievable cash.

They parted from each other and went their own way. Armando spent the rest of the day on the beach, flirting with the young chicks, being friendly with all of the people that hung around the beach and the bar across the street, known as "The Big Wave".

***

The Big Wave was a hangout for motorcycle gangs, groupie girls and people that loved to hear good music and dance. The Bar had a band that had become fairly well known as the "The Renotes", which consisted of a singer and several musical instruments.

When you entered the building you could see the bar along the back wall. There was a large dance floor and a stage on one side where the band put on their shows. On the other three sides of the dance floor were tables and chairs for the customers to sit and drink between dances. This was a very popular lounge and the most popular location within the lounge, at night, was the toilet where everyone could purchase their nightly illegal narcotics.

This lounge was Armando's favorite place, mostly because he knew everyone that hung out in the area and he was as close as possible to all of them and able to still do business.

The owner of the lounge didn't care for Armando or his business and had made derogatory statements to him on more than one occasion, but Armando simply laughed it off.

The next day he planned to go to New Hampshire and meet with his friends in an effort to move his business forward.

~*~

Back at the Hospital 1979

Armando's eyes open slowly; everything was blurred, as he looked up, he saw the florescent lights going by him as he lay there on the gurney.

"What's going on?" he asked in a half-dazed state.

He heard the voice of an angel speak out to him. "Go to sleep, Mr. Kiefer, we're going to the operating room. Don't worry, you will be fine"

Armando was anesthetized so that the doctors could work on him in the emergency room. After hearing a voice that he thought was an angle, he smiled and seemed to take pleasure in the fact that an angel was talking to him. He fell off to sleep again.

While still in his daze, he could hear a male voice saying, "He's in very bad shape", another saying, "I hope you can help him, Doctor." This was the voice of the doctor and the nurse speaking as they walked along with the gurney that Kiefer was on.

Armando went back to his dream where he was reliving his life on the street.

~*~

Monday June 23, 1975 The Dreams Continue

Armando was on the road, it was cool and he had to drive with the windows closed, which surprised him since it was June. The weather should have been warmer. His travels that day would bring him to Lancaster, a small town in New Hampshire.

He drove through the town center and over to Hartco Ave which he followed for several miles. He then came to an unnamed dirt road on his left. There was no identification on this road except the dot. High on a tree, about eight feet off the ground, there was a red dot, about one foot in diameter, on the corner tree. This was the marker. He turned in and drove back in the woods for about two miles where he came upon a cabin. He parked and went into the cabin.

There was no one visible inside. The cabin looked very normal, a kitchen, dining room and a hall leading to the bedrooms. In one corner there was some electronic equipment that is used by musicians for recording. In the middle of the kitchen floor which was a part of a great room, was a trap door that was open. Armando could see the stairway going down to a dug out area below the cabin. He yelled out. "Damian, are you here?"

***

Damian Bordeaux was a white male, forty years of age, five feet nine inches tall, one hundred and forty pounds, dark hair and eyes. He had once been a police officer and while conducting a raid on some bookies, he was shot in the head. This injury caused him to give up the police work, but that was not the worst of the injury. As time went on Damian was on very heavy medication for the pain. When the doctors stopped giving him medication, he went to the street to purchase it. From there he slowly found his way to becoming involved with and then producing methamphetamine. Damian and Gerry Lebeau were the suppliers to Jimmy Orbits.

"Armando, is that you?"

"Yeah."

"Stay up there for a few minutes while I turn the ventilating fan up high."

Armando could hear the fan turn on and roar. "I use it to clear out the methamphetamine dust in the air. OK, It's clear now, come on down."

Armando walked down into the hand-dug cellar area and saw a long table with all types of tubes and chemical paraphernalia spread out, bubbling and cooking.

"Shit, I don't want to be here while you're making that crack shit and cutting the meth."

"Don't worry, I haven't blown up a place in years." Damian stated with a laugh.

"Yeah, bull shit, this dust can go at any time."

"That's the chance we take, Armando. I have good ventilation, don't worry. What do you need?"

"I'm surprised to see you cooking crack."

"Yeah, it's a special order for someone. I don't usually mess with that stuff. The meth I cut down here all the time."

"How long will you be cooking?"

"I'm just about done. What's up with you?"

"I came up to party and see if I can get to the Canadian guy. I have a very good deal to offer."

"How much are you looking for?"

"Multiple pounds."

"I can't do that, I just do enough for myself and a few friends. You need a real chemist for that, with a real lab. You can talk to Gerry about that, he has the people to talk with."

"That's why I wanted to talk with you and Gerry."

"He'll be here later. The party will start in a little while. Speak with him, he's the man you want."

"Great, I need some relaxation."

***

Gerry turned out to be Gerry Lebeau, a white male, thirty-eight years of age, five feet ten inches tall, one hundred and fifty ponds, blond hair and blue eyes. Gerry was a citizen of Canada, singer and musician, who was the owner of the camp in New Hampshire. Damian was the grounds keeper for the camp in exchange for living there and using the place as his own personal lab.

Armando was hoping that he could make a deal with Gerry, who is the big boss. From there he could push his current small business, which is all that existed in the United States, into the largest importer and supplier of methamphetamine from a lab. In Armando's opinion, good laboratory methamphetamine was almost nonexistent in the United States at that time.

~*~

Back at the Hospital 1979:

Armando woke up again. As he came out of his sleep he was dazed and realized that he was dying and may not make it through the surgery. He called to the doctor. The doctor came over to him and told him that he was going to sleep now and not to worry, things should turn out fine.

"I'm not worried Doctor. I just want to say one thing."

"What's that?"

"May God guide your hands."

This was Armando's mother talking, when he was a child. She instilled in him, her religious beliefs which had subconsciously stayed with him. He continued to dream about the big question, "Who did this to you?"

~*~

Back at the cabin in New Hampshire, 1975

Armando was sleeping in one room and Damian was resting in another. Armando heard music. He got up and saw that the cabin was full of people drinking, doing drugs and the music was just beginning to start.

Gerry was playing the guitar and singing, people were dancing. Everyone was having a ball and enjoying life. They could make all the noise they wanted. The cabin was so far out into the woods that no one could hear anything or be bothered by their sounds.

At about three o'clock in the morning the music and the noise began to quiet down. Gerry walked out of one of the bedrooms with two girls and a large smile on his face.

"Gerry, can you spare a moment?"

"Sure, Armando, what do you need? You know I have the best meth around, over ninety percent pure if you're interested and it's at a great price for you."

"Gerry, I'm always interested, but I wanted to speak with you about some business."

"Come into my office"

Gerry opened the door to his room and walked in so that they could speak privately.

"Gerry, I'm setting up a group of clientele for the product. I want to be able to purchase it in large quantities."

"Armando, first try this." Gerry reached into a box that he pulled out from under the bed and pulled out a crystal rock as clear as glass.

"Wow, is that meth?"

"That is the purest meth you have ever seen or will ever see in our life time"

"Is this the Canadian meth that I hear so much about?"

"That's it. Try it and we will talk tomorrow."

"OK, I'll be happy to."

Armando had methamphetamine many times in the past and always got a similar reaction to it, which to him was normal. All of the meth he had previously tried was from people that were making it in their cellars or in a very small lab somewhere. Most of them were not proficient in the analysis of the chemicals. The meth that Gerry gave Armando to try was not yellowish in color and showed none of the impurities. This was crystal, pure crystal.

Armando took the rock from Gerry and went into the other room. He took the mortar and pestle (a cup and crusher used by a chemist), broke off a very small piece of the rock and crushed it into a powder. He then took the powder and mixed it with some dextrose to reduce the potency. After preparing the drug, he ingested it by inhaling the drug up his nose.

Armando sat back on the couch and waited the few seconds that it took for the chemical meth to have an effect on his body in a way that he did not expect.

He could feel the warm and the hot flashes throughout his body as the meth broke through the inner walls, carried by the blood and flowed into his brain. His hair felt like it was standing on edge. He was sliding down the wall, so to speak, deeper and deeper into the ecstasy of this new and purest form of drug called methamphetamine.

Armando fell in love with this new crystal. It was unlike the street stuff that he had experienced over the years called by the name of "drugstore speed". This Canadian meth was the intimate love of his life, it completed him in a way that nothing else would or could.

He would never be able to go back to using the speed that was produced by Damian and sold by Jimmy Orbits and others.

He instantly realized that this Canadian laboratory speed could replace everything throughout the entire area.

He had to make a deal with Gerry. This would place him in a great position to expand throughout the New England area and then who knew how far he could go?

The next morning Armando would speak with Gerry as soon as he came out of his bedroom, which Gerry referred to as his playpen.

Armando fell off into a cloud of sleep, even though he was laying on a couch with a bunch of pillows, blankets and jackets all over it.

~*~

Tuesday June 24, 1975

Armando awakened feeling hungry. He walked over to the refrigerator, which had plenty of beer, but very little food. He was the only one awake. He left the cabin and drove into the town to have breakfast. While there, he purchased fifteen coffees to go and brought them back to the cabin for everyone.

While paying for the coffee he laughed. He remembered how a few months ago he didn't have enough money to pay for one coffee, now he was buying coffee for the whole house. Things were looking good.

He returned to the cabin with the coffee and several people were awake, including Gerry.

"Great idea getting the coffee, Armando."

"My pleasure, can we sit and talk for a few minutes?"

"Armando, let me wake up and have a snort and a shower, then we will talk, but there is very little to say. You'll understand when we talk. I'll take a shower now."

***

About a half-hour later Gerry walked out of his room and looked wide awake, not from the shower, but from a snort of meth which would wake up anyone.

"Armando, what can I tell you? Did you like that shit?"

"I loved it. This stuff must be a thousand times more potent then what is referred to as the drugstore meth. Can you advise me on what I need to do, so that I can get close to the chemist in Canada, so that I can build a good business?"

"It's very easy, Armando. I will take you on, as my partner, if you raise one hundred thousand dollars. Once you pay me that money, we'll be partners and you will have access to everybody that I have access to."

"That's a lot of money, Gerry. I'll need some time to speak with a few people and put it together."

"Armando, you take all the time you need. I can use a guy like you. If you can raise the money and we are partners you can save me a lot of work. Right now I do it all myself with no real help except from Damian, but he doesn't want to be involved at this level."

"What kind of a deal are we talking about, Gerry?"

"Here's the plan. We'll have an even two-way split, you and I. With the money that you bring in and my share, we will become the largest dealers on the East Coast. We'll control the entire northeast, New England and parts of New York. No one will be able to touch us. There is a lot I can't say right now, not until you make a final decision."

"I have a partner that I can't just drop," stated Armando.

"Who, Jimmy?"

"Yes."

"I forgot about him. That's OK. We will make it a three-way deal, one hundred thousand dollars each. With three, we will make even more money. He has good connections that'll help in our protection; he'll be a great help to us."

"Give me a couple of weeks."

"As I said, I'll be here when you're ready."

The two men joined the other people in the camp. Armando finished his coffee and decided to leave and head back to Massachusetts to try and arrange for the one hundred thousand dollars.

***

Armando was not sure who to speak with for that much money. He figured that his partner, Jimmy the druggist, would have a connection.

Chapter 3

The Musketeers

Wednesday June 25, 1975

Armando entered the drugstore and was surprised to see the druggist's wife working behind the counter.

"Hi, Mrs. Orbits, how are you?"

"Hi, Armando, please call me Rita."

Rita Orbits, a white female, thirty-three years of age, five feet six inches tall, one hundred and thirty pounds with long black hair and brown eyes. She had a pockmarked complexion, dark 'Teeth', glary eyes and always was in a hurry, the typical look of a meth addict. Looking at her, Armando knew she was a freak, a speed freak.

"Is Jimmy around?"

"Sure, he's downstairs in the cellar, go ahead down."

Armando walked into the back of the store and down the stairs to the cellar. Once there he saw several stacks of boxes with stock for the store and a table with assorted mixes on it for Jimmy's meth cutting.

"Hi, Jimmy."

"Hi, Armando, how's things?"

"We have a small problem."

"What's the problem?"

"We need one hundred thousand dollars each to get set up with Gerry and become his partner. I don't have a hundred grand, not yet."

"That's a lot of money, Armando. I am not sure that I am interested in getting any bigger. I have the drugstore and the side business. That's enough for me, but I can understand your position, wanting to get involved at that level."

"This is one hell of a break for me and the money would be guaranteed. Once in with him we would control the entire New England area and more for meth."

"Oh, I didn't know you were talking that big, that's extremely big."

"Try this stuff."

"I'll try it tonight. Stop by in the morning and we'll talk"

"OK, I will see you in the morning."

***

Armando left the drugstore and went to his home where his wife Loretta was waiting for him.

"Where have you been for the last few days?" asked Loretta.

"I had some business to take care of. I have an opportunity to work with some real great people and make a lot of money."

"Yeah, I'm sure it's all legal, too."

"What do you want from me? There is no work for a guy like me. No education and no real experience. I can make good money this way."

"One day, you'll come home and the baby and I won't be here."

"You can't take my son."

"We'll see what I can do."

The day ended as usual, Armando was arguing with Loretta instead of enjoying each other's company.

~*~

Thursday June 26, 1975

Armando was up and out before Loretta had baby Francis fed. He didn't say a word as he left the apartment other than, "I'll see you later."

He went for breakfast and then he ordered two coffees to go, one for him and one for Jimmy.

He arrived at the drugstore at about ten a.m. and Jimmy was helping a customer with some prescriptions she needed. He saw Armando and asked him to go down to the cellar and wait for him.

Armando handed him a coffee and went to the cellar. Jimmy had a small area in the cellar, with a couch and a television for his break time. Armando turned on the television news station, sat down and waited for Jimmy.

***

About a half hour later Jimmy came down the stairs and joined Armando on the couch.

"Armando, that crystal that you gave me was fantastic. I've never felt that feeling before, so intense so indescribable."

"Then you agree we should join him and go ahead with the deal?"

"Let's look at it, Armando. Gerry has the "Clean Bloods", a motorcycle gang in Vermont for protection. He's very close to them. They are connected and have chapters all over the country. He also has the Canadians who will only deal with him. They make this crystal and it is the purest I have ever seen or tasted. From our point of view, we can count on my brother, Joe, if we need him for help. He works for mobsters who control the truckers and the Teamsters and that's our connection to the local mafia."

"That makes a great combination, it sound good to me, Jimmy. We have the southern areas and he has the northern areas protected in many ways. Our protection is doubled, since we can both cover."

"There is the other side of the coin, Armando."

"Yeah, we'll have to deal with certain people down here in our areas."

"Yes, the South Boston mob, who is associated with the Boston and Rhode Island Mafia and The Bolos who run the clubs in downtown Boston. They will all want a piece."

"We give up nothing. We deal with them as needed, Jimmy, on an individual basis."

Jimmy sat there for a few minutes and didn't say a word. Armando could tell that Jimmy was weighing all of the pros and cons of this deal.

"Armando, it makes sense; we'll join Gerry. Call him and tell him that we'll get a suite at the Sattler Hotel in Nashua, New Hampshire. We will meet there and discuss everything. Also, have him bring some of that Canadian meth, so that I can have a real taste."

"Great, I'll telephone him"

The meeting was set up for Sunday, June 29, 1975 at twelve o'clock noon.

***

Jimmy brought the cash to the meeting and they discussed all of the complications that could arise. They also discussed their protection, which was varied and very high-placed within the different organizations that ran the underworld of this country through their separate association with different individuals.

"We only have one real problem that I can see," stated Gerry.

"What's that?" asked Jimmy.

"We're fine throughout Maine, Vermont, New Hampshire and Massachusetts, but we can't go into New York and we have to be careful in Rhode Island."

"Why?" asked Armando.

"Because the New York families control New York and Rhode Island and we cannot afford their protection, not yet, nor can we interfere in their business. Maybe in time."

"Why can't we go ahead and deal there anyway, then when they tell us to stop, we deal with them?" asked Armando.

"You don't do that. I know people that are connected with them in Canada. We have an OK in Canada, but stay out of New York was the word, for now anyway."

The three men agreed to stay out of New York.

Over the next year, by June of 1976, The 'Three Musketeers' Armando, Gerry and Jimmy did a total of nine hundred thousand dollars in profit for their first year in business, giving them three hundred thousand dollars each.

~*~

Monday July 11, 1977

They had a meeting at their favorite location, the Statler Hilton suite, where they split the profits for the previous year.

By June of 1977 their product had become one of the most popular items on the street. Because of the popularity of the Canadian crystal, their profits were going up with no ceiling in site. Their second year in business they made almost one million dollars each in profits.

By now they were becoming suspected and known by the authorities as the heads of a large organization that imported and distributed the speed, crank, meth, crystal. all street names for their methamphetamine. They didn't even discuss the authorities; they felt that they were invincible.

They enjoyed the nickname that they had been given by many people on the street. That nickname was 'The Three Musketeers'. They were called this by the street people that became addicted to the crank, the dealers who were dependent on them to stay high. All of these people felt that the Musketeers were life savers. This nickname was taken from the stories of the Three Musketeers that appeared on television and in the movies who actually helped and saved the lives of people instead of slowly killing them.

***

The lives of these three men completely changed. If they wanted to go somewhere or have a meeting they didn't just fly there, they chartered a plane. Dinners cost them hundreds of dollars and clothes were the most expensive they could find. Imported suits, shoes and they would have their hair styled and cut every week. They were on top of the world. The problem with this type of life was that they were becoming sloppy with security. They stopped checking the loyalty of their associates. The operation was becoming too large for the three men to handle. This, in time, would bring problems.

***

The Federal Drug Enforcement Administration and The Federal Alcohol and Tobacco and Firearms Administration were beginning to hear stories about these new upstarts, which opened their eyes to what was apparently becoming a major problem throughout the North Eastern part of the United States.

The United States federal authorities were not the threat that they had to worry about at that time. They had been having a problem with the French Mafia in Canada, who now wanted to take over the entire lucrative operation themselves.

Gerry's brother, Stephen Lebeau, a white male, five feet eight inches tall, one hundred and fifty pounds, brown hair and brown eyes, a citizen of Canada, was the runner for the Musketeers. He was given this job mainly because he spoke French fairly well. The job gave Stephen a great income. Things went smoothly, peacefully and quietly until late that summer when the authorities took notice of them due to their reputation in the meth business.

~*~

Monday August 1, 1977

While at the camp in the back woods of New Hampshire, Gerry could see that Stephen was a little agitated and asked what was wrong.

"Gerry, these Canadian Frenchmen have not been as friendly as they used to be. I think something is wrong, but I can't put my finger on it."

"Steve, don't worry about it, we have a good thing here and they have a good thing through us. They wouldn't fuck this up. It must be your imagination."

"OK, I'll take your word for that, but it still seems a little weird to me."

"When are you leaving for the run?"

"This afternoon."

***

Steve left that afternoon for Canada and when he arrived, he met with his contact within the French Mafia. They spoke in French to each other.

"Bonjour, Marcel, comment sont vous "

"Nous sommes bons, mais vous avez un problem"

"Que voulez-vous dire "

"Je te dis ceci parce que nous nous étions 29verter29 les uns avec les autres pendant beaucoup d'années. Rappelez-vous qu'l n'a jamais indiqué une chose à vous. Mes patrons veulent

assurer vos affaires et ils m'ont indiqué pour vous 30verter de ne pas revenir à Canada"

"Que diriez-vous de mon aujourdui d'approvisionnements?"

"Je ne dois pas supposer à, mais je les donnerai a vous."

"Remerciez de vous."

"Séjour hors du Canada. Ils placeront un contrat sur tous les deux vous et votre brother"

"Pourquoi non nous discutons ceci et venons à un agreement"

"Je demanderai, mais je doute de l'it"

The conversation in English:

"Hello, Marcel, how are you?"

"We are good Stephen, but you have a problem."

"What do you mean?"

"I am telling you this, Stephen, because we have been dealing with each other for many years. Remember I never said a thing to you. My bosses want to take over your business and they have told me to warn you not to come back to Canada."

"What about my supplies today?"

"I am not supposed to, but I will give them to you."

"Thank you."

"Stay out of Canada. They will place a contract on both you and your brother."

"Why can't we discuss this and come to an agreement."

"I will ask, but I doubt it."

***

Stephen took his supplies and made arrangements for transportation. He then drove back to New Hampshire with the disturbing information that Marcel had given him.

When Gerry received the information he smiled and looked at his brother.

"There is always more than one way to skin a cat."

"Skin a cat! We're talking about a contract on us, you and me. These people don't fuck around."

"Did you get the order that we needed for the next week or two?"

"Yes, I got it"

"You will not be going back there. I'll take a trip and talk to the chemist himself."

"Who will do the runs for us?"

"Don't worry about that, I'll handle it. Things should work out."

"OK, you're the brains."

***

Gerry contacted Armando and told him that they had to have a meeting in about a week. Armando agreed and said that he and Jimmy would come up to New Hampshire.

"If I'm not here stay with Damian, he will keep you company until I return."

"Where are you going?"

"I'll explain when I see you."

Armando contacted Jimmy at the drugstore and advised him as to what Gerry requested.

"Why does he need us to come up there?"

"That was my decision because of the way he spoke. I could distinguish some worry in his voice."

Jimmy agreed without hesitation.

~*~

Sunday August 7, 1977

The drugstore was closed on Sunday. This was the best time for Jimmy to travel up to New Hampshire.

During the ride to New Hampshire they had a discussion about Gerry, his brother Steve and Damian that interested Armando very much.

"Jimmy, I know that Gerry is a well known musician and singer and Steve has always worked for him. I don't know this guy Damian very well. He's real quiet and doesn't say much. What do you know about him?"

"That's an interesting and sad story at the same time. He was a police officer in Florida for many years. One day he was doing a raid on a rape and kidnapping suspect. Damian was assigned to go in the front door along with his partner. He was a great cop and loved the job. They kicked in the door and started into the house when the house was quiet. Damian was standing to the right of his partner when his partner saw the assailant with a gun in his hand. The assailant was taking aim at Damian. His partner pushed him in an effort to save Damian's life. As Damian went down he took a hit in his head. His partner killed the assailant."

"Wow, what a story!"

"That's only half of it. Damian was operated on and they saved his life, but he is epileptic now and can't work as a cop."

"How did he wind up in the middle of the drugs?"

"That's the rest of the story. He was in severe pain almost constantly and needed very strong drugs to kill the pain so that he could function normally. After a couple of years, the doctors stopped the medication and said that he had become hooked. They did all they could to withdraw him from the meds, but to no avail. He was in need of meds so he went to the street to buy what he needed. Over time, he met Gerry and they became close friends. He will do anything for Gerry and vice versa."

Chapter 4

The Chemist

Sunday August 7, 1977 Late Morning

It had been a pleasant day when they left Massachusetts, but during the drive the temperature dropped to a cool point; it was chilly enough for a jacket. After the long drive they arrived at the cabin.

"Damian, you make one hell of a French toast sandwich," stated Armando.

"Yes, my mom made these for me as a kid. I love them."

"Yeah, my mom made those triple deck sandwiches for me when we were kids. They had peanut butter, jelly and cream cheese. I could go for one of those."

"That sounds good." Jimmy remarked.

"Do you guys want some biker's coffee or straight?" Biker's coffee is coffee mixed with methamphetamine.

"Straight is good for me" said Armando.

"Yeah, I'll have it straight until I know why we're here," stated Jimmy.

"Why are you guys here?" asked Damian curiously.

"Gerry seemed to have a problem and wanted a meeting," answered Armando.

"Yes, he told me about it."

"What can you tell us, Damian?"

"Nothing, it's a little complicated for me. He'll be back soon and run it by you."

"Do you have any more pain, Damian?"

"I'm fine as long as I do the black beauties three times a day and chase them with a little meth."

"Black beauties, I haven't seen any of them around for a long time," said Armando.

"Yeah, Gerry has a friend that's a chemist. He makes them up for me. They save my life. At least I can survive and live a somewhat normal life."

"I wish you luck, Damian. I hope it all works out for you some day. Maybe the doctors will find a way of helping you so that you don't have to take all that shit," indicated Jimmy.

Just then the door opened and a cool breeze flew in throughout the cabin. It was Gerry coming back from his meeting.

"Hi everyone, are you men doing OK, or what?" Gerry asked, as he walked into the cabin.

"If you mean are we satisfied with the money we're making, yes, very satisfied," stated Jimmy.

"Can I get some coffee, Damian?"

"Sure. Gerry, have a seat."

"Here's what's going down. Steve went up to do the normal run when his contact gave him a tip," stated Gerry.

"Here's your biker's coffee, Gerry?"

"Thanks, Damian."

"What kind of tip?" asked Jimmy.

"There is a French contract out on me and my brother."

"What? Why would there be a contract out on you guys?" asked Jimmy

"We are the only ones that they know about. They know nothing about you two since you have the United States part of our deal and never go into Canada."

"What about the 'Clean Bloods', the motorcycle gang, they're your friends, can't they protect you?" asked Armando.

"This goes beyond them, all the way to the political forum and they have to be careful whose toes they step on. They have multiple businesses to take care of."

"Gerry, if I know you, there is a plan in the works already. What do you have in mind?"

Gerry smiled and looked at Armando, as Armando was ending that sentence.

"I have a plan, you're right. Armando, you will do the runs instead of Steve."

"Fine, I'll be happy to, but how does that keep me alive and protect you guys?"

"I have a guy. I know this is hard to believe, but I don't even know his name, he goes by the initials "JP" and he is a chemist. I have known him on and off for several years through his representative. I've only spoken with him by phone, the rest of the time it's always his representative that speaks for him. I offered him a deal to supply us."

"You're abandoning our other supplier so that it looks like we are out of the business. You have a new supplier that'll produce what we need. I have only one question. How much will it cost us for this change?"

"Nothing more than we are paying now. As a matter of fact we eliminate the middle man and our profit margin goes up, not down."

"That sounds good to me. What's the punch line, Gerry?"

"Not really a punch line. We have to switch for a while. Jimmy can't do it; he has a business to run. The contract is on me and Steve. Armando, you will have to do the runs. When things calm down in a year or so Steve can take over again."

"That's fine with me," stated Armando.

"Good, I'll make the arrangements and get back to you. It'll be a semi-weekly run for ordering and importing," said Gerry.

"Gerry, I don't know exactly what to do and I certainly don't know this chemist," Armando replied.

"That's OK, I'll handle everything. I'll show you what to do, where to go and who to contact. Everyone you deal with will speak English so that you don't have to worry about the French language."

"So, I'll wait until I hear from you?" asked Armando.

"Yes, it will be in a short while."

***

Armando and Jimmy left the camp and began the long ride back to Quincy, Massachusetts, where Armando lived and Jimmy had his drugstore.

They all drove brand new Cadillac's with all of the extras. These men were making so much cash that the word expensive was completely lost in their vocabulary.

"Armando, I was thinking about getting a chauffeur when we do these trips, then we could party and enjoy life, without worrying about driving."

"That's a good idea, but how much attention would you draw? I don't know of any druggist that has a chauffeur."

"Yeah, I guess you're right. It would draw attention that we don't need, especially now with that the French contract hanging over us."

"Fuck those guys, we can work our way around it. Gerry is a brilliant man and can figure things out that we can't even begin to imagine. He seems to always have a backup plan. Have you noticed that?"

"Yes, he is amazing at times."

"If you don't mind I'm gonna get some rest while you drive."

"Go ahead, get some sleep. I'm fine to drive."

~*~

Back at the Hospital in Quincy, Massachusetts May 1979

The doctors were operating on Armando Kiefer and trying to fix the damage to his lungs, kidney and liver when it became apparent that there was just too much damage.

"Nurse, call for assistance. I need another doctor here sewing up some of this stuff. As I sew up one place, another place starts bleeding badly. It's like I am operating on a ninety-year-old man instead of a young man," stated the doctor.

"Doctor, does it look like he will survive?" asked the second assisting nurse.

"I still don't know. I need some help and then we will see. We also need more blood for him."

"OK, I'll get the blood" stated nurse number one.

"Whoever stabbed this man did an ample job. He must have stabbed him at least twenty times; now we're left with the repair. Do any of you know anything about him?" the doctor asked.

"I know one thing. They didn't miss a vital organ. They wanted him dead, whoever they were," said the first assisting nurse.

"I overheard the detectives talking about him and how he is the 'King of Speed'. I think that's methamphetamine," stated the second nurse.

"Doctor, I thought that meth was just a myth now that there is no real medical use for it."

"There are still some rare medical uses for it, but it is not used except in special cases. Women were using it to lose weight for years. We discovered that they were getting addicted to it, so it has been cut down to specific uses only. Did anyone call for some help?"

"I'll call right away, Doctor," said nurse number one.

The operation on Armando's lungs, liver and other areas continued. Armando remained in his dream world as the doctor battled to save his life.

~*~

Back in the Hospital Armando's dream continues

It was late at night when Armando arrived at home to find his wife and child gone. He checked his son's room, empty; he checked his bedroom, empty. He went into the kitchen and found a note on the kitchen table.

> *"Armando, I can't take anymore. You not being home, going on long trips, keeping secrets from me, selling that murderous stuff and keeping guns in the house. I have to protect my child. Your secrets are safe with me, but stay away from me and Francis."*

Armando was broken hearted even though he knew she was right. Then he became angry, so angry that he began to break things all over the house, placing his anger into these numerous objects that meant nothing to him. Things that were purchased by his wife to keep the house in what she called a livable state. He wanted his son back and would get him back no matter what it took.

~*~

Monday August, 8 1977

Armando went to the drugstore to speak with Jimmy. He told Jimmy how his wife had treated him and asked for some advice.

"Hi, Jimmy. I got fucked while we were away."

"What are you talking about?"

"My wife, she up and left me. She took the baby and left this note."

"It can't be that you treated her badly. After all, you have a house now, all the furnishings, all the money you need or she needs. What's her bitch?"

"Read the note."

"I see she is opposed to our business. She will hold that over you, Armando. Be very careful how you handle this."

"Do you have any suggestions, Jimmy?"

"Yes, get a lawyer and work on her through him. Show that you simply want to see her and the baby happy. Give them what they want and maybe she will soften up and come back to you. Let her know that you miss her and the baby."

"Yes, that's a good idea. I'll hire a lawyer to speak with her. Is there anything else that you can suggest?"

"Yes, if you can't convince her, keep her happy. This could place our whole operation in jeopardy if you're not careful."

"Thanks, Jimmy. I knew your calm mind would be able to help me out."

"Anything else doing, Armando?"

"No, do you want some coffee? I'll go and get us a couple of cups."

"That sounds good."

Armando left the store to go for the coffee.

***

While Armando was gone, Jimmy received a call from Gerry asking that Armando be ready to go by Friday.

Jimmy told Gerry that Armando would be there Friday morning early.

When these men talked on the telephone, they were very careful not to mention any specifics about the product that they sold, just in case the police were listening in. This was one of their rules.

Jimmy was taking care of a customer when Armando walked in with the coffee.

"Armando, go downstairs, I'll be down in a little bit."

Armando followed the directions of Jimmy and went down, turned on the TV, opened his coffee and sat back to wait for Jimmy.

***

"Armando, wake up. You fell asleep."

"Good thing I didn't have the coffee in my hand, I would have burnt the family jewels."

They both laughed.

"Gerry called; he wants you up there Friday. I told him that you would be there early in the morning."

"OK, I'll be there. Was there anything else?"

"No, just be there. That gives you enough time to take care of the wife situation."

"Yeah, I will stop by and see my lawyer as soon as I leave here."

"OK, stay as long as you like, I have to go up and tend to the store."

"OK. Jimmy, I'll leave in a few minute. Just finishing my coffee."

"Take your time."

***

Armando left the store and went to see his lawyer. He told the lawyer exactly what he wanted done and the strategy that he and Jimmy figured out.

The lawyer agreed and told him that this may not work out. "What if she just wants a divorce?"

"Give her whatever she wants. I want my kid taken care of."

"OK Armando, I'll do all I can for you."

Armando left the office and went home to the empty house.

~*~

Friday Morning, August 12, 1977

Armando woke in the Boston Motel, just off of Route #128 and outside of Weymouth Ma., not far from Quincy. He looked at the other side of the bed and found a girl sleeping. At first he didn't remember her and then he began to recall that he had been in a lounge and hooked up with this woman. He didn't even know her name.

Armando took a shower and got dressed. He looked at her closely. She was out like a light. Before he left the room, he threw two one hundred dollar bills on top of her clothes, which were on a chair.

He walked outside; the air was chilly as it hit him. Although the temperature was somewhere in the high sixties, it felt cold after the warm bed all night. There was a slight mist in the air, but the sun would eat that up as the morning progressed.

He got into his Cadillac and drove off. It was still dark. He had to be in New Hampshire that morning. He didn't know what woke him, just luck he supposed.

He arrived at the camp in New Hampshire by nine a.m. He entered the camp; it was quiet, almost scary. Everyone was asleep.

Armando made some coffee and waited.

***

It wasn't long before Damian was up and cooking breakfast, then Gerry walked out of his room with some girl that Armando didn't know and Steve came out of his room with another girl. There were so many girls in and out of the camp that Armando was not surprised that he had never seen them before.

Everyone said good morning and they all sat down at the table for breakfast.

Armando was getting a kick out of watching them. They all looked like zombies walking from their rooms to the table.

"Gerry, you awake enough to talk business?"

"No, give me an hour. Why don't you take Laura there and get a blow job? She'll suck the balls off of you."

Laura, sitting at the table, laughed and looked at Armando for an OK.

"Is there still some meth in the bedroom, Gerry?" asked Laura.

"Yeah, there's plenty."

"Come on, Armando, we'll play while he wakes up, then he'll want to play again."

"Hey, Laura, what about me?" asked Christie

"Christie, you come with us, we'll rock his world. After we crank up, that is."

Armando simply followed the girls into the bedroom and no one heard from him again for quite a while.

***

An hour later, Armando came out of the room: "Gerry, can we talk this over now?"

"Sure, Armando thanks for the time to wake up. Those two are not the best, but they will do in a pinch."

"They were fine by my standards," answered Armando.

"Wait a minute, Armando. All you girls get the fuck out of here for a while. Go downtown and have some breakfast. Here's a few hundred, do some shopping, take all day, that should cover it. Take your time, we have business to discuss."

The girls got dressed and took one of the Cadillac's from the yard and drove into town as directed by Gerry.

"OK, Armando, I have everything all set for you to make the runs."

"Gerry, where do I go, who do I see and more importantly, how do I get the shit back?"

"Oh, I forgot that you never did this part of the operation before. We'll have to go over everything slowly to make sure you have it all."

"That's fine with me. I want to do this correctly. I don't want to get screwed. After all, I'm going across international borders."

"Don't worry, Armando, if you go down, our entire operation goes down and we lose a million a year each or more. You do what I say and you'll be fine."

"OK, Gerry, I trust you, I just had to express my concern."

"I understand. First you go to Nashua and rent a car, then bring it back here. Do that today, then we will move to the next step."

"OK, I'll leave now."

"Armando, don't get anything flashy, very simple. Something your grandmother would rent or buy."

"I'll take care of it."

***

Armando left the cabin and two hours later he returned with a 1971 Chevy Impala, two-door hardtop and maroon in color with a white top.

As he pulled up to the camp, Steve was out on the porch and called Gerry.

"Who's this coming down the road?"

"That must be Armando."

Armando pulled up and parked the rented vehicle.

"I knew it was Armando. Hi, Armando, nice wheels. They're perfect for the job."

"OK, now what, Gerry?"

"Steve will show you."

"Armando, you don't do anything until you get to Canada and pick up the crank."

"When I get there, what do I do, Steve?"

"We will go through it once here. Take the molding off of the inside of the car and the felt covering. Then you stretch out the felt covering over this reinforced wooden sheet. Now you place the entire felt covering inside the car and back up on the ceiling with the reinforcement."

"OK, that's done, now what?"

"That gives you enough room to store about fifty pounds of meth in the roof of the car. The reinforced wood holds the ceiling up and you're good to go. You can place another fifty pounds in various areas like the inner walls of the doors, twenty pounds inside the spare wheel well. Take this spare, it's the one we use all the time. You notice that it opens at one end."

"But I have to go through this every time?"

"No just this time. You normally leave the back window trim without the metal rim until after you load the roof then you put the rim back in place and that seals the inner roof as well as the window."

"OK Steve, then I'll drive back here. It seems simple enough."

"Believe me, it is. I've been doing it a long time."

"Now, who do I meet and where?"

"Just one tip, lease a car. A few months at a time, then you only have to set this up once, in the leased car. We can afford it. Let's go inside and speak with Gerry."

"He's all set, Gerry. He needs to know who to meet and where to meet them."

"Thanks, Steve, for showing him. Armando, you go up to 340 George Street North, Peterborough, Canada. Go to the top floor and ask for Adrian Leflore, he is the only Adrian in the building. He'll direct you from there after you ask him, "Where are the babies' bottles with the whisky in them?" Then you laugh and shake his hand."

"Where are the babies' bottles with the whisky in them? I understand and I know where that is, I used to make runs up there years ago for marijuana, so I do know that area."

"Then you're all set."

"What about the payment?" Armando asked.

"Once you are there, meet him and see the product, call me and I will release the funds to an offshore account that they set up."

"I'm meeting the Chemist?" asked Armando.

"No, you are meeting his representative. This guy will handle everything for you. Call me once everything is OK and just say, "The baby is in the carriage."

"The baby is in the carriage. No problem."

"I will leave tomorrow if that's OK, Gerry?"

"That's fine, let's get crank'in. I'll get some product and we'll have some fun tonight. I have a few girls coming over from a show that I did last week in New York. We'll have a ball."

"Which bedroom can I use, Gerry?"

"Armando, those last two are empty, take your pick."

The rest of the night was spent doing speed and partying with the girls. At one point, Gerry got so high that he was creating some music that sounded like a cat crying. To him it sounded great. Everyone else was running away.

Chapter 5

Death

Saturday August 13, 1977

Saturday morning, Armando woke up in bed with a couple of girls. This would become a normal way of waking up while at the camp.

He went to the kitchen and found Damian making breakfast for everyone.

Armando grabbed a cup and poured some coffee.

"Damian, you seem to do all the chores around here. You amaze me, you never complain about them."

"Armando, I have a serious problem because of an injury that I received years ago. If it wasn't for Gerry I would be out on the street. He helped me out and gave me a place to live. He also gives me what I need for the pain. Gerry never asked me for anything so this is the least I can do."

"So you guys are just real good friends?"

"Yes, we became friends years ago, when I was on the other side of the line. When I got hurt he was there to help out."

"Most people don't have a friendship like that in their entire lives."

"Yes, I'm very lucky. You know, he pays me. If anything happens, I'll have money saved until he gets out of jail."

"I'm gonna take a shower and then take off on my trip. By the way, Damian, where the fuck did those broads come from?"

Waking up with two girls, especially girls he didn't know was something new to Armando.

"Who the fuck knows, they chase Gerry around like he's a God or something. Most nights its different women that show up. I told him, he must have a monster hanging, but in reality, it's the music that they chase him for. He's still famous and they love him for it."

"Thanks for the coffee, Damian."

***

Armando walked outside and the cool air surprised him. He realized then that the farther north he went the colder it would be. The entire day was spent driving up to Montreal, Canada. The roads were quiet and he saw plenty of moose crossing the roads. At one point he saw a deer; it actually surprised him because of the way it blended in with the trees.

After driving for over five hours, it was two o'clock in the afternoon when he arrived at his destination. He didn't have any problems crossing the border, but he didn't have any contraband in the car so there was nothing to worry about.

He parked in the back, entered the office building and walked up to the front desk.

"Hello, sir, I do not speak French. Do you speak English?"

"Yes Sir, how can I help you?" the clerk asked in broken English.

"I have a meeting with Mr. Adrian Leflore. Can you direct me or contact him?"

"Yes Sir, and your name?"

"I am Armando Kiefer."

The concierge picked up the phone and dialed a number.

"A Mr. Kiefer to see you, Sir", a pause and then he said, "Yes Sir."

"Mr. Leflore has asked that you join him in his office, Sir, room 433."

"Thank you."

Armando got on the elevator and went up to room 433. He entered the office and observed a woman receptionist who was sitting at a desk with the door to another office just behind her.

"Mr. Kiefer, go right in, Mr. Laflore is waiting for you."

Armando walked past the receptionist and opened the door to the back office and was amazed. This was a corner office with windows on two sides that extended from the ceiling to the floor. The view was of the bay with ships and boats sailing up and down. The office was meticulous. Everything was in the correct place. There was a large fish tank on one side with what appeared to be tropical fish. Armando looked at the main desk and was stunned. It was as large as his bed at home. All he could think of was what a great piece of ass he could get on that desk. The room was carpeted and had what appeared to be very comfortable chairs strewn about the around.

Armando was standing there in amazement, looking out those windows when he heard his name.

"Mr. Kiefer, what can I do for you?"

"Mr. Leflore, I was hoping that you could help me find out where the baby bottles with the whisky in them are?"

"Thank you. Your name is Armando, I understand?"

"Yes Sir and you are Adrian?"

"Yes, do you speak French, Armando?"

"I can say hello which I believe is bonjour and that's about it."

"That's OK. I will be your translator while you are here."

"When do I pick up the product?"

"It's almost three now. I was thinking that we could have a nice late lunch or early dinner and then take care of business. What do you think?"

"That sounds good to me. I'm a little hungry anyway."

***

The two men left the office and Adrian took Armando to the "Shekz" Restaurant that was located at #7272 Boulevard Duple in an out of the way area of Montreal.

Armando noticed that Adrian Leflore was a heavyset man with a dark complexion, he weighed about two hundred and seventy pounds, was balding on top with grayish black hair and brown eyes. He dressed in a suit and had the appearance and conversational expertise of a lawyer.

"This restaurant seems to specialize in French sauces, Adrian?"

"Yes, it is one of the best. The sauces here are known all over, they are the most delicious that I have ever tasted. You should enjoy your dinner; at least I hope you do."

They finished dinner and left the restaurant.

"Adrian, that was fantastic. I may have to stay over a night just to rest from that meal; and the flavor, it was unbeatable."

"I am glad you enjoyed it. Shall we complete our business?"

"Yes, let's do that."

***

Adrian drove to his office building where he dropped Armando at his car and asked Armando to follow him. Adrian drove to a warehouse about four blocks away where they could both pull their cars off the street and inside of the warehouse so that they would be out of site of the public.

They parked and Adrian signaled for Armando to follow him to a staircase in the back of the warehouse. They went up the long staircase and Adrian unlocked a steel door which opened to an office. It was an average office with a desk, chairs and some furniture spread around the room, nothing special except a large safe in one corner.

Adrian walked over to the safe and opened it. The safe was about six feet tall and three feet wide with two doors. As soon as it was opened, Armando could see stacks and stacks of one pound packages of methamphetamine. There had to be over a thousand pounds in that safe.

"Armando, here are your two hundred pounds; take your time, check them out and I'll help you load them. Then we will call for the release of the money to our account."

"Thank you, I would appreciate the help."

Armando brought his McDonalds spoon with him. McDonalds had a spoon that they gave their customers for coffee and other things. On the back end of the long handle of the plastic spoon was a very small spoon shape which the drug users discovered held the perfect amount for one hit of cocaine, heroin or methamphetamine. The back end of the spoon held about a quarter of a gram.

Armando tested the meth; he snorted a hit and waited to feel the effect as he loaded the car. He began to feel it, he was in ecstasy. He telephoned Gerry and gave him the code to release the money. He had to wait a while before he could drive back to New Hampshire. Armando and Leflore waited for Adrian to receive a call verifying that the transaction went through. It was after nine before he decided to drive back to the cabin.

He was traveling with two hundred pounds of methamphetamine that the chemist created in his lab. He had to go through the border and he was worried that he may look suspicious. His mind kept turning the question over: *What if they notice my worry? What if they stop me? I'll go to jail for twenty years the way the courts are treating dealers today. No, I'll make it. I'll get through with no problem.* He was determined to get through. He would shortly see what would happen.

***

When Armando pulled up at the crossing, he had his identification ready. He was now going to enter the United States.

"Hi, here is my license."

"Thank you sir, I see here that you live in Massachusetts?"

"Yes, all my life."

"Are you visiting Canada on business?"

"Yes I am, my company has me consult here from time to time, more often lately. I hate the drive, though."

"Yes it is a long drive. OK, sir, go ahead."

Armando had crossed the international border with two hundred pounds of meth hidden in his car. That would convert into over one million dollars each of income after it was cut and distributed. He smiled and was proud of himself.

***

Once across the border without a problem, he drove directly to the camp and arrived at about three o'clock on Monday morning. He parked and entered the camp.

There was a large party going on which probably started after Armando left the camp to go to Canada on Saturday night. Armando knew that Gerry was known for these types of parties with plenty of speed, cocaine and plenty of booze and broads.

"What the fuck are you doing here?" yelled Gerry

"What do you mean? I just got back from my trip. You remember my trip, don't you?"

"I told you that you don't come here. You go to the shack," Gerry stated.

"What shack? Nobody told me anything."

"OK, calm down, I must have forgot to tell you or assumed that Steve told you. Did you have any problems?"

"I had no problems until now. You know, you tell me to relax, but as soon as I opened the door you started yelling at me. I drive for hours on this trip and you're yelling at me, fuck you."

"I'm sorry Armando, I thought you knew. We never bring the stuff here. I have two hundred acres here. I have a small shack that looks like nothing about a mile back in the woods.

That's where you go with the product and we unload there, directly to the lab that I have set up."

"OK, I'll take it back there," Armando said.

"Next time, stop and telephone us when you are a few minutes away from here. We'll meet you at the shack. I'll ride with you and direct you there this time."

***

They drove out of the road that led to Gerry's camp, took a right on the main road and entered the next dirt road. They drove for about a mile on the very heavily treed, dirt road until they came to an old shack.

As they drove up, Armando saw the shack and was surprised. "What the hell is this? That place looks like it is falling down."

"That's cover, Armando. You remember the money I spent and didn't say where it went except that it was for everyone's protection? Wait till you see where that investment money went."

"We just trusted you, Gerry, to do what was necessary."

"I did. Follow me."

They went behind the shed to an area that was covered with leaves and dirt. Gerry grabbed a broom through the window of the shack. He began sweeping the area below the window. Armando could see a bulkhead begin to come into view. After he was finished sweeping, Gerry reached down and opened the bulkhead.

They walked down to what was an underground lab, furnished, ventilated and out in the middle of nowhere.

"This is perfect, Gerry."

"Thank you Armando, I'm proud of this lab."

"Gerry, what if you get busted?"

"They could hit this place and I would never be involved. This land is under a holding company that is owned by another holding company and it goes on and on like that. They can never tie me to this land. The land that I live on with my camp is a separate parcel altogether."

"We always knew you were smart."

"We, who is we?"

"All the guys; don't get crazy on me, Gerry."

"OK, I understand. Let's unload this shit and I can start on the cuts tomorrow."

Armando and Gerry unloaded the car and counted out the two hundred pounds of meth.

***

For the next few months, Armando did his runs to Canada and never ran into any problems. He became well known in that country as a representative of a US company, by the border people and others.

Armando was comfortable in his new role as the main importer of methamphetamine to the United States. He began to know certain people at the border and would go to their booths. These men knew his cover story of being sent to Canada quite often by his company on consulting jobs. What was even more perfect for Armando was that they believed every word of his story. Everything was working perfectly.

~*~

Back at the Hospital, 1979

"Nurse, did you say something about this man being involved with illicit drugs?"

"No, Doctor, I said that I overheard some detective's saying something about methamphetamine in relation to this patient."

"I want you to take some blood and have an analysis for narcotics right away."

"OK, Doctor, I will take care of that."

The head nurse took the blood and had it quickly analyzed.

"Doctor, the blood shows heavy concentrations of methamphetamine."

"That's why we are having so much trouble," answered the doctor. "Nurse, we're going to stop this operation. We're having too many complications sneaking in on us. I'll close him up. We'll have to give his body twenty-four hours to get rid of that crap. It is causing his arteries to open under the slightest pressure. We will lose him if we don't wait."

"OK, Doctor, any bed orders?"

"Yes, no visitors. Keep him asleep, quiet and take his vitals regularly. I will schedule the operation in about twenty-four hours. He should be much better by then and his system should be rid of those drugs. One other thing; please notify the police department. That detective, what was his name? Oh, Detective Lijoi, we've worked with him before. Tell him that tomorrow afternoon he can have a few minutes with him and advise him about the drugs in his system. I want the patient sleeping until then."

"That's fine, Doctor. I'll write up the orders and get him a room."

***

Armando continued to dream about his life and what led up to his being stabbed in the back, while at the beach.

~*~

Tuesday May 22, 1979

Armando Kiefer while in the hospital was on and off the operating table to clear his system of methamphetamine; the drug that kept him happy was now killing him.

The doctor agreed to allow the detectives to speak with him for a few minutes before his next operation, possibly the last he would ever have. This operation may kill him.

***

Detective Ernie Lijoi Sr. was working for the City of Quincy, Massachusetts as a Deep Cover Investigator (DCI). Deep cover, in this case, is when the undercover agent lives different two lives. The normal life of a man with a family , a home, children and all the daily ups and downs that go along with those benefits of life. Along with that he lives a street life. Ernie lived under the guise of Eddie Pannoni, a cover name with a different address in a deferent town from where he actually lived, different street friends and a complete identity in every way with all of complications that are found on the street. These were the two lives of Detective Ernie Lijoi as Eddie Pannoni.

Ernie under the name of Eddie Pannoni had become well known and respected on the street as a buyer and dealer in guns and drugs. It was also well known that he was not a user of drugs. His excuse was that he put the money in his pocket, not up his nose or arm. His street story was that he sold the drugs he purchased in New York when he returned there on his regular trips, very much like a dealer that gets his drugs in another state or country.

Because of being raised in a New York neighborhood that was run and controlled by the Mafia, he had developed an attitude and accent that represented New York as did his style of speaking and dealing with people. These were his largest assets on the street.

Detective Lijoi was a white male, about thirty-four years of age, five feet eight inches tall, dark brown curly hair in an afro style and a dark brown beard. He dressed in a way that fit into the situation or case that he was working on at the time. It was working well for him, the department and any and all agencies, federal or local.

During this particular time, Ernie and his team of detectives from the Quincy Police Department were getting ready to close in on a group of drug people believed to be involved with the smuggling of illicit narcotics.

Ernie had been doing surveillance and investigating this group of methamphetamine dealers and other cases for several months. He would receive a break in the case during his upcoming conversation with Armando Kiefer, a victim of a multiple stabbing which happened on the beach in Quincy.

***

The two detectives, Lijoi and Griswold were directed to the room where Mr. Kiefer was sleeping.

"Detectives, he's still asleep, but the doctor said that you should speak with him before he goes in for the operation, in case he doesn't make it. I'll give him a shot that will make him aware of you men for a few minutes."

"Thank you, Nurse."

The nurse gave Armando the shot and within minutes he began to wake up. He spoke in a slow, easy and soft tone. He was still a little drowsy.

"Who are you guys?"

"I am Detective Lijoi and this is Detective Griswold."

"Lijoi, that sounds familiar; I've heard of you."

"That's possible, but we are here to find out what happened to you. Who did this to you?"

"Look, I don't know exactly who did this, but I have a few suspicions and suspicions do not help anyone so I'll keep them to myself."

"If that's the way you want it, Armando that's fine with us," stated Detective Lijoi

Detective Griswold then asked; "By the way, we have your car. Are you aware of what we found hidden in the door walls of the car?"

"I guess it was inevitable. We couldn't keep going forever. Yes, I know what you found."

"How would you describe it, sir?" asked Lijoi

"Methamphetamine, probably more then you have ever seen," stated Armando

"Yes, you're right about that. Thirty pounds to be exact," stated Detective Lijoi.

"How did you get a legal search warrant to search my car?" asked Armando.

"You were stabbed by an unknown assailant. We applied on the bases of the odor of marijuana coming from your car when we found it. From there we found the meth and that was enough to confirm who you are."

"OK, that sounds legit. I was smoking grass in the car. I guess you got me," Armando said.

"To the tune of twenty years at least," said Detective Lijoi.

"How can we work this out?" asked Armando.

"There is nothing that we can do for you, Mr. Kiefer."

"How about my doing something for you?"

"What do you mean?" asked Lijoi

"I can bring down the largest crank or methamphetamine, as you call it, operation that you have ever seen, one that spreads from New York to Canada and all the states in between."

"Mr. Kiefer, Armando, that sounds very good, but you have to get well first and you have a very serious operation to go through."

"Yeah, but after the operation and when I'm well enough, I can work with you guys instead of going to jail."

"Yeah, we can do that later. You take care of yourself first. Get yourself well and then we will see if you are serious."

"I'll show you how serious I am. Have you ever heard of a man called Mr. Enrique Risotino, aka, the Musketeer, half Spanish and half Italian guy? He lives here in your city."

Det. Lijoi looked at Det. Griswold because this is the name of the man that they were building a case on and only needed confirmation from an informant that he was seriously involved in distribution of meth.

"He has in his possession several pounds of meth right now."

"That's easy to say about anyone. How do we know that you are close enough to him to have this information? Can you describe him? His car? His home? What does it all look like?" asked Lijoi

"That's easy. His house is a large two-story red home with white trim and a black roof, a very wide driveway with two Corvettes', one red and one black. He has two guard dogs that are well trained and vicious as hell. He is half Spanish and half Italian, thirty years old, six feet one inch tall, one hundred and eighty pounds, black hair and brown eyes and he lives at #12 Federal Street in Quincy."

"Where does he keep the drugs?" asked det. Griswold

"That's the best part; he has a large safe in the cellar where his lab is and he keeps his supplies and meth in that safe."

Armando was beginning to get groggy again and the detectives could tell.

"Armando, you rest now, we will talk when you are better able to speak. Get yourself well."

Armando closed his eyes and fell off to sleep quickly. The dream of his life continued.

Chapter 6

The Search

Tuesday May 22, 1979

As soon as the detectives arrived back at the office, Det. Lijoi took out the file containing all of the information gathered by him and his team on Mr. Enrique Risotino. He confirmed the information from Mr. Armando Kiefer and added him as the third informant on the search warrant application.

According to this information, Mr. Risotino was connected to a group or part of a group that was importing methamphetamine through the Canadian border. Mr. Risotino was in some way associated with or tied into the French Mafia. Much of this information was supposition and would be confirmed at a later date. The current facts were there and confirmed by others. That's what gives the warrant its strength. Kiefer's confirmation of the facts on hand would make him a reliable informant, usable in the future, if he lived.

***

The French Mafia consists of Frenchmen and Italians who live and grew up in Canada. They were believed to be connected to the Boston and Rhode Island Mafia and thereby connected to the New York Families of the Mafia.

Most of this Mafia information was merely supposition that would someday be checked and verified by the federal agencies. At least that was what Ernie thought at the time. Ernie had no idea how far this upcoming search and arrest would take him into the world of myths about the drug that made up the world of methamphetamine.

Methamphetamine is a difficult drug to deal with. Depending on the source for the drug it can be a yellowish crystal to as pure white and crystalline as cocaine, cheaper to purchase and even more addictive.

***

The detectives were parked outside of the home of a Mr. Enrique Risotino, aka, the Musketeer, half Spanish and half Italian, thirty years old, six feet one inch tall, one hundred and eighty pounds, black hair and brown eyes. He had no criminal record and lived at #12 Federal Street in Quincy. The night was calm, the sky was clear and the weather was perfect for working. The temperature in the mid sixties was comfortable and nice to feel after the long cold winter.

The house was a large two-story, painted red with white trip and a black roof. A very wide driveway that had two Corvettes' parked on it, one red and one black. Kiefer stated that there were guard dogs, although they did not see them.

Detective Jerry Gibson, the fingerprints expert and Detective Jack Wade, the photography expert were in one car. Detective Rick Bradshaw, the electronics expert was in another car with Detective Carl Robinson, the expert on locks and safes. Detective Ernie Lijoi, the narcotics expert and Detective Henry Griswold the firearm expert were in the third car.

They each had their own call sign to be used for their radio communications, designated by an "N" to represent narcotics and called November on the radio with a number for each man.

Ernie contacted the group, "November 7 to the team, give me one key of your mike, if everyone is ready."

Ernie heard the microphone key from each car click, one after the other: *click, click.*

The other two cars were ready to hit the house. "Does anyone see any dogs?"

No reply, no one could see any dogs.

"Henry, I forgot to ask for some dog officers to come along."

"Just call and request them. It shouldn't take long."

Ernie switched the radio to the normal police frequency and requested the men he needed.

"Nov. 7 to control."

"What can I do for you, 7?"

"I need at least two dog officers here a. s. a. p., I forgot to call them."

"You're on that thing you gave me the info on?"

"Yes."

"Stand by, I have someone here now."

The radio went back to its normal discussions and coverage while Ernie and the team waited.

"Control to November 7."

"7."

"They're on the way. You know the vehicle that they will be in, right?"

"Yes, thanks for the help."

***

A few minutes later, two men pulled up in a small van. They spoke with Ernie, said hi to the other men and began getting all dressed in padding. The padding was to prevent injuries in the event they were confronted by the dogs when they hit the house. Ernie had been told about these dogs and several of them had observed them on the property during surveillance.

They had a plan that Ernie constructed and they hoped that it went smoothly.

Two of the detectives and a dog officer went to the back of the house, walking through the seventy-five feet of forested trees that separated the house from the main road.

The second car of detectives would hold back for a few minutes until the third car was ready for them.

In the third car was Ernie, Henry and the second dog officer. They would drive up the driveway and calmly walk up to the front door and ring the bell.

Once at the front door, the second car of detectives would join them, giving them back-up as needed.

They saw that the first car of detectives was in place.

Ernie drove up to the house and parked in a way that blocked both of the Corvettes from backing out and no cars could get out of the garage.

Ernie and Henry approached the front door, rang the bell and waited. They could hear people in the house talking and music playing. The sound made Ernie and Henry think that a party was going on. This was good for the detectives. Maybe the resident would think that they were more guests coming to the party.

The door opened. A man was standing there who fit the description of Enrique Risotino, aka The Musketeer, aka Ricky.

"Who are you guys?"

"Mr. Risotino, we have a search warrant for your home, cars and any and all property present in the home or on the property."

"Shit, what the fuck is this about? I have guests here. Can't we do this another time?"

"Sorry, sir," the officers walked into the house. Ernie contacted the other teams via portable radio and told them to come in, that the area was secured.

"Will everyone in the house please gather in the living room?"

The officers walked around the interior and exterior making sure that everyone was there in the living room.

"Henry, will you search everyone, please?"

"I'll have to get a female officer to come down."

"That's OK, take care of it, will you?"

"It's done, boss."

"Mr. Risotino, where are the dogs?"

"Oh, they won't bother you, they're in the cellar."

"Is the door to the cellar unlocked?"

"Yes, it is. They will not bother you. I give you my word."

"Thank you for your word, but I think those dogs are guarding your most precious possessions."

"No, no, look I have a gun collection, I have collectable's coming out of my ass."

"Will you control the dogs for us or do we have to do it?"

"Fuck you, control them yourself if you can."

Ernie spoke with the dog officer for a couple of minutes. The officer left the house temporarily. After two minutes he returned with a dart gun.

"Good, that will work."

They approached the cellar door, opened it slightly and saw that the dogs were standing at the foot of the stairs. They looked up and began to come up the stairs fast, barking and angry.

The two dog officers took care of the dogs by allowing one dog to get his head through the door while they shot him with the dart. He went right to sleep. They followed the same procedure with the second dog.

After the dog officers took the dogs out to the van and placed them into cages, they were able to remove their protective padding. The house was now as safe as possible.

***

Ernie believed that Risotino was a speed dealer, but was not sure how large a dealer he was. Ernie didn't know if he would find grams, ounces or pounds of the methamphetamine in the house. Each weight would indicate how large a dealer he actually was.

One team of officers stayed with the people on the first floor in the living room. They would be responsible for keeping the written list of evidence gathered. This list would later be attached to the affidavit and would become a part of the court records. The second team went up to the second floor to search. Ernie and Henry went to the cellar to search and they would also search the first floor when they finished the cellar. The two uniformed men had their job to do. One covered the front door and the other assisted whichever team needed any help.

As soon as they entered the cellar they could see tables with shelving above them. On the shelves were bags and boxes of what appeared to be a cutting agent.

"Henry, it looks like we hit a cutting lab; this guy must be bigger than I thought."

"I think so, take a look over there," Henry pointed to the back wall.

Standing against the back wall was a six foot tall safe, about three foot wide with two doors.

Ernie walked over and checked the door to see if it was unlocked. It was locked tight.

Ernie called up to the first floor and asked the uniformed officer to bring down Mr. Risotino.

"Mr. Risotino, what is the combination to the safe?"

"Does your search warrant include the inside of the safe?"

"Yes sir, it does where it indicates, "Any and all storage areas."

"I don't agree that includes the safe."

"Look, I'm not screwing around anymore with you, asshole. Open the safe yourself and I'll put in my report that you were cooperative. Make us spend the money and time for an expert to come down and open it for us, you become uncooperative. It's up to you."

"You give me your word that it will go in the report?"

"Yes, I'll state in my report that you opened the safe freely and were cooperative. That's the best I can offer now."

"I have a better offer." Stated Mr. Risotino

"What are you talking about?" asked Ernie

"Can we talk privately?" asked Risotino

"No, speak and we will listen" stated Ernie

"There is two hundred and fifty thousand dollars in that safe, in cash and gold ingots. Let me go and drive off. I will go to New Jersey and I will never come back here to Massachusetts."

"I bet you wouldn't come back, but that's bribery." Said Ernie

"That's all I have going for me at the moment." replied Risotino

"We will take the money, the drugs and you. We don't play this game in that way. We may also add an additional charge of bribery if you decide to be any more of an asshole."

Risotino reached over and unlocked the safe. It was obvious that he was upset about his mistake of offering the bribe.

Ernie and Henry looked into the safe. They saw at least three pounds of methamphetamine which was probably cut into three from one pound by Risotino.

"Henry, cuff him and give him his rights. He's under arrest for distribution," stated Ernie.

Risotino turned to Ernie and asked what could be done for him.

Ernie looked at Henry, "What can we do for him?"

"Ernie, we can give him a comfortable cell until he has his preliminary hearing and then we can let the state house him in one of their comfortable cells."

"How does that sound, Mr. Risotino?" asked Henry.

"OK, guys, I guess I'll wait for my lawyer."

Ernie replied, "Now that's the smartest thing you have said yet."

"Your lawyer will be the best person to speak for you," replied Henry.

Risotino stated: "Yeah, but I still would like to make some kind of a deal."

Ernie said, "Look, you're better off waiting until you speak with your lawyer. Once you do, if you still want to make a deal, we can talk. To show good faith, here's what I am going to do; I'll release all of your guests that are not holding on their person. That's my first move. It's your turn, but wait for your lawyer before you speak."

Besides the three pounds of methamphetamine that was found in the safe, the detectives found the cash, two hundred and fifty nine thousand dollars, more cutting agents, two scales and packaging material. In the house the detectives found three pounds of marijuana and eight grams of cocaine, each gram in a separate area of the house.

Henry observed a box on a shelf in the basement. He opened it and found thirteen needles and syringes which are commonly used to inject cocaine, meth or heroin. The detectives confiscated all of the weapons and narcotics in the house.

One guest had four additional grams on his person; this guest was arrested. The rest of the guests were released after the officers obtained and verified their personal information such as names, addresses and dates of birth.

A list was made of the evidence and the two prisoners were transported to the station, booked and placed in cells.

***

While the officers were taking care of the evidence and doing preliminary reports for the morning court case, Enrique Risotino was booked and allowed to make a phone call to his lawyer.

Shortly after the call to his attorney, the lawyer, Mr. Jonathan Dubois showed up at the station asking to speak with the arresting officers, Detective Ernie Lijoi and Detective Henry Griswold. He was asked to wait a few minutes.

Once the detectives had all of the evidence cataloged, checked and locked away in the evidence room it was time to speak with Mr. Enrique Risotino and his attorney.

After explaining the basic charges to the attorney and advising him as to the evidence gathered at the home, the attorney demanded to speak with his client privately. The detectives left the room.

"Enrique, when did you get into this kind of shit?"

"I have always been dealing."

"I can probably get you a deal, but you may have to do a few years. What do you think?" asked Dubois

"I don't want to do a day."

Dubois said: "I'm afraid that this guy Lijoi has you pretty good. He's not the type to give in easily."

"I want to speak with them. I have information that will make them drop my charges if I help them. I know it goes on all the time, why not for me?"

"I know you. I know that you are gonna do what you want in spite of my advice. I have to tell you not to speak with them and to let me handle it." stated the attorney.

"Yeah, sure, I'll pay you twenty or thirty thousand and then I'll wind up working with them anyway. I may as well cut some of that out. You draw up the agreement after I make the deal."

Dubois said: "I'll do whatever you want, but I am opposed to what you are planning."

"Call that detective in, will you?" asked Ricky Risotino.

The attorney walked to the door, opened it and asked the Detectives to join him in the room.

"Are you gentlemen all set?" asked Ernie.

"No, we're not in agreement. My attorney wants me to go through the process. I figure I save money by cutting the process down."

Detective Lijoi asked, "Mr. Risotino, two things; first, you should listen to your Mr. Dubois. Second, how do you expect to save money?"

"By cooperating with you in exchange for jail time." answered Ricky Risotino.

"An interesting offer; do you agree with this as his attorney, Mr. Dubois?" asked Ernie.

"No, not at all, I think he should wait it out, but he's paying the bills. I only do the work."

"If that is so, then you are only required to set up the parameters of the deal such as whether or not he serves time in exchange for information." stated Ernie.

"That's true."

Ernie said: "Risotino you should speak with me and Henry privately, now that we have established your intent."

Dubois: "That's fine with me."

"Mr. Dubois, I will advise the District Attorney. You and he can work out the details on your end. Now it would be better for your client if you have no knowledge of exactly what he is doing." stated Henry.

"I'll agree to that and I will speak with the D.A. tomorrow," Dubois replied.

"Thank you, sir," Ernie said.

Mr. Dubois left the room and the station house and had no more contact with either Lijoi or Griswold until the trial.

***

"OK, Mr. Risotino, we will talk for a while, but in a couple of weeks we'll get even deeper into it. For now just give me a brief summary of what you can do for us in exchange for jail time?"

"Have you guys ever heard of the 'Clean Bloods'?" asked Risotino.

"The motorcycle group?" asked Henry

"Yes, they're all over the country, different chapters in every state. Have you ever heard of the Three Musketeers? Have you heard of the Devil's Angels?" asked Risotino.

"Yes, the Devil's are another motorcycle group, but not the Musketeers. Who are they?" asked Ernie.

"The Musketeers are a small group of three men that import all the methamphetamine into this part of the country from Canada."

"First, are you a musketeer? Second, how do the others fit in?" asked Ernie.

"Risotino laughed: "No, I'm no Musketeer." I know they say that about me on the street, but no, I wish I was. In answer to your second question, these groups are the protection for the Musketeers and for the Italian Mafia that works from Canada and throughout the States."

"OK, that's some information that we have. How can you help us with that?" asked Ernie.

Ricky stated: "I can cut you into the Musketeers. They need people to help them during the war that is going on and you would fit right in."

Henry stated: "That sounds pretty good, but I would have to bring the Federal Drug Enforcement Agency in on something like this and you wouldn't be off the hook until it was all over."

"I don't care who you bring in, as long as I don't do any time," stated Ricky.

"We'll discuss this further, after your arraignment," Ernie said.

Risotino was taken back to his cell and the officers made a few notes about their discussion with him, then left the station for the night.

***

Henry expected the next day to be a day of conferences, negotiations and checking out information from Mr. Rosotino.

"We don't have to worry about him for a while, Henry."

"Why's that, Ernie?"

"He'll be arraigned tomorrow morning and then the D.A. will have to speak with his attorney before we get a crack at him again, but it will happen."

"That's good; I'll do some reports tomorrow."

"OK, see you then. Listen, Henry, let's stop by the hospital and see how Armando is. He seems to know what he's talking about and he is now a reliable informant under the law since we confirmed all that he told us was fact."

"OK, Ernie, we can check on him sometime tomorrow. Anything else that you can think of?"

"No, I guess we have done enough for today. I'll see you in the morning."

Chapter 7

The War

Tuesday May 9, 1978 Armando's Dream Continues

Armando had been doing his runs into Canada for over a year. He and his partners were making more money than he ever imagined. However, there were rumblings of the French Mafia trying to find out where they were getting their methamphetamine. This could present a problem if they found out, but Armando didn't let it bother him.

"Armando, are you sure you feel safe going up there? Those frogs will be looking for you," stated Gerry.

"They don't even know me, but if it makes you feel better, I'll take Steve and we can check in with his friend in the French Mafia while we are there."

"That may be a good idea. Maybe he can give us some insight into what's going on since he speaks the language."

That afternoon Armando and Steve took off for Canada.

***

Armando had developed some habits over the past year. One was to stay at the Mount Royal Hotel in Montreal whenever he had to make a trip to Canada.

After checking in they met at the bar. They had a few drinks and smoked a few bones. They did a few hits of meth and were crankin.

About three hours later Steve decided that he wanted to see his parents' farm/camp which now belonged to him and his brother Gerry.

"What kind of a farm is it?"

"It was an animal farm with one hundred acres of crops, but when my parents were alive they also used it as a summer camp for kids. We always had a lot of kids to play with."

"Sounds like a good idea to get away from the bar for a while and take a break. Let's go."

Steve explained that the farm had a nice house and sat on three hundred acres of land. There are also three bunk houses and two barns with a bunch of rusty farm equipment. If needed, the property could accommodate a couple of hundred people. They drove to the farm which was a short distance outside of Montreal.

"Turn here and stop. I'll open the gate" said Steve

Armando turned onto a short road and stopped at the entrance gate to the property.

Steve got out of the car to open the gate and all hell broke loose. Steve was hit. Shots were ricocheting everywhere.

Armando got out of the car and ran into the tall weeds.

Steve was laying on the cold ground bleeding. Armando could see him from the weeds and he could hear him moaning for help. The moans kept growing louder and louder until he heard another two shots and then there were no more moans.

Shots were still being fired. Armando could feel and hear the bullets whizzing by his head. They hit the ground all around him. Armando moaned a couple of times then yelled out as though he were hit and laid on the ground quietly.

Armando could barely see the car because of the glare from the headlight, but then some men stepped into the light and he could make out that there were three of them. The three men began to speak, but they spoke in French and Armando didn't know any French.

***

Armando remained in the field for two hours after the men who were doing the shooting left the area. He was cursing himself for not learning the French language. He may have been able to pick up on what those men said. It was well after three in the morning when he finally decided it would be safe to try and get away.

Armando crawled back toward the car and as he moved closer he could see Steve's body riddled with bullets, laying on the ground in front of the car like a bloody rag. Armando got to the car and the first thing he did was open the glove compartment where he had his .357 magnum handgun.

He cheeked it to be sure it was loaded and then he went around the car to check on Steve. He could see the blood surrounding his body, seeping into the ground slower then water. Steve was without movement, Steve was dead. Along with the numerous holes in his body, he had a large hole in his head. The blood was no longer escaping. It had all come out and there was some gray matter lying on the ground which Armando thought was Steve's brain.

Armando got back into the car and drove back to New Hampshire. He didn't want to telephone Gerry. He wanted to tell him in person. It was Wednesday morning, May 10, 1978 and he had to wake Gerry and tell him that his brother had been killed. Armando would never forget that day.

He made it to the border and pulled up to the booth of one of the border guards that he knew.

"Hi, you look strange, like you have been through a battle."

"Yes, I have been. This job I'm working on in Montreal is driving me crazy."

"Well, go ahead home and get some rest, you look like you need it."

***

Armando got through the border safely and continued toward New Hampshire. He arrived at the camp and walked in.

Gerry was sitting at the table going over some music notes when he looked up at Armando.

"Hi, Armando, where's Steve?"

"I have some bad news, Gerry."

"Did you guys have a damn accident?"

"No. There's no easy way to say this. Steve is dead."

"What did you say?" as Gerry almost fell off of his chair at the kitchen table.

"They caught us at your mother's house. Steve was going to show it to me. When we pulled up to the fence he got out and all hell broke loose. They shot him and I am sure that they think they shot me too."

"Where the fuck is he?"

"He's still there in the grass."

"Let's go and get him. We're going back up there. I have a friend that will fly us up, he owns his own plane."

***

They went in the friend's plane and flew directly to the farm in Canada. They landed in a field beside the house. Armando walked in front of Gerry to the gate where the shooting took place.

"Get my brother out of there, please. Clean those bugs off of him." Gerry began to break down in tears.

"Gerry, do you have a shovel at the house and maybe some plastic?"

"Yeah, yeah" as he wiped his eyes.

"Where are they?"

"The barn, I want to stay with him. You go and get what we need."

"No problem, I'll be right back."

Armando went up to the barn, got what he needed and returned.

"Gerry, you stay in the car. I'll bury him."

"No, I'll help you. You see that hill over there about five hundred feet?"

"Yes."

"We'll take him there. We used to play together there when we were kids. I never thought I would be burying him there."

"I really don't know exactly where you are talking about. Let's wrap him with the plastic and carry him. You go first."

They picked up the body and Gerry directed them to the area where he wanted to bury Steve. When Gerry was satisfied that they dug a hole that was deep enough, they placed Steve in it and covered him up. ***The body they buried that day has never been recovered.***

***

"This is a pretty spot Gerry, he will love it here."

"Armando, this is a war. You realize that, don't you?"

"Yeah, I do. What do you want to do?"

"First, we speak with some friends of mine. I have a car for emergencies in the barn. We'll use that car and go to some friends of mine. I'll tell the pilot he can go, to leave us here."

"Gerry, shouldn't you give yourself a couple of days to rest, after all this is quite a shock."

"Armando, I know you mean well, but I have watched my father die, my mother die and now my only brother. Someone is going to pay for this one."

"OK, Gerry, I'm with you no matter what it takes."

"Good, now let's get the car from the barn and take off."

"Who do we speak to first?"

"We will see my brothers-in-arms, the 'Clean Bloods'. They'll know who did this or have a better idea than you do. You said that they spoke French, that's all you could hear, you couldn't make out the faces of anyone because of the lights coming from the car and your position. I have to be sure of the information that we have."

"That's exactly what happened."

***

They got into the car and Gerry directed Armando to a small tavern, located outside of Montreal City. Armando parked and Gerry got out.

"Armando you wait here a minute. These guys don't know you."

Armando nodded in agreement.

Gerry entered the tavern. After a few minutes he walked out and signaled for Armando to come inside.

Armando entered a large room with tables and chairs spread around the floor. The bar was located on the back wall. It was long and narrow with men standing along it, drinking and enjoying themselves. The juke box was playing "The Great Pretender" by the Platters. Armando for some reason thought to himself that this was an appropriate song.

Armando followed Gerry to a door behind the bar which opened to a small room. Three men were sitting waiting for Gerry to return with Armando.

These three men were bikers, the chapter leaders, the president, vice president and (tête de l'escadron de la mort) the head of the death squad for the 'Clean Bloods'. They all spoke in broken English with a French accent and they had that Italian look about them; dark hair, eyes and skin tone. They even used their hands when they spoke.

They were introduced to Armando as "Brute", "Whiskers" and "Tat". Their nicknames were all that they used. Anyone that began inquiring about their real names was considered a danger and a threat. They eliminated this type of person, no matter who they were.

The three men that were sitting at the table questioned Armando extensively. They asked what kind of cars? Did they have lights on top or window lights? They asked many other questions that Armando could not answer because of the gravity of the situation at the time. They indicated that they understood his position

After the questioning, Brute began telling Armando and Gerry his opinion.

"Gerry, here's what we know to be fact. There's an elite, nameless group known only as "The Hit Squad" that is run and controlled by the Canadian Mounted Police. They are very effective in keeping people from out of the country under control and their specialty is narcotics dealers, although they do not limit themselves to that. They are not above creating a rift between groups and picking up the pieces that are left over. There is a good possibility that they saw your brother and Armando at the hotel and passed on the information to the French Mafia. We heard that there was a contract on your brother a while back. We have not heard a word about Armando, not yet."

"Why would they get involved in protecting the meth business?" asked Gerry.

"The Mounties don't get involved unless they are unable to prove you wrong in the Canadian Courts. When that happens, things are turned over to The Hit Squad."

"My brother was told by a friend that the French Mafia was after him and had a contract on him. I should have mentioned that."

"Yes, you should have. So let's say the Mafia did this. How do you want to handle it, Gerry?" asked Tat, the head of the hit squad.

"That's why I'm here. We're supposed to support each other's effort. The same way we support each other financially by turning in a percentage of our profits every year to the organization. We are one of the largest supporters that you men have," stated Gerry.

"We know that and we are very comfortable protecting our interests, you know that. You're placing it in our hands. Don't get all upset. You just lost your brother, try and relax we know it's not easy. This will be taken care of." promised Whiskers and the other men agreed.

"We don't want to give you a lot to do right now, but go back to New Hampshire and close up the camp. Reopen the house at the farm. Those 300 acres, the large barn, the bunk house and the main house will be of use to us. We have time to set up," stated Brute.

Gerry and Armando decided to drive back and follow the directions of the group.

~*~

Thursday May 11, 1978

Armando and Gerry got out of bed, had breakfast and packed up a few things including ammunition and all the guns in the camp. This included three 12 gauge shotguns, four 9mm handguns and a 357 magnum.

They told Damian what they were about to do and he wanted to go along, but Gerry wanted him to stay behind and look after the camp.

"Damian, you're the closest thing I have left to a brother and I don't want to see you involved with this shit. You have enough problems with your seizures and all."

"OK Gerry, I'll stay here and do as you ask."

Armando telephoned Jimmy before they left for the farm and told him what was going on. Armando told Jimmy that he would not be hearing from Gerry or him for a while, not until this was taken care of and Steve's death was avenged.

Armando and Gerry packed up the car and left for the farm. When they arrived, there were at least two hundred men hanging around, all packing guns of one kind or another.

They were all ready to go to war with the French Mafia. The farm location would be the headquarters until a solution was found.

***

The set up was that the French Mafia was associated with the New York Mafia Families and the motorcycle group called The Devil's Angels was the strong arm for the New York Families.

The Devil's Angels would fight on behalf of the Mafia in this war, the Mounties would be in the middle and the Musketeers would be with the 'Clean Bloods'. The sides were figured out and the war began. There were many killings on both sides most of which Armando would never forget.

While this was going on, Jimmy the druggist contacted his brother and told him that they would need all the help that they could get. His brother, Joey Orbits, was associated with the Teamsters Union and good friends with the head of the Italian Mafia in Boston and the head man, Mr. Johnny Anettano. Joey stated that he would do whatever he could.

Because of Joey's associations, a warning went out to the French Mafia to lay off or there would be grave consequences. These types of warnings went out on both sides in an effort to stop an all-out war. The next step would be a possible sit down to discuss the disagreements.

Gerry would have nothing to do with a sit down. He wanted blood. His brother's death affected him in a very strong way and Gerry wanted the men that did it.

***

That night they had a meeting and it was decided that Armando would continue the deliveries in New England, USA. He would make a trip the next day.

Chapter 8

Dy-No-Mite

Friday May 12, 1978

Armando had several locations to deliver to. He was about to leave to go and pick up the pure meth from the chemists' representative, Adrian Leflore, when Gerry asked him where he was going.

"I have to make the pickup."

"Oh, I forgot, with all that's going on. We have it here. Adrian loads a remote rocket and sends it the two miles over the trees and the river to the farm, from the roof of his building. While we're here, we'll get the deliveries that way. It's safer for the time being."

"You're kidding me? He must have to send a ton of rockets?"

"No, why would I kid you? He sends a total of ten rockets, each containing five pounds then we return the rockets to him and he does it all over again. That guy is a genius he comes up with more ideas than anyone I have ever met."

"How often does he send them?"

"As often as we need them. We deliver the cash and he delivers the goods over the trees."

"Is it all cut and ready to go?"

"Yes, I think it's all done. Here, take it".

Gerry opened the refrigerator and handed Armando a six pound jar of speed as crystalline as it could be.

Armando separated and cut the six pounds into eighteen pounds in no time.

"Gerry, I would love to see one of those rockets come in."

"Next time we get a delivery."

"I'm out of here."

***

Armando left and made a first stop in Vermont where he met with Sam Roller who was the main man in Vermont. He supplied all of the dealers in Vermont after he cut down the meth. Roller was a white male, five feet eight inches tall, one hundred and thirty pounds, with a dark beard and mustache, was balding and had brown eyes.

Armando made all of his deliveries in that one day and his last was at the home of an old friend, Charlie (Red) Wilson. Red was a major distributor of meth. He also dealt with heroin and cocaine, selling to numerous dealers in the southern part of Massachusetts. He lived in Taunton and had an unassuming home in a quiet area.

Red was a white male, forty years of age, five feet nine inches tall, one hundred and forty pounds, red hair and eyebrows, light complexion and light blue eyes.

Armando got there late that day, it was his last stop. He walked in and crossed the living room then entered the kitchen. Sitting at the kitchen table with Red was another old friend, Billy (Nutty) Slipka.

Billy (Nutty) Slipka was a white male, thirty-four years of age, five feet eight inches tall, thin, one hundred and thirty pounds, dark hair and brown eyes. Nutty, as he was called, was a little crazy at times and at times very logical and sensitive, a complicated man.

"Nutty, how the fuck are you, man? I thought you were locked up," exclaimed Armando.

"Yeah, I was in jail, Armando, not any more. It's good to see you."

"Red, do you have some room for me here tonight? I don't want to impose, I can get a room, but I'm real tired. I've been driving all day. I delivered to Vermont, New Hampshire and several places in Mass."

"No problem, Armando, you can take the small bedroom unless you need the bigger one," offered Red.

"That's fine. I plan on just sleeping, no broads," stated Armando.

"Not me, man, I just broke out. I need to get laid!" exclaimed Nutty.

"Just be quiet, I gotta get some sleep. What do you mean you broke out?" asked Armando.

"I didn't think you were going to acknowledge that."

"What happened?"

"You know that broad, Maria? The one I was banging before I was arrested for attempted murder?" asked Nutty.

"Yeah, I know her, we spent a few interesting nights together," said Armando.

"Yeah, that's her. She said you had a small dick," Nutty laughed.

"OK, what happened with the break?"

"She brought in a .25 semi and I hid it. You know how lax they are in the local jail. I would have never gotten away with it at one of the state prisons. I hid it in back of my neck, under my collar with my hair hanging over it and on the way to court I broke away. I pulled the gun on one of the guards while we were alone. I took off with the cruiser he was transporting me in. Then I dropped the cruiser in an alley and stole some clothes off of a clothesline in the alley and left. I ain't goin back either."

"So now they want you for assault with a dangerous weapon and stealing a car as well as escaping."

"I don't give a fuck; they will never take me alive anyway."

"Did Red tell you what's going on in Canada?"

"Yes, he did, and I was thinking maybe I can be of help to you guys."

"Why not, you can drive up with me in the morning," stated Armando

"It's a deal, Armando, and thanks for the help," Nutty said

"No, thank you for offering to help us out. While you're in Canada and after things settle down I'm sure we can find a job for you with the organization."

"Hey, that shit is right up my alley," stated Nutty

"I'll see you guys in the morning."

"Armando, what about your wife, you didn't even mention her like you usually do, where is she?" asked Red.

"She took off with the kid. She got fed up with the business. I have a lawyer on it."

"Good luck with that. I lost mine and my kid for the same reason. I miss my kid."

"Yeah, I miss my son, but I'll fight to get him back."

"Be careful, women can be dangerous," cautioned Red.

"Yes, I know, that's why I'm staying out of it and away from it. The lawyer will handle everything."

"See you in the morning. Whoever gets up first goes and gets some coffee and donuts at Dunkies (Dunkin Donuts) as soon as they are awake." stated Red.

Armando and Nutty agreed.

~*~

Friday May 13, 1978

Armando was the first one up that morning. He dressed, got in the car and got plenty of Dunkin Donuts and coffee.

He returned to find everyone still sleeping. He wanted to get on the road so he began trying to wake Nutty up. Finally, after knocking and calling Nutty, he opened the door and saw Maria sitting at the edge of the bed trying to wake up.

"Maria, get him out of bed. I have to get on the road."

"OK, he may be a few minutes. He was talking about some plan he has to help you and your friend out in Canada."

"First of all, he should never have told you that he was going there. What you don't know you can't talk about. Secondly just get him going I want to get on the road."

"OK, give him a few minutes."

Armando walked back to the kitchen and Red was sitting at the table eating donuts. "Hi, Armando, did you get any jelly filled?"

"Yeah, I should have, I told her to give me a couple of dozen mixed."

"Oh, here's one. Listen, Nutty has changed, he's even crazier. Watch him, make sure he doesn't get himself killed. He's not a bad guy and maybe he'll pull out of this crazy attitude that he has."

"I'll do my best, but this is a war I'm in. They don't fuck around. The kids stuff is all over, these guys play for keeps."

***

Half an hour later Nutty walked out of the bedroom with Maria on his arm. They had some coffee and donuts before he kissed Maria goodbye.

"Maria, you come and visit me once I'm settled in. I'll call you in about a week or so."

"Is there some speed up there?"

They all laughed at her question. "There is enough to fill your mouth and keep going."

"Wow, call me as soon as you're settled. Armando, take care of him for me."

Armando shook his head, "I'll do the best I can." He and Nutty left the house and Nutty had what looked like a very bulky jacket. Armando didn't question him at that time. He was in too much of a hurry.

***

While on the road to Canada the two men discussed the weather and old times.

"Nutty, remember when I escaped from Plymouth?"

"You did, what happened? How did you do it?"

"It was a crazy and funny situation now that I think about it. At the time it was very serious."

"Tell me about it, we have the time."

~*~

Summer of 1970 Armando's Great Escape

"I was driving along peacefully, minding my own business, when I was stopped by a Plymouth Police Officer for a broken tail light. The officer ran my papers and came up with an arrest warrant for an Armando Kiefer. The officer informed me and placed me under arrest for a speeding ticket that was never paid.

"I was transported to the station and they towed my car. They booked me and I tried to tell them that it was not me. It must have been my father's ticket and he just forgot to pay it. The police would not listen to me. They said that the court would have to decide.

"From the police station, they took me over to the Plymouth Court House to appear before a judge. I was standing before the judge and he would not listen to me. He just told me that I would have a trial and the jury would decide. This was getting ridiculous. I blew my top with the judge and said, 'You asshole, I'm telling you this is not me and you're still gonna tie me up in the jail. In the end, you'll find out that it is not me. I have a life too.' The judge stood up and began yelling at the guards and they subdued me and cuffed me. I finally shut my mouth and decided that I was not gonna let this asshole win.

"I set up a plan.

"The court officer had to drive me to the jail where I was to stay until the trial. We got in the car and he was an OK guy. On the way there he bought me some cigarettes and even stopped to buy me a bottle of wine which I drank and he had a few pops from it. When it was empty, I placed the empty bottle under the car seat. The officer knew that the charges would eventually be dropped.

"At one point he pulled up to a stop light and stopped. I reached over, pushed the gear into park, opened the door and began to get out.

"The court officer stopped me by yelling at me. Not that he wanted me to stop and not take off, but he actually surprised me by saying: 'Please, don't hurt me, please, please don't hurt me.'

I turned to him and said: 'Hey, I wouldn't hurt a hair on your head. The court is wrong in this case and I am not sticking around to go through their bull shit', then I took off.

"During my travels, while I was running, I saw an old red truck with a tool box inside. I broke in and got a hammer, some other tools, a hacksaw and later I was able to get the cuffs off. That steel that those cuffs are made of is hard; it took forever to cut through it.

"I was an escapee for four days. Then I got word from a friend that the Sheriff had someone look into the case deeper and found that I was correct. The guy they wanted was my father.

"I was told not to worry and to turn myself in to the Quincy Police who would transport me to Plymouth and they would take care of the case.

"At the time, I was living on Fairview Street. I went home and called the Quincy Police.

"All Quincy knew was that I was an escapee. Four cruisers showed up and they cuffed me and took me back.

"When I arrived at the court house in Plymouth, the clerk was there and demanded that I be placed in FBI body cuffs which I never heard of before. They cuffed me around the waist down to my ankles and my hands. I could barely move. The court officer that I escaped from gave his orders from across the large room we were in. He was afraid to come near me.

"Once the court officer was satisfied with the way I was cuffed and chained up, they took me before the judge. The judge threw out the charge on the ticket that was my father's, but said that he could do nothing with the escape charge and I would have to go to court. He said that I escaped from an officer of the court, his clerk and the case would have to go to a trial."

"That must have pissed you off," said Nutty.

"It certainly did, but instead, I kept my cool and talked to the judge."

"I can almost imagine what you said, go on, tell me," stated Nutty.

"I said, Judge, 'I never harmed him. He was good to me. He stopped and bought me cigarettes and a bottle of wine before I went to the jailhouse for the night.'

"'Mr. Kiefer, you are telling me that he purchased a bottle of wine for you, a criminal, in a case before me. A criminal that he was transporting, he allowed you to drink the wine in his car prior to your escape?'

"'Yes, we both drank it and I placed the empty bottle under the front seat.'

"The judge turned to the officer standing there. 'Go down and search his car for the bottle of wine.'

"A few minutes later the officer came back carrying the empty bottle of wine. The judge ordered that it be checked for prints and they found both mine and the clerk's prints on it.

"Once the results came back the judge had the clerk arrested then looked at me and said: 'Look, you have to do the trial on the escape, but you will not have a problem in view of the evidence that just came to light, along with the fact that the citation was not yours.'

"That upset me, but what could I do? The case finally got cleared up a year later."

"Wow that is one hell of a story, Armando."

"It's true, every word as best as I can remember it. Do you want to stop for some lunch?"

"Good idea."

"By the way, Nutty, how come you're so bulky? You're not fat, what's up?" asked Armando

Nutty opened his jacket and Armando could not believe his eyes. "They're not taking me alive," Nutty exclaimed.

Armando slowly pulled the car over to the side of the road. He got out, walked to the passenger side, opened the door and yelled at Nutty, "Get the fuck out of my car."

"Armando, what's the matter? I figured this would be of some help to you and your buddies."

"Are you crazy? We have to go over an international boarder. You carry dynamite strapped to your body!"

Nutty was sitting in the car, with about 20 sticks of dynamite strapped to his body and rigged to a detonator. All that had to be done was that he or someone presses the button. He, and anyone around him, would blow up. With this dynamite crazed bastard in front of him, Armando was yelling at him as loud and hard as he could.

"You asshole, were you planning on taking me with you?"

"No, Armando, I would never do that."

"Where the fuck did you get the dynamite?"

"After I broke out, I ran across a construction site. I stayed there for the night. There was no one there, not even a guard. In the morning, when I woke up, I saw boxes of this shit in that little building, where I hid. So, I had the idea of taking a few with the detonator. I have three detonators."

"Can you take it off?"

"Sure, but I don't want to. I don't want to be taken alive."

"You will not be taken as long as you let me run this show."

"What do you mean?"

"I can get you across the state line, don't worry about that. Take that dynamite off."

"Ok, I'll trust you. I wouldn't trust just anybody, but you I trust."

Nutty took off the dynamite, deactivated the detonator and handed it to Armando. He placed it in the well with the spare tire and placed some papers over it, put the spare back and then took off for Canada. They were not far from the border.

"You are nuttier then a fruit cake."

"No, I just want to die if they try and take me, rather than serving any more time."

"You don't have any guns or knives on you, do you?"

"I have a pen knife, and I have my baby, that all."

"Who or what is your baby?"

"My .38, that's all, I swear."

Armando pulled the car over to the side of the road again, got out and walked to the other side, opened the passenger door and told Nutty to stand up.

Armando frisked him for the gun and anything else.

Nutty began laughing and kidding around.

"Hey, Armando, I didn't know you were like that. I don't want a blow job, ha, ha."

"This is no joke, Nutty. I need to be as clean as possible going over that border. After that you can do what you want."

When Armando was satisfied he returned to the driver's seat. They took off.

"Listen, Nutty, when we arrive at the farm, you are going to have to follow orders. You cannot go off on these tangents of getting dynamite and things like that. Gerry will be in charge up there and the 'Cold Bloods'. You do what they ask and no more."

"No problem, Armando, you can count on me."

***

They decided to get a hotel for the night instead of walking in on everyone in the dark, especially where no one knew Nutty.

~*~

Back at the Hospital May 22, 1979 Later That Afternoon

Armando had been on the operating table. They stopped the operation due to complications from his abuse of methamphetamine, which was interfering with the anesthesia and causing unsafe bleeds throughout his arteries. Detectives from the Quincy Police Department were allowed to speak with him for a few moments.

"Good afternoon, Doctor," the nurse said, greeting the case doctor.

"Good afternoon. How's he doing?"

"He seems somewhat better. His blood is clearing according to the lab and the internal bleeding has slowed. His pulse and blood pressure seems to still be a little erratic."

"OK, keep him sedated, I want him to sleep. He needs the rest."

"He doesn't know how lucky he is, doctor."

"What do you mean?"

"Well, he is getting a complete withdrawal from the drugs while he is out. That's much better than while he is awake."

"We're clearing some of the physical chemical out of his system, but the psychological effects take several days or longer. When he wakes up, his addiction problems start over. Due to the psychological effect, we may have to send him down to the drug rehab unit, if he'll go."

"Yes Doctor, did you write the order?"

"All done, we're ready for him in the operating room. He should be able to finish the operation by now."

"Yes, Doctor, I'll bring him in."

The doctor walked out of the room, the nurse checked Armando and then walked out herself.

***

Armando was still dreaming about those things that had happened in his life that led up to his being stabbed and left for dead on the beach in Quincy, Massachusetts.

Chapter 9

Nutty

Sunday May 14, 1978

Armando got up early and tried to wake Nutty, but he was not hearing any of it.

"Get outta bed"

"Yeah, yeah, I'm gettin' up'"

About an hour later, Armando was able to get Nutty out of bed and over to the diner for breakfast. As they entered the diner, Armando's eye was caught by a headline in the newspaper. ***"Drug War takes Lives."*** He bought the paper and began reading about people that he had met and people that he knew for a long time that were being killed by one side or the other, some of them tortured and then murdered.

"Nutty, this war is getting bad. People are being tortured as well as being murdered. You should read this article."

"Armando, what do I care? I'm happy to be on my way to Canada and whatever happens, happens."

"Nutty, you're getting yourself into a group that you have never been associated with before. These guys don't fuck around. You better be careful, I can bring you in, but you have to tow the line or they will kill you as fast as the enemy."

"Why would they kill me?"

"They don't need people taking off on their own and screwing up their plans and they ain't gonna tell you their plans, they only tell you the part that you are assigned to do."

"OK, OK, I'll take orders, don't worry."

"I hope you do."

***

They left the diner and drove towards the farm where Gerry and the other men were set up. They continued driving and crossed the international border into Canada with dynamite and guns in the car.

"I can't believe that they didn't even question you, Armando."

"They know me. They know that I am here on business. They just don't know what kind of business. They never seem to question you if you are dressed in what is perceived to be a professional manner and present yourself that way."

"Yeah, I noticed your entire person seemed to change and you were very respectful towards the border guard."

"All part of the game, my man. All part of the game."

"I can see, I'm gonna learn a lot from you. I would love to buy a nice suit, like yours, once I get my hands on some cash."

"Any suit will do. This suit was a thousand dollars. It's all handmade."

"How come the guard didn't ask about me?"

"He did. Didn't you see him nod toward you questioningly?"

"No, I didn't even look at him."

"That's why you heard me say that you were a cousin taking a ride. It gets lonely traveling alone. He smiled and agreed with me."

"Yeah, I remember hearing something about being lonely on the trip. I was kind of nervous."

"You should be, with all that power in the trunk."

***

They both laughed and kept driving. Later that day they arrived at the farm gate.

"Nutty, open the gate, will you?"

"Sure" He got out and walked towards the gate.

Armando watched him. He didn't see Nutty; his mind's eye was observing Steve, the night he was killed, in that same spot. The pictures of Steve doing the same thing started running in his head. He grabbed the door handle and began opening the door; he began sweating profusely. He wanted to get to him, to help him and was frozen to the door handle. His body knew that there was nothing that he could have done for Steve. It all happened too quickly.

Nutty opened the gate and signaled Armando to drive through. Armando did not respond at first.

"Armando, you OK?"

"Yeah, I'm OK, I just had a little déjà-vu, I guess."

"Yeah, I heard about the murder. Was it here?"

"Yeah, you walking to the gate caused me to start sweating and it all came back."

"Are you all right? You look like shit."

"Yeah, I'm fine. Get in."

They pulled up to the farm house and parked alongside the cars and motorcycles already parked outside. The large number of cars created a barrier for cover, if needed.

"There must be at least two hundred men here. You guys don't own all these cars and bikes, do you?"

Armando laughed "No, these are our friends. You'll meet a lot of them; just remember what I told you. Come on in."

They entered the farm walking past the two biker guards at the door, who were watching for unknowns.

"Hi, Armando. Who's the stranger?"

"Hi guys. This is Nutty, an old and dear friend; he may be of help to us."

"Nutty? I like it." said one of the biker guards.

Armando and Nutty walked into the farm house and stepped into a house of mattresses lying on the floor all over the place. The only room that was clear of mattresses was the kitchen. Gerry was in the kitchen and could see that Armando had come in.

"Armando, come in here."

Nutty followed Armando into the kitchen.

"Gerry, this is Nutty, an old friend from way back. A little crazy, but knowing that crazy is what we need right now, he can be of some help. He just broke out of jail in Massachusetts."

"Welcome, Nutty, but what's your real name?"

"My name is Billy Slipka, but I like Nutty instead."

"That's fine with us, we can use the help and you can use my house as long as you like."

"Gerry, can I ask a question?"

"Sure, this ain't no jail, my man."

"Armando mentioned the French Mafia. Who are these guys?"

"Don't let that French part fool you. They are Italian Mafia with all the Italian connections all the way to Italy and to the families of New York. That's why we need all the help we can get."

"They are so big and you guys are much smaller. Why do they want your operation?"

"Three million a month, that's why and if you join us, you'll get a piece of that, a very small piece, but a piece comparable to your value."

"Who are the heads of this branch of the French Mafia? Does it run like the Italians that I'm familiar with in Boston, Rhode Island and New York?"

"To paraphrase the Montreal Gazette*, it is believed that Joseph (The Lime) Ticatto was alleged to be part of a four-man committee that made key decisions on the organization's activities. He is believed to be the man that orchestrated the shift in power in the late 1960's and 1970s that saw the Ticatto organization take control of an existing Mafia organization run by mob boss Vincent (Nickel) Busoni. Three other men, Peter (The Switch) Banenda, 69, William (Numbers) Stoncadi, 54, and 60-year-old Richard (The Beast) Cronsito were also alleged to be part of the Mafia's committee, based out of the former Bonstenata Social Club on St. Leonard Street in Montreal. These are the type of guys that we're up against. This is gonna be one hell of a fight. We have already lost several men."

Found on The Boss, Thursday, September 18, 2008, at 4:32 pm. Found on www.mafiatoday.com under Canadian Mafia

"Wow, you know a lot about these guys, Gerry."

"Nutty, learn now about us. We believe that the more you know about your enemy, the easier the fight will be for us."

"I will remember that."

"Armando, tonight The 'Clean Bloods' are gonna hit a joint frequented by the mafia. They will drive by and throw a bomb. You and Nutty go along because they are going to another hang-out of theirs right after. That will give Nutty a chance to get familiar with what's going on."

"No problem, but I think you should see what Nutty brought to the party."

Armando went out to the car, got the dynamite out of the trunk and brought it in to show Gerry.

"How the fuck did you get that across the border?"

"My old ingenuity; you know I've made friends with some of those guys guarding the border. They never question anything."

"That will certainly come in handy, Armando. Thanks."

"Nutty brought it. He originally had it under his coat."

Gerry looked at Nutty questionably.

"Yes, that's right. I had it under my coat. I don't want to be taken alive, that's all."

"I can understand that, Nutty," commented Gerry.

"Gerry, where do I sleep?"

"Nutty, like I said, we lost five guys so there are five empty mattresses. Take your pick. Armando you are upstairs with me in my room. You have a bed there."

"Great, that's great, thanks," said Nutty

"Armando, we can use this stuff. I'll form another team to go with you guys and they can put this dynamite under a couple of specific cars."

"Armando, you're one of the three bosses here and also my partner; we have to treat each other right."

"Who does the cooking around here, Gerry?" asked Nutty

"Damian does most of it, but right now we have a professional cook or at least that's what Joey Butler went to school for. He's a biker now, but he loves his sauces and so does everyone else, we call him Sauce. He's a damn good cook."

"Great, I can eat a horse."

"Just yell for him and he'll do whatever he can for you."

***

That evening Armando got together with a few of the bikers and set up a little strategy. They would take three cars. One would follow about three hundred feet behind the first. The first would send the bomb through the front window, the second would check the damage as they drove by the club, and they would meet some of the other bikers at the club where the Devil's Angels hang out, The Sloppy Soda Lounge just outside of Montreal. The third car will take Nutty's dynamite and attach it to a couple of specific cars and then blow them up when they're ready.

"Armando, why are we going to a Devil's club?" asked Nutty

"Because, Nutty, the Devil's do the dirty work for the Mafia all over the area. We have an opportunity to eliminate a few of our enemy. We can cut into their power by eliminating a few Devil's Angels as they have eliminated a few of us."

"OK, I was curious. As Gerry said, try to know your enemy."

"That's OK, I never mind questions."

***

The men were all set and getting anxious to go. They were drinking whisky from a few bottles, passing them around and building the courage to do the job ahead. Meth was being passed around for energy. ***(another myth: author)***

"Men, it's been a long day. It's nine o'clock and there should be plenty of people hanging around the club in Montreal. It's time to start our attack."

The bikers pulled three cars up in front of the house, parked them and waited for the men to come out and pile into them.

"Wait a minute, where did these cars come from?"

"They're stolen, Gerry, redone by Armando's guys; they're the best at that. If we lose a car the Mounties will never know who it belongs to."

"OK, as long as we know it doesn't connect to us here or anywhere else."

The men piled into the cars and the bikers revved up the motorcycle engines.

"Everyone knows what to do and where to go?"

Armando replied, "Yes ,Gerry, Mother dear, we have it all in hand."

"OK, I just want to be sure it all goes OK."

"We'll be fine. We'll see you in a few hours."

The cars and the motorcycles left the farm. All of the men were half lit up from the combination of whisky and meth that they were ingesting.

Armando was in the second car so that he could estimate the damage from the bomb that they would throw at the social club. Nutty was riding behind one of the bikers and would go to the Sloppy Soda Lounge where they would all meet later for the purpose of eliminating some of the enemy's army, the Devil's Angels.

The two cars arrived within a few blocks of the Mafia social club and the first car made its run. They approached the social club and prepared the bombs. They threw one from the front window of the car, a second from the rear window of the car and then drove off.

There were two very loud and large blasts within a few seconds of them throwing the bombs. They watched, through the rear view mirror, as they escaped. They could see rubble fly out into the street and smoke coming from the club. They headed for the Sloppy Soda Lounge as planned and were all excited that they had done a great job.

A few minutes later, Armando's car drove by and could see several men laying on the street and near the doorway; that were not moving, possibly dead. The damage was horrific. He could see into the social club and saw that the furniture was turned upside down and bodies were laying everywhere. There were flames shooting into the air. His only thoughts were of those poor injured people. He wanted to stop the car and get out and help them, but he didn't. He realized that it was his upbringing from his mother's religious teachings that made him want to stop the car and help. He resisted the temptation and told the driver to drive on. They headed for the Sloppy Soda Lounge to meet up with the other men.

The third car had gone to a private home address where there seemed to be a party going on. One of the men sneaked into the middle of the nine cars in the driveway and placed a bomb under two of them. They drove about a block away and set off the dynamite with a remote detonator. They didn't go back to check after they heard the two blasts.

Back in Armando's car it was quiet, no one spoke. They all waited for Armando to start the discussion.

"We put a dent in their plans, men. Good job."

They all began talking about the bomb and what they had noticed and they were very proud of themselves for finishing that part of the job. Now the second half of the job lay ahead.

***

As Armando entered the Sloppy Soda Lounge, all he could hear was music coming from the juke box. The bar itself was stretched out along the back wall and there were tables on the right and tables on the left as he walked in.

He could see his men on the right side of the bar and sitting at the tables on the right side of the room. On the left side of the room and the left side of the bar were the Devil's Angels, with a long space between the two groups along the bar.

It was fairly quiet. No one spoke. Armando sat down with a few of his men and one man got up to get Armando a drink from the bar.

"Listen, men, I don't think we should start any trouble. Just being here, in their bar, is enough of an embarrassment to them."

"Whatever you say, but I don't agree."

"What's your name?"

"I'm called Sleazy."

"Sleazy, we'll do this my way. If they start something, that's another story then we'll follow through."

"OK, this is your war. We're only here as protection and to assist."

Suddenly a knife came out of nowhere. It was as though it fell from the ceiling and stuck into the table at almost center.

Armando, Nutty, Sleazy and the other men were stunned for a second then they heard one of the Devil's.

"Oh, I'm sorry; I was lobbing my knife and I lost control of it," the Devil was apologetic.

Everyone waited for Armando to say or do something. He didn't acknowledge the Devil's knife or comment.

The Devil then turned back to the bar and commented to his friends: "You see, guys; I told you they were nothing but a bunch of pussies."

Sleazy was a large man, three hundred pounds, six feet tall, with a beard; the type of man that looked like he would kill everything in his path.

Sleazy got up from his seat and turned to Armando.

"Sorry, Armando, but I don't take that kind of shit," he said, and the fight started.

Sleazy picked up a chair and hit the big mouth over the head. He then felt a sting in his back, someone stabbed him and he went down.

By this time, everyone was fighting and knives were showing up.

***

After a few minutes of fighting and a couple of stabbings, Armando and his men got out of there, back to their cars and left the area.

When they arrived back at the farm, Gerry was waiting on the porch of the main house.

"How did the bombings go?"

"They went perfect, but we have some casualties."

"What the fuck happened?"

"We went to the Sloppy Soda Lounge and a fight broke out. We stabbed a few of them and they stabbed a few of us. I don't think any of the cuts are life-threatening."

"Armando, where's Nutty?" asked Gerry

"He must be here somewhere. Did anyone see Nutty?"

"I saw him; he was fighting with some guy and fell through the kitchen door. I figured he was all right so I kept on fighting," stated Big Bill, another member of the 'Clean Bloods'.

"That's funny, I could have sworn that he was with us," stated Armando.

"He's not here, man. Get another car and you and I will take a ride and look for him,"

Armando and Gerry spent the entire night looking for Nutty to no avail.

***

At 6:00 a.m. they stopped to pick up a newspaper to see what type of news their night of mayhem had created.

The headlines read; ***"The Drug War Continues. Numerous bodies found dead and maimed."***

Armando read some of the article out loud.

"One of the bodies discovered in a ditch turned out to be an escapee from a jail in Massachusetts, U.S.A. This man had been tortured for information and then killed by slowly cutting off parts of his body. His body was discovered in six parts, strewn all over the ditch."

Neither Armando nor Gerry said a word all the way back to the farm.

Once they arrived at the farm, Gerry said he was going to bed.

"I'm sick of this killing," Armando said.

"So am I, Armando, so am I." They both went to bed.

Chapter 10

Transformation

May 23, 1979,Back at the Hospital
Armando's Second and Hopefully Last Operation

"Dr. Steinberg, what do you think?"

"He seems to be much better. It's amazing how the human body can heal itself, the rest is psychological."

"I'm glad. I took a liking to him, even though he's rarely awake. He was easy to help."

"That's good, nurse, He's going to need a lot of help in the future. He'll be recovering for at least a month, maybe more."

"At least he's alive and someday can tell his grandchildren about what happened to him."

"I have a funny feeling that his story is not going to be one of those family tales."

"Yes, on second thought, I think you're right."

"Yes, I'm sure of it."

"Detective Lijoi left a message asking to be notified as soon as he is awake after the operation. Is that OK?"

"Sure, I think he will be able to think and speak clearly once he's out of recovery."

"Thank you, I'll telephone him when the time comes."

The operation continued and about three hours later, Armando was taken off of the table and placed into the intensive care unit, ICU, where he could be watched closely for a while.

Later that evening he was awake for a while, but still a bit groggy from all of the medication. He fell off to sleep again and continued his dream about how and why he got stabbed at the beach and his separation from the Musketeers.

~*~

Sunday April 22, 1979

Armando had been making his runs for another year; it was now 1979. He was making plenty of money and watching numerous men die in his defense. It was bothering him so much that he decided to speak with Gerry.

"Gerry, we have to talk. This shit is too crazy, I can't live like this forever."

"OK, Armando, let's go up to our room and we can talk privately."

The two men went up to the second floor room that had been their home for over a year. They sat on the beds facing each other. The same way that they would plan strategies they now would discuss their future.

"Gerry, you were brought up here, you're a Canadian, your family is buried on this property, and you can speak the French language. I could go on, but that's enough for now."

"Armando, I sense that you're bothered by those things. Do you want half of the farm?"

"No Gerry, not at all. I want out. I want to go back to Massachusetts and simply work as a supplier from there. I have a wife who left me and I have a child, a son that I've only seen a couple of times. I'm American, I speak American and I live in America. I want all that back."

"Armando, I didn't know that you felt this way. I have no problem with you getting out. I'll miss you. We will always be friends and you will always be welcome here."

"Thanks Gerry, I hate leaving you with this war on, but I miss home."

"You go ahead, don't worry about me or this war. It may go on for a couple of years."

"I'll stop up and make a pickup from time to time."

"Whatever you need, buddy, it's all yours, available to you anytime you want it."

"Thanks, I'm glad you understand."

***

A few days after this conversation, Armando left the farm and returned to the apartment that he kept in Quincy, Massachusetts where he made arrangements to speak with a couple of the dealers that he knew and supplied.

He contacted Pauli Jameson, Charlie (Red) Wilson, Stewart (Stew) Vigiliano and Martin Zackary, the four major dealers that worked for Armando in Massachusetts. They had the state broken up into four quarters and each took his own section.

He also contacted Johnny (JZ) Zales, who took care of a large portion of New Hampshire and Mr. Enrique Risotino of both Quincy and Vermont; this man sold a lot of Meth and cocaine in both states.

These six men would become his main team. He would continue to supply them and rake in the cash. Things were about to change for Armando although he had no idea in which way or how much they would change.

~*~

Thursday April 19, 1979: Armando's Dream Continues

It was two p.m. and everyone was sitting at the private table in the restaurant on Wollaston Beach in Quincy.

"OK, guys, I'll tell you why I asked you here, I'm going independent. You men have made a ton of money with me and that'll continue. I'll continue to supply you. I want you to know exactly what is going on."

"All I care about is getting the supply that I need. You've always been there when I needed a reload, as long as we've been doing business. That's enough for me," stated "JZ".

"JZ" would later be identified as Jonathan Zales, a.k.a. "JZ" a white male, five feet nine inches tall, one hundred and forty-five pounds, blond hair and brown eyes. "JZ" was a Boston resident who lived in the Baker Hill area of Boston, in a home located at 2400 Midland Ave.

The rest of the men agreed and Armando was all set to run his own operation.

"Thanks, men, the night is on me. Enjoy yourselves," proclaimed Armando.

***

For the next few weeks things went fine for Armando. April turned to mid May and the weather was getting warmer and warmer.

~*~

Sunday May 20 1979: The Night of the Stabbing and Armando's Hospital Admission

Armando was at the Big Wave Lounge on the beach enjoying a beer and conversation with a hooker that he knew.

"Armando, can I buy some crank from you?"

"What makes you think I sell crank?"

"It's pretty much common knowledge around here that you're the boss."

"I'm sorry, I don't deal to your level, but I'll give you a taste, free of charge."

"Are you sure it will be free of charge?"

Armando leaned over and whispered in her ear, "As long as I get what I want for free, you get what you want free."

She leaned into his ear, "I suppose you want your normal polishing done?"

"You got it, baby."

"You want it right now?"

"Can you do me under the table?"

"Sure, I can do you in a phone booth, anywhere."

They proceeded to finish up with the sex and Armando reached into his pocket and handed the hooker a small white folded piece of paper containing two grams of his best meth.

"This should last you a couple of days," said Armando

"Thanks, Armando, anytime you feel the urge come and see me."

"I will. You're good at what you do."

Armando finished his drink and ordered another beer when he saw Pauli Jameson standing at the bar, across the room. A white male, five feet nine inches tall, one hundred and eighty pounds, thirty years of age, blond hair and brown eyes a known speed, marijuana and cocaine dealer.

"Hi, Pauli, what's up?"

"It looked like you were up from here, you sleazebags."

"Oh, you could see my party?"

"Yeah, I saw it and so did everyone else. You better slow down on that crank you take. You're beginning to slip by not caring about what's going on around you."

"OK, ok, I've had enough insults, you done?"

"I'm done and you should listen. You've been on top for too long. It may be time for you to step down and let someone else run the operation," stated Pauli.

***

Later that night when the Big Wave Lounge closed, everyone was leaving. The place was getting quiet. Armando took the beer bottle that he had sitting on the bar and walked out. By this time, all of the cars were gone, the street was quiet and the beach across the street was not noisy at all; you could barely hear the surf.

Armando walked across the street and was standing at the wall having his last snort for the night and enjoying the dark view of the beach, sky and surf.

He couldn't hear a sound, not even the little rat that was combing the rocks below the wall for some food.

Armando dropped some beer on the animal and watched the beer go from his bottle to the back of the rat. Then the rat jumped and ran off. Armando laughed at the rat. Then he felt that sting in his back, several times. He fell forward and slouched forward over the wall. *What the fuck is going on?* he thought. Someone lifted his legs to finish his drop from the top of the wall onto the rocks. He was left for dead.

~*~

Friday May 25, 1979 at the Hospital in Quincy.

Armando had been operated on twice. He was unconscious and dreamt most of the time. His dreams were about his past life and the things he had done over the years.

He woke with a new feeling, a feeling of remorse. He didn't understand his feeling at that moment, but knew that eventually he would pull himself together. He had to get well first.

As he was remembering, he recalled that Pauli Jameson had all but threatened his life that night. This was important to him. His feelings suddenly changed to rage and he wanted to get even with that bastard Pauli.

***

That afternoon Detectives Ernie Lijoi and Henry Griswold arrived at the hospital and were directed to the new room for Armando Kiefer.

"Good afternoon, Armando, how do you feel?"

"I feel like shit warmed over a few times."

"You're sore; I mean you're body is sore from the operations", stated Lijoi.

"Did you say operations, plural?" asked Armando

"Yes, they had to stop the first time because your system was so cranked up from the meth. You rested for a day and they gave you something to clean out your system and then operated on you again. If they didn't stop when they did you would be dead," Lijoi replied.

***

Detective Ernie Lijoi was a clean-shaven Italian male, five feet eight inches tall, one hundred ninety-five pounds with short brown and very wavy hair and brown eyes. This was as he looked until a case came up that required his guise Eddie Pannoni to reemerge.

Detective Henry Griswold was a white male, five feet nine inches tall, one hundred and eighty pounds, light brown hair and brown eyes. He was the key man that covered Ernie's back when Ernie went into deep cover mode.

***

"Wow, I didn't realize what had happened. I just have vague glimpses."

"Do you remember speaking with us? Do you remember us at all?" asked Detective Griswold.

"Yes, that's about all I remember regarding you two detectives."

"You don't remember telling us about Mr. Enrique Risotino or his stash?" asked Griswold.

"Yes, yes I do, it's coming back now and I meant what I said about getting out of this business and cleaning it up."

"You must have dreamt that part. You never said that to us, but we are glad to hear it," said Lijoi

"I'm serious; maybe it's the fact that my system is clean. I still feel the urge, but I can work that out in time. I want to work with you guys and do some good. God knows I've done enough bad things. I want to help."

Detective Lijoi told Armando, "If you're saying what I think your saying, I want you to get better and completely free of the meth and any other drugs. When a doctor can tell me that you are clean, we can talk. Also you will have to sign an agreement that you wish to speak with us without your attorney. We still have the meth case on you."

"What meth case?"

Lijoi told Armando, "When we found your body on the beach we found your car and searched it for evidence as to your probable murder, which is the way it looked then. When we searched the car we found a shit load of meth. You have to be charged with that, but maybe we can speak with the District Attorney. If he agrees, he can hold off the case until you and I have a chance to talk and look at what you have."

"OK, give me a week or two and I'll be ready. I'll prove to you that I'm serious."

"OK, get well. If they let you out before we can get together again, contact me at this number."

"One quick question before you men leave. Do you know a guy named Pauli Jameson?"

"Yes we know him, why do you ask?"

"I can't prove it because I didn't see the guy that stabbed me, but I think he did it because he came very close to threatening me earlier that night."

"Did he actually threaten you?"

"No, he walked around it; he said I should retire, let someone else take the reins, things like that."

"Those are suggestions, not threats."

"Yes, you're right, but he tried to kill me once before. He tried to shoot me."

"We can look into it right now or we can wait until you are better and see if he took over for you."

"OK, let it go for now. We will talk in a week or two."

The men all shook hands and Det's Lijoi and Griswold left the hospital. Their expectations were very good because of the conversation with Armando.

***

Lijoi and Griswold went back to the (BCI) Bureau of Criminal Investigation where they prepared reports for the District Attorney regarding Kiefer and for the courts to cover the recent search warrant at the home of Enrique Risotino. They then delivered the reports to the appropriate locations, the court and the DA's office in Dedham, Massachusetts.

The weekend was going to be three days long because of Memorial Day on Monday May 28th, 1979. The detectives left the station looking forward to the long weekend.

Ernie arrived home at 5pm and asked his wife Teresa if she wanted to go up to the cottage in Maine for a couple of days.

"That sounds like a nice idea. I'll pack after dinner and we can leave in the morning as long as you don't have anything pending?"

"No, nothing for me. Why don't you call the kids and see if they want to come up? I can open the camp tomorrow when we get there and then we'll be all set for the summer. I have to remember to bring my soldering tools with us in case there are some leaks in the pipes or breaks from the winter cold."

"Yes, someday when we build a new house there and knock down that one hundred-year-old camp, you won't have to worry about that anymore."

"Yes, if that day ever comes."

"We'll leave in the morning."

~*~

Saturday May 26, 1979

Teresa and Ernie got out of bed their normal time around 7am. They packed the car and stopped for breakfast in town at the diner.

Teresa, an Italian female, five feet six inches tall, one hundred twenty-five pounds, with very dark wavy brown hair and brown eyes, she was a very pretty girl with an easy going personality.

During this trip Ernie would prepare his wife Teresa for his upcoming deep cover investigation. His problem was finding a way to tell her so that she wouldn't get upset. She disliked undercover work because of the injuries that she had seen Ernie go through over the years, but she accepted the work that he did without much complaining.

After breakfast they started out towards Augusta, Maine and the camp.

"Teresa, I have to talk to you about something."

"That sounds strange, what's wrong?"

"Nothing is wrong. I am working on a case that may, not definite yet, but may require that Eddie Pannoni comes out of the moth balls."

"That means that you're going deep cover again?"

"The case may require it. I think it will definitely require my going back as Eddie so I would rather look at it as a definite possibility."

"Ernie, I have always gone along with you in the past. I sit home, I worry and I get scared every time someone comes to the door when you're undercover. I don't know if I can go through that again."

"Honey, you surprise me. By now, I would think that you would be used to my being undercover."

"Sitting home alone can create ghosts in my mind, like the times in the past when you came home shot, stabbed and cut up in different ways. How long do you think your luck will hold out?"

"I don't believe in luck. I believe that you make your own situation and you may as well accept it."

"Yes I know how you believe and the different things you believe in."

"Then how can you worry?"

"Maybe I'm not as strong as you."

"I've never met a girl, mentally, stronger than you. I think that you complain, but you can handle it. You know, when I was in the service we had a saying, 'When your number is up, your number is up and that's the way it is'."

"I guess I won't be able to stop you if this job comes to a head."

"It's not that I want you to stop me. I would like you to understand that I have to do this. If I don't do it there is no one else in the department that will do it. I picked this life and you were right there when I decided to get into it. Now I'm one of the few that can handle the case that is coming up. We can't give this to a novice, he would get killed. I want your support, before I go forward."

"Ernie, you know that I will always be with you in anything you do, but it's hard to be the one that has to worry all the time. You're doing the job so you don't have the time or the inclination to worry about your situation at any given moment. I do have the time."

"That's true; by the way, you don't think that I will ask you to do the reports like you used to when I worked out of the house, do you?"

"I hope not, I can't take all that bloody stuff you have to report."

"No, you won't have to do that."

"That's one consolation. At least I don't have to know everything that's going on."

"Thanks, I knew you would understand."

"You said that this may not happen, right?"

"Yes it's only a possibility right now. If it comes to that kind of a job, I'll give you a heads up."

"OK, let's have a nice quiet weekend and forget all about that stuff."

"Yes, Teresa, that's exactly what I had in mind."

***

They arrived at the camp in Maine. Ernie got a fire going to take the chill out of the house. He put his fourteen-foot boat in the water and tied it to a post until he could get the dock set up the next day.

The next few days they spent happily, not bringing up the subject of undercover work. They were in their little piece of heaven with a view of the lake, a twenty-foot sandy beach which Ernie created himself after moving boulders out of the way with his car.

The camp was an old creaky house that was so off level that when his brother-in-law rebuilt the fireplace they had to place a level on it and leave it to show that the fireplace was level, but the rest of the house was leaning to one side.

On the second floor you had to sleep with the head of the bed on a certain side of the room. If you didn't do that and slept on the opposite side, the six inch drop in the room from one side to the other would cause the blood in your body to rush to your head.

Everyone thought that the house had a certain charm and they all had a lot of fun there.

On Monday afternoon they left to return to Massachusetts.

Chapter 11

The Hot Foot

Thursday May 31, 1979

The weather turned back to the feel of winter. It was a cool morning in the high fifties, with a slight mist in the air which added to that winter feeling, even though it was the end of May.

Ernie was on his way to the station to research some information that he received from a reliable informant. The informant stated that he knew a man named Jacob Rabino. The informant stated that Rabino was dealing cocaine and marijuana out of his home at 222 Water Street. The informant also described the perpetrator as a white male, five feet nine inches tall, one hundred and seventy pounds, brown hair and brown eyes, a sharp dresser with a likeable personality. He also gave Ernie the registration number of the car that Mr. Rabino drives as being HTP-3345.

Ernie ran the registration and the listing came back to a Mr. Jacob Rabino of 222 Water Street, Quincy, Massachusetts.

Because of this information, Ernie and Henry set up surveillance and watched the house for traffic and other activity. On this date, they would watch the house again and hopefully get enough information for a search warrant and an arrest warrant.

After coffee, they set up to watch the house while they waited for the crowd to start their visits to Mr. Rabino for their weekend supplies of illicit narcotics.

The two detectives pulled up to 222 Water Street and made sure that they had a good description of the house for a search warrant and the correct unit. Henry walked by the house to confirm the resident's name on the mailbox.

They were all set and ready for the action to start. They didn't have to wait long. An hour later a car pulled up, the passenger went into the house for about three minutes, came out, entered the car and left the area. The parade had started.

A few minutes later, a second car pulled up, but when they ran the registration plate, it turned out to be a known user and addict named Robert Anderson of Quincy.

They contacted a cruiser and advised the cruiser of their plan. The cruiser was to watch for him and when he left the area follow, stop and hold him. Detectives Lijoi and Griswold would do the rest.

A few minutes later, Anderson came out of the house, got into his car and drove off.

"November 7 to Charlie 6."

"Charlie 6."

Charlie was the designation for the cruisers.

"The bird is flying."

"I see him at the corner. I'll stop and hold."

"Wait for a few blocks before you stop him."

"That's affirmative."

Ernie and Henry drove away from the area in the same direction as Anderson who went up Water Street and took a left onto Pleasant Street.

The cruiser named Charlie 6, stopped Anderson at the corner of Pleasant Street and Fort Street, a small square at that intersection, and waited for the detectives to pull up. This location was about a quarter of a mile away from the house, far enough not to be associated with the residence in question, 222 Water Street.

Ernie and Henry pulled up and asked the driver to exit the vehicle.

"Mr. Anderson, nice to see you again. Are you carrying any weapons?" asked Detective Lijoi as he checked the pockets of Mr. Anderson.

"I don't carry weapons. Why are you guys hassling me?" asked Anderson.

"Where have you been during the last hour or so?" asked Lijoi.

"Have you been juicen (taking drugs), Robert?" asked Detective Griswold

"I'm straight, I'm straight. You guys know I need to be there."

"Be where? Explain that, so that these young patrolmen will understand your lingo."

"Be there, be at that high place. For me to be there, that's when I'm as straight as you guys, you know that, Detective Lijoi, you know me for years."

"Yes, Robert and you have been a junkie for years. You should change your habits. Now look at this."

Ernie was checking Anderson's pockets for a weapon and felt a hard object. He placed his hand in the pocket and took out the hard object which turned out to be a half ounce of cocaine.

"Shame on you, Robert, don't you know that this is illegal? Is it blow or juice?"

"No, it's only blow. I do very little heroin anymore."

"You're under arrest and you know the game. You can cooperate and we speak to the District Attorney or not. It's up to you."

"If I give you my supplier, can you do something for me, Lijoi?"

"I can make no promises except that I will talk to the District Attorney on your behalf, but you have to give us the man."

"OK, 222 Water Street, I just left there. I paid him for the quarter and he had plenty on hand, plus a load of smoke."

"What's the guy's name?"

"All I know is Jacob. I don't ask questions. In this business no one asks questions. You live longer that way. You know that, Detective Lijoi."

"Is there anything else that you can tell us, Robert?"

"He always has a gun on hand when he is dealing, I've seen it. He has a nice clean house, he's a neat freak. He lives with a broad, but I don't think she's involved in his business."

"What's her name?"

"I don't know, I've only seen her once."

***

Ernie walked away to speak with the patrolmen, while Henry stayed with Mr. Anderson.

"Officers, would you take him down and book him, please? The charge will be possession of a controlled substance. Have his car towed and taken into the station garage for a total search. Be gentle with him, he's not a bad guy, just hooked."

The patrolmen agreed. Ernie and Henry left the area and returned to the office to complete an affidavit for both a search warrant and an arrest warrant.

Upon arrival at the station, Ernie immediately contacted the duty sergeant to inform him about the upcoming search and to request that the prisoner Anderson be moved through the system as quickly as possible.

Ernie didn't want Jacob Rabino to see that Anderson had been arrested. Rabino's first thought would be that Anderson ratted him out. That type of information could cost Anderson his life.

It would take several hours of work to complete all of the paperwork required to do the search and arrest at Mr. Rabino's location. This would give the duty sergeant plenty of time to move Anderson out of the station.

***

Ernie sat down with a cup of coffee and plenty of paper to do the search and arrest warrant. He included his informant's information, the surveillance information and the confirming information received from Anderson without divulging the informant's names. Then to finish the affidavit, he added the arrest of Mr. Robert Anderson after he left the home on Rabino while under surveillance, indicating that he could not have obtained the drugs anywhere else. The last part indicated that the drugs were field-tested and identified as cocaine.

Then he filled out the paperwork for the arrest warrant of Rabino and the application for the search of the house. He put all the paperwork together. He and Henry went to the court and submitted the information. They were sworn to the affidavit and the warrants were issued.

They were ready to hit the house. They had to contact the entire team and have them all available for the search.

***

They returned to the office that they used, which is in a different part of the city. They used a third floor apartment in a three-family building. This building is owned by the City Hospital and used to store equipment. The hospital allows the Special

Services Unit of the Quincy Police Department to use the third floor apartment as their office.

From the office, they telephoned the team members for support and backup. Det. Gerry Gibson, fingerprint expert, his call sign was November #8; Det. Jack Wade, photography expert, his call sign was November #5; Det. Rick Bradshaw, Electronics expert, his call sign was November #2; Det. Carl Robinson, locks expert, his call sign was November #6 and the boss Captain Donald Richards, the man in charge with a call sign of November #1.

It was seven p.m. when the detectives arrived at the office. They waited for Captain Richards who arrived shortly thereafter.

***

Ernie briefed everyone on the entire case and the probability that there may be at least one gun involved, maybe more. The informants both stated that they saw a handgun each time they were in the house.

"Captain, do you have a preference as to how you want this done?"

"It's your case, Ernie. You and Henry know the layout, you call the shots."

"Thanks, Captain"

All of the detectives knew their assignments to get into the house and do their jobs as per the warrant, once they had control of the house. These were the experts, the top men in the department. This unit did most of the search warrants, arrest warrants and all of the wire taps that were needed in Quincy. They advised and assisted other departments in many ways.

The detectives piled into a few cars and the captain arranged for three marked cruisers to go with the team for backup and assistance. The men in the cruisers knew their job and what to do. The cruiser teams made the job a little easier to handle.

***

Upon arrival at #222 Water Street, Quincy, Detective's Lijoi and Griswold approached the front door with two uniformed men. Det. Lijoi knocked and announced their presence. There was no answer so they used "BIG MOE" to knock down the front door.

Big Moe was a four feet long, six inch wide steel pipe filled with concrete. It had handles on both sides so that two men could swing it and knock a door in easily.

Everyone standing on the front steps stepped to the side, for safety sake, before the door went down. As the door was falling to the floor they heard a gun go off.

The detectives and patrolmen pulled their weapons. Ernie, crouched very low in the doorway, took a quick look into the house. He saw nothing and signaled to the men that he was going to try and go in as far as a couch that was just inside the doorway.

Henry signaled for him to wait a moment. Henry directed the patrolmen and detectives to set their sights on the windows, ready to cover Ernie if needed.

Everyone was set and ready. Ernie started in and quickly stopped at the gray couch, slouching along the side, using the arm as cover. The house remained quiet.

"Henry, nothing, I don't see anyone? Come in but stay down."

Henry and another officer came into the house and used the back of the couch for cover while the other men covered the windows.

The radio signaled which was not the usual procedure, "Guys, I see a pair of feet by the bed in the back bedroom. Someone is down," said the officer covering the rear window of the house.

Ernie looked at Henry as he answered the call from Detective Wade, "Received."

"Think he killed himself, Henry?"

"I'm sure we'll find out, my turn to go first."

Henry moved to the upholstered Lazy Boy chair on the other side of the room. The house was still calm.

Ernie crept to the edge of the wall which led down the hall to the bathroom and the bedrooms. The house was still and quiet.

The other officers covered their movement. Henry joined Ernie on the opposite corner and the backup officers joined them as Ernie and Henry covered their move.

Ernie and Henry went down the hall, one on each side; the two patrolmen covered their progress. They checked the first closed door; Henry opened it while Ernie got down on all fours and went in at a low level near the bottom of the door. It was the bathroom and no one was there. They continued down the hall and opened the doors one at a time finding them all empty, until they came to the last door in the hallway.

Henry turned the knob on the door while reaching from the side of the door and a shot went off. Then another and a third shot rang out. All of the shots except one went through the door and would have hit someone, had they been standing directly in front of the door.

"You want some more, motherfucker?" came from inside the room.

Then another shot and someone was yelling at the top of his lungs, "You motherfuckers, you assholes."

The radio sang out, it was Det. Wade again: "Ernie, I shot him in the foot."

Ernie and Henry rushed into the room and found and took control of the gun which was on the floor next to the subject who had just been shot by Detective Jack Wade. He was sitting on the floor holding his foot and calling everyone assholes.

The officers removed his shoe and wrapped his foot in some towels to help control the bleeding, which was not very bad.

Ernie stooped down so that he was eye to eye with the subject and smiled. "Mr. Rabino, we may be assholes, but you're under arrest for two counts of attempted murder of a police officer, two counts of firing a weapon within city limits, and if you don't have an FID card, we'll add illegal possession of a handgun. That's all before we start the search. God only knows what your charges will be after that."

"Fuck you!" said Rabino

"Yes, that figures," replied Ernie

***

All of the men were called into the house. One man was assigned to look over the exterior and then stand at the door. Everyone else was assigned to different areas of the house.

One of the patrolmen was asked to call an ambulance and stay with the prisoner. "When he's OK, take him down to the station for booking, unless he demands to be present during the search."

"Are you Mr. Jacob Rabino?"

"Yes, that's my name."

"And drugs is your game," answered Henry with a chuckle.

"We're going to get an ambulance to come down and look at your foot. It doesn't look too bad to me, but we'll call for one anyway. Do you want the ambulance to take you to the hospital to be checked out or do you want to stay here?" asked Det. Lijoi

"I want to go to the hospital, but I want a detailed report of what you take."

"You or your lawyer can obtain that at the station after it is written up, Mr. Rabino"

Mr. Rabino was left to the officer's care as they waited for the ambulance.

The men had their assignments and fanned out within the home. Ernie and Henry took the basement, knowing that this was the common area for labs, materials, cutting and the safes that held the cash.

As they walked down the stairs they observed a homemade table of wood.

"We have an artist, Henry; he's a builder of tables."

"Yes, and take a look over there."

Ernie looked and in the far corner he saw a small safe about three feet by two feet which was cemented into the cellar floor.

"Think he was afraid someone would rob his safe?" Ernie asked with a smile.

On a table they saw cutting powder: "He certainly had enough cutting material, this is a three gallon container of it," said Henry.

"Yes, he was doing quite a business. I'll call in to get the safe opened," Ernie stated.

Ernie used the telephone that was hanging on the wall in the cellar instead of putting the information over the air on the open channel that anyone could hear.

"Hi, Lieutenant, this is Lijoi. This guy has a safe and I need someone to open it."

"I'll send a locksmith; I think Kirsch is an expert with safes. He was a safecracker in his youth."

"That's fine, whoever you can get."

Ernie hung up the phone and they continued to search the house.

In the master bedroom where Rabino had been hiding and waiting for the cops to come in, they found an ounce of cocaine in the dresser next to the bed. In the kitchen they found a couple of ounces of marijuana in a cabinet on the top shelf.

The rest of the house was clean except for some meth in the living-room, which was spread out on the coffee table as though it was waiting for someone to walk into the house and snort a couple of lines.

Shortly thereafter, John Kirsch the locksmith pulled up to the house and was directed to the safe in the basement.

"John, is it true that you used to be a safecracker in your youth?" asked Henry

"Yes, when I was in my thirties I got into it for a while, but it didn't last long. I always had an interest in locks ever since I was a kid."

"Someone mentioned it and I thought I would ask to confirm it."

"Well, now you know. I did my bit when I got caught and decided to go straight. For thirty years I have been clean as a whistle."

"Thanks, a lot of guys wouldn't admit that."

"I'm not ashamed of it. I made a mistake. We all do that from time to time. At least I learned by mine."

"That's great, thanks for helping us out."

"Not a problem, anytime."

It took him about twenty minutes and the safe was opened. The detectives took all of his information for their reports before Mr. John Kirsch left the area.

"Thanks, John, we appreciate your help."

"Anytime."

Ernie and Henry took a good look inside the safe and observed four stacks of cash on the bottom, amounting to one hundred and six thousand dollars. On the second shelf there were four one-ounce bags and a one-pound bag of speed or meth, some cocaine and a quantity of paraphernalia such as mixes or cutting agents as well as needles and syringes.

Two shotguns and two handguns were confiscated and added to the search list. These weapons would be sent to the firearms lab to be checked out by Detective Griswold the firearms expert.

Ernie contacted the duty sergeant at the station, again by phone, and advised him to add possession with intent to sell cocaine, and the same for meth and marijuana. He also asked him to add illegal possession of drug paraphernalia to wit needles, syringes, cutting agents and packaging materials.

"Sounds like you got this asshole by the balls. Anything else, Ernie?"

"Yes, we do, we got him good. If there are any other charges I'll let the DA know. Is he there yet?"

"Yeah, they brought him in. He's yelling and screaming. I think he's hopped up."

"Yeah, that's the impression I got. Let him sleep it off and maybe he'll be more amicable in a couple of hours."

"That's exactly what I'm going to do."

"We'll talk with you later."

"Later."

Ernie hung up the phone and turned to Henry.

"Did you hear the charges, Henry?"

"Yeah, no problem, is he still high?"

"Yeah, they'll let him sleep it off. He'll be fine in a couple of hours."

The detectives finished with the house and returned to the office to complete their preliminary reports for the court in the morning, after which they all left for the night.

~*~

Monday June 11, 1979

Ernie got up, had breakfast on the porch and watched the early morning animals enjoying the sun and the warmth of the day, which felt as though it was in the high sixties with a clear sky.

The squirrels were chasing each other up and down the trees. Schools of bait fish were jumping in an effort to get away from the larger fish deeper in the lake that were feeding on them. The smaller animals were sniffing around the trees and bushes looking for an insect breakfast.

Ernie smiled and realized that no matter what animal there were, life was the same basic thing, try to survive and not be hungry.

He finished his breakfast and left the house after kissing his wife goodbye for the day, then drove to the office.

***

Two weeks had passed since he spoke with Kiefer who was still in the hospital. He had not heard from Kiefer and decided that today he would visit him again and see what he had on his mind.

Ernie arrived at the office and met with Henry.

"I would like to stop by and talk to Kiefer today. I want to see if his head in still in the same place."

"Yeah, it's been about two weeks. I think that's a good idea, Ernie."

"We'll stop at the diner for coffee and then go up."

"Let's do it."

***

The two men drove to the diner to have some coffee and start their day.

"Henry, I just remembered, we have that guy Risotino to talk to, also. How about running down to see him after Kiefer?"

"Why not? I think that when we see him we should ask Kiefer about that Musketeer nickname that the other informants used for Risotino"

"Great minds think alike. I had that same question on my mind, assuming that he still wants to work with us."

"Is he in a bed or detox?"

"He was transferred to the detoxification center at the prison hospital. He still has those charges for the drugs pending, but no one can do anything until he is in good health."

"OK, we'll see Risotino after Kiefer. If we're lucky, we'll have two good informants."

"I don't think so. I bet it turns out that we use Kiefer instead of Risotino. I could be wrong, but I have a feeling."

"Your instincts are usually very good about these things, we'll see. By the end of the day we'll probably know exactly where we stand."

***

After coffee they started out for the prison detox center. While in route they drove down Franklin Street and Det. Lijoi observed a white male standing in the street holding a shotgun with both hands.

"Stop the car!"

Henry pulled the car over to the side of the road and looked at Ernie: "What's wrong?"

"Henry, I could be wrong, but I think I just saw a guy standing in the street with a shotgun, as we passed Kendrick Ave."

"How do you want to handle it?"

"I'll get out here and walk around the corner. You take the car and drive down the street slowly."

"Agreed."

Ernie walked back to Kendrick Ave. and turned the corner. He had his gun in his hand behind his back.

Henry turned the car around and drove down the street slowly.

In the middle of the street, about half way down the block, was a white male, holding a shotgun.

Henry stopped the car and got out, using the car door for cover.

Both Ernie and Henry held their weapons, covering the man standing in the street.

"This is the Quincy Police, drop the shotgun", announced Ernie

The man standing in the street put his hands over his head and raised the shotgun high over his head.

"Place the shotgun on the ground."

The man placed the gun on the ground and then Ernie and Henry approached him. Henry had already called the situation into the station and two cruisers were pulling up as Ernie and Henry were approaching the subject.

Henry picked up the gun.

Ernie asked, "Why are you standing in the street with a gun?"

"A bobcat was trying to get into my house to get my rabbit. I have a rabbit as a pet for the kids."

"Say that again?"

"A bobcat tried to get in and he cut my back door. He wanted the rabbit I have."

"Thanks, that's a new one on me," said Ernie

"Henry, will you check inside the house and back door please? I'll stay with this gentleman."

"One of the cruiser officers walked over to tell Ernie that they were called because someone called in stating that a wild bobcat was trying to get into the house."

Henry yelled to Ernie, "Ernie, he has a rabbit and his wife said she just called the station for help with the bobcat. He has a little girl here also."

"Sounds legit, sir, let's go inside and join my partner."

They went inside where Ernie returned the shotgun and asked the gentlemen to please not go on the street like that. They checked the area out with the cruiser men. Once they were sure it was safe, they got together to talk.

Ernie asked the cruiser men to get the information needed and leave it for him or with the desk sergeant. He would pick it up later and do the reports.

The cruiser officer asked, "You'll do the report?"

"Yes, I'll do it unless you want to?"

"No, no, you do it and thanks."

"No problem", Ernie replied as he and Henry walked out of the house.

"Henry, I'm tired, how about talking to Armando in the morning after coffee?"

"I was hoping that you would say that, if you didn't I was going to suggest it."

"Good I'll see you in the morning at the office."

"See you then."

***

Ernie drove home and during the drive thought about the upcoming meetings with Armando and Rabino. He wanted to be sure that he knew what he wanted to ask. He knew that these guys could be tricky. They were not novices at informing to the police. He was sure they had done it before or they would not have been so quick to offer their help.

The next day would come soon enough and he would see how it went at that time.

He arrived home, went into the condominium and had a quiet night with his wife Teresa.

Chapter 12

Naked

Monday June 4, 1979

Ernie entered the kitchen and made some cereal for himself. It was early, he didn't want to wake Teresa, but he made too much noise with the dishes and she woke up.

He went into the living room and turned on the TV to hear the news. He didn't usually listen to the news, too much negative discussion and he saw enough of that on the job.

The news people always exaggerated the story with words that were meant to make you watch, but the public was getting tired of that nonsense. Someday they would smarten up and realize that the public were not a bunch of children.

He listened as he ate his breakfast and he heard a very short story about a drug war that was going on in Canada. They stated that the war had been going on for several years and the Canadian authorities were doing all that they could to curtail the problem. Ernie had no idea, at that time, how much this short story would affect the cases that he was working on.

It was getting late; he had to go to the office. He looked outside and could see that the sky was clear and it looked like a nice day. He heard the weatherman state that the high for the day would be in the mid sixties. It would be a comfortable day with no precipitation. He kissed Teresa and left the condo.

***

Ernie entered the office and went directly to his desk and began looking over his reports on Armando Kiefer and Jacob Rabino. He wanted to be ready for the meetings that he and Henry had planned for that day.

Henry arrived and he picked up the reports and read them, for the same reason that Ernie read them.

"Henry, you ready for coffee? Then we can go and speak with these guys."

They went for coffee, then to the detox center at the county jail where they would meet with Armando.

They signed in and turned in their weapons, which were locked in a gun safe. Then they were allowed to meet with Armando.

"How are you feeling, Armando?" asked Ernie

"I feel pretty good. I can remember a lot more now that my head is clear."

"Do you remember who stabbed you?" asked Henry

"No, I never got a look at him, but I have a suspect."

"You mean Pauli Jameson. At least that's who you mentioned before."

"Yes, I think it was him."

"We can't go on suspicions, we need evidence," stated Ernie

"Yes, I understand, no problem. He's one of the men that I want to do something about, anyway."

"Before we go any further, if you wish to speak to us on a different matter other than your stabbing, you have to sign this paper indicating that you agree to speak with us without having your attorney being present to advise you," Ernie said.

"I'll be happy to sign. I want to do the right thing for a change."

"We investigated Jameson a little and he is an interesting subject. That's all I can say right now," Henry stated

"Yeah, no problem."

"What did you want to tell us, Armando?", asked Ernie

"Here's what has happened. I got so fucked up on this meth that I forgot and didn't care about anything else. I know you guys got me good, but for some reason this experience has turned me closer to God. I would like to be of help instead of a major part of the problem, how about my working with you and cutting you into some of the top people?"

"What are you looking for?" asked Henry

"I know I have to do some time, maybe I can do a little less if I help you out. That's not my main concern. I want to help stop this stuff from ruining the people that take it."

"So you have found religion. Now you want to save the world, all because you got stabbed?" asked Henry.

"No, not just that, there are several things that bother me now that I am alive again and free of that crap."

"OK, let's say we were able to convince the judge and the D.A. that you're worth putting some time into. What would you expect from us as officers?" asked Det. Lijoi

"I would expect to be protected and I would want to work with a streetwise, experienced man like you, Detective Lijoi. I can tell, just speaking with you, that you have been there before."

"That's reasonable. Let us speak with the District Attorney and get back to you in a couple of days."

"Look, they will place me back into the main population in a couple of days. When that happens I can bail myself out. That will cost me fifty thousand dollars, but at least I will be on the street. When I'm out how do I get in touch with you men?"

"I think we'll see you before that, but here's my card. Detective Griswold's name is on it also. We have the same contact numbers."

"Thanks, if I don't hear from you as soon as I get out I'll contact you."

"OK, we'll be waiting for a call."

"Oh, one thing we meant to ask you about before you go back to detox?"

"What's that?"

"This guy Rabino is known on the street as one of the 'Three Musketeers'. Who are they and what are they so famous for?"

"Detectives, that's what I mean. He's full of shit, he's no Musketeer. He's using that name because it has power. I am one of the 'Three Musketeers'. The name was given to us by the people on the street because we are fair and we get them what they need, we take care of them."

"Now you're talking about methamphetamine, correct?" asked Ernie

"Yes, and that's what I want to stop. I don't know how far up the ladder I can get you, but we'll give it one hell of a try, if you're willing, Detective Lijoi."

"We'll discuss that at a later date. For now, get well, heal your body."

Armando was taken back to the detox center and Det's Lijoi and Griswold left the meeting room and went to the front desk.

"Here are your weapons; will you sign for them please?"

"No, sorry, we have to meet with another prisoner of yours."

"Who would you like to see, officers?"

"We want to speak with Mr. Jacob Rabino of Quincy."

"Will you wait in the meeting room, please? I'll have him brought up. He's a bit of a problem so he'll be in body irons while he's up here."

"OK, that's fine"

Det. Lijoi and Det. Griswold went back into the meeting room and waited for Rabino.

After a few minutes the door from the prison side opened. A prison guard came through the door and then Rabino shuffled in with a second guard behind him.

"Detectives, do you want us to stay in the room with you and the prisoner?" asked the guards.

"No, that will be OK, just lock him down the way you normally would and we'll speak with him for a few minutes."

"Mr. Rabino, I see you have not been a good boy," stated Lijoi

"These idiots can't take a joke."

"A joke, I don't think they are afraid of your jokes. You said that you wanted to talk to us, we're here." said Henry

"Look, I'm looking at about a five to seven year stretch at least and that's if I get a decent judge."

"You'll be lucky if that's all you get, based on the evidence we gathered."

"Yeah, maybe you're right."

"You can bet on us being right. Look, we didn't come here to listen to you cry. Why did you want to speak with us?" asked Henry

"I'm looking for a deal on this case that you built against me."

"You should have your attorney speak with the D.A."

"Yeah, I can do that, but I want to get some agreement on the basics of a deal."

Detective Lijoi advised Rabino, "If you're going to speak with us without your attorney, you must agree to do that in writing. Sign this agreement and we can talk."

"OK, I'll be happy to, but if we can't come to an agreement I want this paper destroyed."

"Your attorney can get it from the D.A.", stated Lijoi

"OK, then I will sign."

"What can you offer us that will make us go to bat for you?"

"I can give you several of the people that I supply. They buy from me or from someone else when I don't have it."

"I'm not saying no, but we have you, why would we need the people that you supply? You're the source for them."

"That's all I have. Those people have other sources. What do you want?"

"We want the people that supply you."

"You're fucking nuts, they'll kill me and I'll be lucky if they leave me in one piece."

"That's fine, I'll be nuts and you enjoy your time in prison. A nice looking young man like you will do well in there as soon as you are decided on."

"Decided on?"

"Yes, the men in prison that haven't seen any women for a while will fight over your ass. I hope you wind up with a nice guy."

"Fuck that, you and I have to work something out."

"When's your bail hearing?"

"Next week. My attorney said he can get me out on personal recognizance."

"Let's see if that happens. You contact me or my partner Detective Griswold once you are on the street and we'll see what we can do. We can make no guarantees, but we can talk and present our opinion to the D.A. Here are our numbers."

"OK, that's a deal. I'll let my attorney know what I'm doing."

"That's a good idea. We'll wait to hear from you."

Det. Griswold called the guards and told them that they can take Rabino back to his cell.

***

Detectoves Lijoi and Griswold left the county jail and did not say much until they got into the car.

"What's your take, Ernie?" asked Henry

"If this works out correctly we can use Rabino to enhance a cover story and grab a few medium dealers on searches. At the same time, we'll come in with Armando who seems more sincere than Rabino and we can use him for the top people."

"That sounds perfect, but can we get it done without any injury? That's the question."

"We can't worry about that now. Let's see how it all goes. I may be all wet on my plan; it may not work out at all."

"Ernie, if I know you, this plan of yours will work out, one way or another."

***

They returned to the office, made a report on their meetings for the files and the day ended.

Henry left the office and went to visit with some family while Ernie drove home.

"Hi, Teresa, what's for dinner?"

"I'm making a pork roast. I'm cooking it a little different tonight. I chopped up garlic, some seasoning and pepper, then rolled the roast in it. It's in the oven now."

"How much pepper did you put on it?"

"Don't worry; I think you'll like it."

"I'll wash up for dinner. Why don't we eat on the porch?"

"That's fine; I'll set the table out there."

***

About a half hour later the food was ready and they ate out on the porch. It was a moon lit evening and you could see the fish rising and hitting the top of the water looking for bugs and anything they could get for dinner.

"Honey, it looks like that discussion that we had about the deep cover work will be happening. It will start in a week or two."

"Let's not spoil a perfectly good dinner discussing that right now."

"OK, I just wanted to give you a heads up."

"Please, Ernie, let's not discuss it now." stated Teresa

"Look at that bass jump. He must weigh seven pounds," Ernie changed the subject

"Yeah, I saw it. Are there a lot of those in there?"

"There are tons of bass, but not too many that size. Once you get over five pounds in this part of the world that's a very good size."

"But you catch a lot of other fish, don't you?"

"Yes, we get pickerel, pike, yellow perch, trout and more, you know that."

"I'm just trying to get your work out of my mind. I guess I can't. When will you start this new job?"

"I am not sure yet, but I think within a couple of weeks."

"Will you work out of home or the office?"

"There are a lot of decisions that have to be made. I'll let you know when I know exactly what's going on."

"Who is making the decisions?"

"Henry and I will set up the operational parameters and decide on how to operate. Then we will get the Captain's OK, who is usually in agreement with whatever way we want to run the operation."

"You'll keep me in the loop, right?"

Ernie smiled, "Yes, I'll keep you in the loop as much as possible."

"For now, I guess that will have to do."

***

The rest of the evening was spent with Ernie taking care of six tomato plants that he planted next to the condo while Teresa was inside cleaning up the kitchen.

~*~

Wednesday June 6, 1979

Ernie and Henry arrived at the station about the same time. After checking messages they decided to go for coffee and plan out the day.

"I hate mornings like this, Henry."

"Yeah, me too, this mist in the air is real shitty, but it'll dry up by ten a.m."

"Where we going for coffee?" asked Ernie.

"I'm glad you asked, there is a new joint that just opened up, let's try it out."

"Where is it located?"

"It's over on Sea Street by Broad Meadows. It's called the Mug and Muffin. I wonder if it is as good as the one in Dedham."

"I bet it is."

***

They went to the Mug and Muffin in Quincy and enjoyed their coffee. They agreed that it was as good as the Mug in Dedham where the District Attorney's offices are located.

Their plan for the day was to do surveillance of the locations where this subject Pauli Jameson was hanging out. They wanted to get as much information as they could about him. They figured that since Armando mentioned him, he must be a fairly large supplier.

They left the coffee shop and began driving toward Jameson's home when Henry stopped the car in the middle of the road.

"Ernie, look at those shoes, lying on the street."

"'I see them, but I also see a piece of clothing about fifty feet ahead."

They continued driving and observed a jacket, a woman's jacket laying half in the street and half on the sidewalk.

Ernie got out, grabbed the jacket and placed it in the back seat. Just as he did, he noticed a skirt in the road. They continued driving and they saw a bra, then a set of panties and about two hundred feet ahead of them was a young female about twenty eight years old, walking in the street naked as a jaybird.

Ernie called into the station: "November 7 standing by."

"Go ahead November 7."

"Start an ambulance rolling, we have naked girl walking the streets. We're at 209 Sea Street."

"On the way."

Ernie looked at Henry and realized that he made a big mistake calling in for an ambulance like that on the public channel. Henry looked at him and laughed.

They heard the sirens; there must have been eight of them all rolling in the direction of the naked girl. All of the cruisers in the city showed up to try and give some assistance.

"Hey Henry, think they want to look or gaze?"

Henry simply laughed in response.

"Let's get her covered. I'll get a blanket out of the trunk," stated Ernie.

They took out the blanket and approached the girl. She didn't want to stop.

"Leave me alone, motherfuckers."

"Miss, you're naked."

"I'm hot, I'm hot all over."

"Miss, it's only in the sixties. There are children around," Ernie told the girl.

She kept walking as she answered, "I don't give a fuck."

"Miss, I'm going to have to take you into custody."

"Fuck you," as she kept walking

Ernie and Henry looked at each other. They didn't want to hurt her, but were forced to grab her. She tried to fight trying to get away, but the detectives overpowered her and covered her with the blanket and then cuffed her until the ambulance got there.

A few minutes later the ambulance arrived and every cruiser in the city responded for back-up purposes.

"You guys can go back to your area, there's nothing to see here. It's all under control."

The ambulance men took the girl, strapped her to the gurney, took all of her clothing and transported her to the emergency room where an assessment would be made of her condition.

Ernie spoke with the ambulance men, "Guys, she's on something, look at her eyes. She may need detox. Give us a call if you need us for anything. I'd like to find out who she is."

"Thanks, Detectives; we'll tell the doctor what you said."

The ambulance took off with the girl as Ernie and Henry continued on their way.

***

"I hope we don't see much of that in the future, Henry."

"I agree, but it was funny how the whole department showed up to assist."

"Yeah, if we were in a shoot-out, we couldn't get that many people. I don't know where they all came from."

"I know they meant well, though."

"True."

***

The two detectives searched around the city looking for Jamison or his car and were unable to find him anywhere. They spent the entire day looking to no avail.

The day was coming to an end when they received a message via radio from their office.

"November 1 to November 7."

"Nov. 7 standing by, what's up, Captain?"

"Ernie, you have a message here from that guy you spoke with recently."

"We'll be right in."

"OK."

***

Henry and Ernie returned to the office where the captain was going over reports from the last few days.

"Hi, Captain, who was it that called?"

"That guy, Armando Kiefer. I told him to call back in a half hour. He should call any minute."

"Henry, do you want to wait for the call or go home? I'll let you know what happens in the morning"

"You take it. He seems to have taken to you. Let me know tomorrow what happens. I'll be on the radio for a while if you want me to come back."

"OK, Henry. We'll talk tomorrow."

A few minutes after Henry left the office, the captain left the office, telling Ernie that he could be reached at home if needed.

Ernie remained and waited for the call.

He didn't wait long, the phone rang.

"Pete's Pizza, what-a-you-want-a?"

"Sorry, I must have the wrong number."

"Armando?"

"Detective Lijoi? "I called earlier and the guy that answered said it was a fish house."

"Yeah, we use different things on this phone. How are you feeling?"

"I'm feeling much better, thanks. Can we meet and talk about what I think that I can do for you guys?"

"Sure, when do you want to meet?"

"You're the boss, you tell me?"

"Why don't we meet at the Mug and Muffin in Dedham at ten a.m. tomorrow?"

"I'll be here."

"See you then" Ernie hung up the phone and left the office for the night.

Chapter 13

The Jail House

Friday June 15, 1979

After breakfast at home with his wife Teresa, Ernie left for the office. He had Armando Kiefer on his mind and wanted to meet with him on that day.

He arrived at the office and Henry was already there putting together a separate file with some points of interest to bring up in the event that Armando wanted to work with them.

"Good morning, Ernie."

"Good morning, what are you doing?"

"I made a file for the meeting with Armando. It's at ten a.m., isn't it?"

"Yes, let's grab a cup of coffee and then we can drive over to Dedham, stop in to see the D.A. before we meet Armando. We can speak with him about both Armando and Rabino."

The two detectives drove to the coffee shop had a quick cup of coffee and then drove to Dedham, Massachusetts.

"Hi, I'm Detective Lijoi and this is Detective Griswold. We would like to speak with Mr. John Hageman, please."

John Hageman came out from his office after being notified that the detectives where there to speak with him. He was a white male, balding, green eyes and blondish, gray hair, five feet tall, one hundred and eighty pounds and dressed in a suit and tie. He was ready for court.

"Hi, Ernie, Gerry; you wanted to see me?"

"Yes, do you have a few minutes?"

"Sure, come on in."

They entered the office and closed the door.

"John, we have a meeting with Armando Kiefer this morning, in a few minutes. We met with both Kiefer and Jacob Rabino the other day. Armando seems to want to work for us and so does Rabino. Do you have any information or objections that we should be aware of?"

"I can tell you that the DEA (Federal Drug Enforcement Administration) seems to have an interest in Armando Kiefer. They're not certain, but his name keeps coming up in relation to a Canadian group that is tied into some Mafia families. They have been trying to find out more, but were not very successful. Rabino they say is a local dealer, good size, but local."

"Who are you speaking with, maybe I should call them?" asked Ernie

The D.A. indicated that he was speaking with the DEA and the ATF. Ernie said that he or Henry would contact them.

"Two things, John; can we keep Kiefer and Rabino on the street for a while if we come to an agreement and can you cut them a break assuming that they do a good job?" Asked Ernie

"What kind of breaks are you speaking of?"

"We haven't really discussed it with them, but I was thinking about maybe cutting their time in half, but only if they deserve it," stated Henry.

"All I can say is, I'll speak with the judge and he will have to decide on the appropriate action. I would rather leave it to him. You men would have to submit statements including your recommendations and why you made those recommendations. It's better for you that the judge decide instead of you making promises in advance."

"That's fine with us, John. We're not interested in getting them off completely. Just saving some time if they do a good job," stated Ernie

"I understand and I think you're right. You two men have more than enough experience to be able to make a call like that. As long as your logic is sound and I am sure it will be, I will back your play."

"Thanks, John, that's all we needed to know at this point."

John Hageman gave Ernie all of the information that he had from the DEA. Ernie and Henry left the office to attend the meeting with Armando Kiefer.

***

They walked into the Mug and Muffin coffee shop and saw Kiefer sitting alone in the back corner, sipping on his coffee.

Henry and Ernie had agreed that Ernie would do the talking and questioning.

"Hi. Armando, are you feeling any better?" asked Ernie

"Yes, I am, thanks for asking."

"Look, we can't pull any punches with you. We just left the D.A.'s office and spoke with him. Here's the story, assuming that you do a good job for us, we will be able to make a recommendation. I have never seen the judge deny one of our recommendations," Ernie told Armando.

"I'm not going to do this for your recommendation, although it will be appreciated. This will be a kind of repentance for me. I was one of the first to start this meth epidemic which is so widespread and now I want to do all that I can to try and stop it."

"You sound repentant enough, but talk will not do it," Ernie replied

"Here's what I can do; I can give you people that have grown as suppliers to a point where they have the ability to obtain the meth themselves through my old partners."

"OK, how many people are we talking about?" asked Ernie

"I would say six to eight men in Massachusetts, New Hampshire and Vermont."

"If these men are suppliers, are they also users?"

"In most cases yes, as long as it doesn't interfere with the business of selling drugs."

"How many people do these six to eight people supply?"

"Probably in the area of one hundred to one hundred and fifty people each."

"So you're telling us that from you alone, the supplies get to one hundred and fifty people and spreads out from there?" asked Ernie

"Yes, those six to eight dealers are probably responsible for supplying, through smaller addicts and suppliers, over a thousand people. There's no way that I could know the exact number."

"That's close enough", stated Ernie

"I would like to be part of stopping it or at least slowing it down."

"We would have to set up some parameters," indicated Ernie.

"What do you mean?"

"Do you know my first name?" asked Ernie

"No, all I know is you're a police detective named Lijoi"

"OK, that's actually good. This is Henry, he is our contact man and will take care of any assistance that we need. For that matter my whole team will help us, but Henry is the key man," stated Detective Lijoi.

"OK, do you know what you want to do?" asked Armando

"Yes, you and I will cruise the city for a while. You will introduce me around to a few people. This will start in about two weeks. I grew this mustache and beard and let my hair grow, into an afro for this purpose. We will make some contacts and see how things go."

"That's fine with me, but some of these people may know you."

"Don't worry about it. I have arrested several people more than once and they still can't describe me. It's a little specialty of mine, changing my appearance."

"Will we have some sort of a story so that I can set it up in advance?"

"Yes, I was getting to that. My name is Eddie Pannoni, get to know it. You can tell people that we knew each other in New York many years ago. That takes me out of the area immediately and puts space between us in time factors. We're old friends and I'm a supplier in New York, looking to make some new contacts for my supplies," Ernie instructed Armando.

"How come I'm not supplying you, that will sound a bit crazy?" asked Armando.

"Didn't you tell me that you broke up with your partners and you're not doing anymore dealing?"

"Yes, that's right."

"We can say that you took care of me until now, or something along those lines. That can change as time goes on. All I need is the initial contact and then we can go from there and do a few different things, if it all works out" stated Ernie

"I suppose you'll help me out when the time comes?" Armando asked.

"Based on how we do, yes, Henry and I will help you out as best we can."

"Is there any other information that I should have?"

"Yes, one very important thing. I have the final say in all matters. If you cannot agree to that and stay with the agreement, then we are simply wasting our time here. If I become incapacitated then you contact Henry before you make a move," demanded Ernie.

"Why is that?"

"Armando, if you're honest and forthright with us, we want to be sure that you are safe. We have information from sources that you know nothing about. Any decision has to take those sources into consideration and at the same time protect you from any danger," indicated Ernie.

"OK, I guess that makes sense"

"Good, then you understand how things will be?"

"Yes, I understand."

"Henry, do you have anything to add?"

"One thing, make sure you become the back-up for Detective Lijoi. In other words if he gets into trouble out there and we can't get to him, he will be counting on you to back his play until we get there," instructed Henry.

"I understand, and he can count on me."

"There is one other thing that I should mention. The DEA may become involved at some point as well as the ATF. They are Federal agencies; I work closely with them at times. They are always helpful in my major cases, in many ways," stated Ernie.

"Whatever you think, I just want to be a part of stopping these drug dealers as best I can. I found religion again while I was on that operating table. I don't want to lose it again."

"Armando, how are you fixed for money, you have to live?" asked Henry

"I'm all set in that area. I have several accounts with plenty in them for a while, enough to take me through this and more."

"We want to make sure that you are not forced back into dealing because of financial needs." stated Henry

"If you like I can show you my accounts; I have a quarter of a million cash on hand, that's in just one account if I need it and at five percent interest I'm doing OK."

"Good, you're all set. We don't have to worry about that," stated Ernie

"I'll be happy to show you guys."

"No, that's not necessary, you just stay straight and keep the case going strong with Detective Lijoi," answered Henry.

"You mean with Eddie Pannoni don't you?"

"Yes, that's correct, Eddie Pannoni, your old friend from New York," stated Henry as he smiled.

"If you men don't have anything else, I'll take off. How do we make contact?"

"I will telephone you in about a week or two. Give me your number", Ernie replied.

Armando gave the detectives the information that they needed; his name, address and telephone number and then left the coffee shop.

***

It was Friday afternoon and Ernie was thinking about going to the camp in Maine for the weekend. He brought up the subject with Teresa when he arrived at home.

"Hi, Honey."

"Hi, how was your day?"

Ernie smiled, "Mine was fine why, what happened?"

"Oh, nothing, everything seemed to go wrong today."

"Like what?"

"Well, the vacuum cleaner didn't work at all, no matter what I did. Finally I decided to check the fuse box and the fuse blew. I went back to the vacuum, tried to turn it on when the wire made a flash and the fuse blew again. I remembered how you fixed the wire on the hair dryer so I got your tools and I cut the wire and reattached it. Now it all works."

"That's great. Did you wrap each of the three lines separately with tape and then the entire section together?"

"Yes, I think I did a good job. It's right there, take a look."

"This looks like a professional job, except that you used a whole roll of tape. If that happens again you should use a lot less tape, but it may be better if you just wait until I get home."

"I had to vacuum the house. I just fixed it. It worked, that's all I care about."

"OK, as I said, you did a good job"

"Thanks"

"What do you think about driving to Maine after supper? We can drive up and be there by ten or eleven tonight."

"Wouldn't it be better if we went in the morning? We'd have less traffic to contend with."

"Then we'll have the change-over traffic. People that rent for the week, they take the camps over on Saturday afternoon."

"Yeah, but we can get up early and beat the traffic."

"OK, we'll leave in the morning.

***

They got up early, went out for breakfast and left for Maine. They stopped at their normal spot, the Trading Post in Kittery, Maine. When they finished, they went on their way and arrived at the camp in the late morning.

The weekend was quiet. Ernie fished and Teresa worked around the camp cleaning, planting and prettying up the place.

Ernie fished and caught a few trout that he cleaned and filleted. They had them for supper late Saturday night.

Sunday morning at breakfast Teresa looked at Ernie. "Your deep cover job has started, hasn't it?"

"That's true, but out of curiosity, how do you now?"

"Ernie, when you let your hair and beard grow wild, I know what's coming."

"I guess it's obvious by now."

"Can you tell me about the job or is this going to be a big secret?"

"All of these cases are secret, there's a strict need to know policy, but as I learn more I'll tell you what I can. Remember, whatever I tell you is for you to know only. My life could be on the line."

"Ernie, we've been married for a long time and I have been through this before, I know how dangerous it is."

"I know you do, but I have to say it for my own peace of mind. The only people that will know what is going on is you and my team members. Henry is the main man. He will only let the others know what is necessary for the case at any given moment. The men on the team expect that."

***

Sunday afternoon they locked up the camp and left the area until the next trip.

That night they arrived at home in Massachusetts. They purchased a pizza on the way and upon arrival, sat back watching television while they ate the pizza.

~*~

Monday June 18, 1979

On Monday morning, Ernie had his breakfast of cereal and milk on the porch while he looked out over the lake. The sky was clear, very few clouds, the weather was warm, close to seventy degrees. This was a peaceful setting and a wonderful place to have breakfast.

After breakfast, he kissed Teresa goodbye for the day. He left the condominium to arrive at the office about a half hour later. Henry was there waiting for Ernie.

"Hi Ernie, should we speak to the captain and run what we have by him?"

"Yeah, do you want to go for coffee first?"

"Yes, I need some coffee. I was up late last night. A couple of old friends stopped by, one pop after another and you know how that goes."

"Yeah, I can see it in your face, you look like you've been through a tough day already and it's only nine a.m."

"Man, I'm beat."

They left the office and went to the coffee shop where Henry had several cups of coffee.

"Henry, if you feel that bad why don't you take a sick day?"

"No, we have to run this by the Captain."

"I can do that, go ahead home."

"No, I'll be fine, don't worry. If I start heaving, then I'll go home."

"OK, then don't just drink coffee, have some food, it will help settle you down"

"Yeah, you're right"

***

Henry ordered a large breakfast and ate every bit of it. After the breakfast he looked and felt much better. Once they were finished with breakfast, they headed towards Captain Richards' office in the main station.

"Hi, Captain, do you have a few minutes for us?"

"Don't be ridiculous, I always have time for you guys."

"Thanks.'"

"What's going on?"

"We want to run something by you and see if you have any suggestions."

"Yeah, sit down, go ahead."

"As you know, we have Rabino very solid with the evidence from the search warrant," said Ernie.

"Yeah, I read the affidavit and the return. Nice haul."

"Thanks, we also have Armando Kiefer on the meth in his car," indicated Ernie.

"Go ahead."

"It appears that they both want to work with us," alleged Henry.

"You guys met with both of them, what do you think?"

"Armando seems to be the more serious one. I think that after he was detoxed, he found God or something like that. That's not uncommon as you know. He wants to do suppliers. Rabino is merely a local supplier, willing to give up the people he supplies."

"OK, so that gives us both ends of the spectrum, from Armando up the ladder to Rabino who wants to go down the ladder."

"That's exactly correct."

"Ernie, I assume you're going to do this as deep cover?"

"That's how we were thinking about handling it."

"Do you think that you can handle both ends at the same time?"

"With the team behind me I can do it. We have to take it slow and easy, that's all."

"Henry, what's your opinion of this case?"

"I think he can do it. I can run the back-up and between us we'll get the job done. As Ernie says we have to take it slowly for a while, we have to speak with the DEA and the ATF who will be of great help to us in a lot of ways."

"OK, then I will agree with you guys. Ernie, what do you need besides the men for back-up and coverage?"

"Captain, I need a little time off with the wife before I do deep cover."

"OK, Ernie, take the week, you go to that place of yours in Maine for a week so that you're out of sight. Henry, you handle the DEA and the ATF meetings. You can take your time and let them know what's going on. Tell them that Ernie will be the lead on this, they certainly know him and they've all worked together many times. They are usually very cooperative, you should have no problems."

The two detectives thanked the captain for his help and they started to leave the office when the captain stopped them.

"Guys, one thing; be careful and if there is anything that I can do to make the job easier, let me know. Also, keep me in the loop."

"Will do, Captain."

Ernie headed home while Henry went back to the office to speak with the men on the team before contacting the federal agencies and advising them about the cases.

***

Ernie arrived home and told Teresa that they were going to Maine for a week which made her smile. She enjoyed going there.

"Ernie, my cousin Walter and Rose are visiting from Italy. They are staying with my mother. What do you think about inviting them to the camp?"

"They're a lot older then us they're in their sixties, aren't they?"

"Yes, we'll keep a good eye on them."

"That's not the reason I'm asking. They don't speak English very well either. Maybe we should take your mother with us as well. She loves going to the camp and we love having her with us."

"Yeah, that's a good idea. I'll call her and see if she wants to come along."

Teresa contacted her mother by telephone and she agreed to go along on the trip. They would leave the next day.

Chapter 14

DEA & ATF

Tuesday June 19, 1979, At The Camp

Ernie, Teresa, Walter, Rose and Teresa's mother all drove up to the camp in Maine together.

Walter was able to speak English, Italian and German fairly well. Ernie understood and spoke a little Italian and a little of the German language from his days in the Air Force. He had been stationed at Rhine Maine Air Base in Germany. This made things a lot easier and besides that, Walter loved to fish. Two fishermen do not need a specific language; they can communicate in many ways. The two men made a good team for the week in Maine.

That first morning at the camp, Walters's wife Rose was cooking something strange. She had picked the flowers from Ernie's zucchini plants back at the condo before they all left for the house in Maine. She took the flowers with her in a paper bag. That morning, those zucchini flowers were in the frying pan covered with egg batter. This was a new dish to Teresa and Ernie.

They all sat around the kitchen table and Rose served the flowers. They were not only delicious, but after a lot of conversation Ernie and Teresa understood that the flowers were very healthy for humans. Walter explained that they were the male flowers only. The female flowers are the ones that make the zucchini and those would be left on the plant.

At about nine o'clock that morning Ernie took Walter fishing. Walter was all for it.

They took off in the small boat and slowly went around the edge of the lake. Ernie gave Walter a fishing rod and lure to troll with. As they went along, Ernie told Walter to be sure and hold the rod tight. Some of these fish are capable of pulling the rod out of your hand if you're not paying attention.

As Ernie finished making that statement Walter felt a hard pull on his rod. He fought a seven-pound bass and successfully got it into the boat. He looked at Ernie with a big smile.

"I'm sorry, Walter, but you have to throw that fish back in," Ernie communicated.

The smile disappeared. Walter wanted to know why.

"We have a conservation law here and there is only a certain size that we can keep."

Walter kissed the fish and threw it back in the water, saying only a few words, "I'll meet with you again, I hope."

They took off again and they caught fish after fish. Walter wanted to keep everyone. Ernie told him that they would only keep a couple to have for supper.

"I don't understand?"

"Walter, I can catch them anytime I like. Why keep them and put them in the freezer?"

Walter agreed and understood. He told Ernie about the fishing where he lives.

***

Switzerland

Walter was living in Switzerland, in the city. During the summertime he had a small apartment that he rented in the mountains alongside a large lake. The government put ten thousand trout in the lake each year. By the end of the summer there is not one fish to be had. He indicated that the idea of the conservation is a good idea, in his eyes.

He and his wife traveled to the lake for two weeks each year and did as everyone else did. They caught as many as they could and froze them for later consumption.

***

Back at the camp

The next day they traveled to Booth Bay in Maine, where they had lunch at a very nice country restaurant. That afternoon, on the way home, they purchased five chicken lobsters which were steamed and packed in a Styrofoam box. They took them back to the camp and Teresa made some side dishes to go along with the lobsters. That evening they rested.

The next day, Ernie and Walter went out fishing again. While trolling with lead line and a minnow for bait, Walter hooked onto a trout. This trout gave a hard fight, taking line and Walter reeling line back. This went on for about fifteen minutes until Walter got the fish close enough to the boat to get her into the net.

Walter rested for a while and believed that he had to throw this eight-pound brown trout back into the water. He picked up the trout by the tail preparing to throw it back into the lake.

"What are you doing, Walter?" asked Ernie

"I will throw the fish back. It's too large."

"No, not this one, we can keep this species and we'll all enjoy it."

Walter was thrilled; he placed the fish on a line, hung the fish over the side, in the water and tied it to the boat to keep it fresh.

"Ernie, do you think we can take my wife out fishing with us?"

"Of course we can. I didn't know she liked to fish."

"Yes, she would love this."

"OK, Walter, it's four o'clock, let's go back to the camp and get her. I'll take you both somewhere where you'll catch plenty of fish at dusk and after."

They went back to the camp. Rose joined them in the boat and Ernie took them to an area where they could catch white perch by the hundreds. Ernie usually threw them back or used them for bait for large bass, but Walter and Rose would not hear of it.

They caught over one hundred perch in the course of four hours, while sitting in this one cove on the lake. Walter and Ernie had to fillet every one of them. They were out on the dock until 11:30pm being bitten by every kind of bug imaginable. They had a lot of fun and would never forget this trip for white perch.

The rest of the week was spent traveling around Maine visiting sites, fishing, eating and watching Ernie's beard grow in, thick and full. By Friday he was ready for work back in Quincy.

Saturday morning the women cleaned up the camp for closing, while Ernie and Walter took the last morning for fishing. They caught plenty of bass, trout and a few pickerel.

That afternoon, Ernie cleared the water lines of the camp and made sure the car was loaded with the belongings of everyone going back to Massachusetts. They all loaded into the car and headed back.

They stopped at a restaurant in Kittery for dinner and then continued on their way home.

They had a wonderful week at the camp in Maine. When they got back to the condo, Teresa invited their guests to stay with them for the night, saying that she and Ernie would drive them home the next day after lunch.

That night they used the pool at the condo and relaxed talking about the fish that Walter and Ernie caught. Walter's seven pound bass was growing and had reached nine pounds by that time. Ernie wondered how large it would get by the time Walter returned home to Switzerland.

~*~

Back at the Office that Same Week:

Henry was not alone that week. He had the rest of the team to work with and plan the upcoming investigation when Detective Ernie Lijoi would again dig into his trunk of tricks and recreate his guise, Eddie Pannoni.

Henry began Monday morning by contacting the DEA, (Federal Drug Enforcement Administration), who was very interested in Armando Kiefer. They didn't say anymore than that over the telephone. They asked Henry to come into their offices for a meeting on Wednesday morning at ten. Henry agreed.

He then contacted the ATF, (Alcohol, Tobacco and Firearms Administration), who also showed interest in Armando and wanted to have a meeting.

Henry mentioned that he was meeting with the DEA on Wednesday and the representative from the ATF said that he would contact the DEA and arrange to see Henry at that same time.

Henry thought that this Armando Kiefer must be a much larger fish then they originally thought. All of the federal agencies that he usually worked with were interested in Armando.

All he had to do was mention Armando's name and they wanted to meet. He felt that the meeting on Wednesday would be enlightening and helpful.

Tuesday was an average day. The streets of the city were quiet, no major arrests and everyone did their job the way they were supposed to, efficiently and with a lot of expertise.

~*~

Wednesday June 20, 1979

The day's weather began in the sixties, but quickly shot up to seventy, with clear skies and that hint of summer hanging in the air. Henry arrived at the office early. He went to breakfast with the team members. After he returned to the office, he gathered up his reports and information on Armando Kiefer and Jacob Rabino, then left for the DEA meeting.

While driving into the city to attend the meeting, he wondered if the DEA or the ATF would have any interest in Jacob Rabino. He would ask about him at the meeting.

Henry arrived at the federal building in Boston, parked in the underground garage and entered the elevator to go to the floor where the DEA offices were located.

He arrived at the office and approached the front desk.

"Hi, I'm Detective Henry Griswold from Quincy."

"Yes, Detective, they are waiting for you in the conference room. I'll direct you there."

Henry followed the young man to a room where everyone was having coffee and talking. They barely noticed Henry walk in. He got himself a cup of coffee and sat down to wait for the meeting to start.

A few minutes later, two men walked into the room. Both men were known to Henry as Alexander Dribblesky, the regional manager of the DEA for the Boston area and his first assistant, Agent John Slater, who supervises everything and oversees all investigations. Both men saw Henry and made a gesture for him to come to the head of the table and have a seat.

Agent Dribblesky called the meeting to order and began by introducing Detective Henry Griswold.

"Here is what has happened; Henry and his partner, Detective Ernie Lijoi answered a call for a stabbing. We now know that the victim turned out to be one of the subjects in our Canadian investigation, Armando Kiefer."

"Is Kiefer alive?" asked an agent.

"Yes, he is. I'm going to turn this meeting over to John Slater who will be running this case in conjunction with the Quincy officers."

"Hi, everyone knows me here. To answer the question again, yes, Kiefer is alive and is now doing well after a couple of operations. The best part of this is that Henry and his partner, Detective Lijoi, got him with a good load of meth and he is willing to work for Quincy. When Quincy is finished we will use him on the federal cases that we have if he wants to stay out of jail. In the Quincy case, Lijoi will be the lead deep cover man"

"Lijoi, isn't he the guy that uses the Eddie Pannoni name? I worked with him once." an agent remarked.

"Yes, why, is there something we should know?" asked John

"No, not at all, he is one of the best that I have ever seen," the agent stated.

"You'll see him in action again, because we will be assisting Quincy with the case."

"Now I'll turn the floor over to Henry who will let you know what is going on at this point."

"Thanks, John. Right now Ernie is changing his looks and identity to Eddie Pannoni. He had to grow his beard and his hair. On Monday we will have our first get-together with Kiefer on the street. Ernie wants to feel him out and make sure he is a viable asset. After that we will begin our investigation. At that time, we'll need surveillance assistance and possibly financial assistance. I will be calling on you men, especially when this runs out of state."

"Has he given you any idea who he has for you?" A question from a team member.

"He has mentioned a few people, but you know how this goes, you start with a few here and wind up with ten or more over there. We have to wait and see where this takes us."

"How many men do you have committed to this case?" asked a team member.

"We have our regular six members. We can get more at the take-down in the end, but we also have other cases. We will definitely need your assistance. Let me ask if there is an ATF agent here?"

"Yes, I'm Agent Paul Surillo. I think you'll understand why I wanted upi to be here by the time this meeting is finished."

"OK, Agent, thanks. It couldn't be that there are guns wherever there are drugs in quantity, could it?" Everyone laughed at the seriousness and truthfulness of the question. "Are there any other questions?"

"Is Ernie aware of whom he is going to be dealing with? These guys are vicious."

"We haven't discussed particulars. That's one of the reasons I contacted you guys. I was hoping that if you knew this guy you would let us know what type of a situation we are getting into."

"Henry, why don't you let me explain? We'll give you a copy of our reports to go over with Ernie. You'll see why the ATF is here with this explanation."

"Sure, John, the floor is yours."

"We believe that this guy Kiefer got started about four or five year ago. He created a team that called themselves the 'Three Musketeers'. They are suppliers of meth to all of New England and some parts of New York. We got wind of them about a year ago, but we haven't been able to get much else, except that we know they are currently involved in a drug war in Canada that we don't want spilling into the United States"

"Drug war?" Henry questioned.

"Yes, Henry, there have been over twenty-five people murdered and a hundred injured, some of whom were innocent bystanders. The French Mafia wants to take over the lucrative business that the 'Musketeers' have and they will do anything to take over that business."

"Like what? What have they done that you know of, besides killing each other off?"

"One of the 'Musketeers' is a Frenchmen who lives in Canada, known only to us as Gerry. He seems to be the brains of the outfit. We just got word from one of our biker people that he received a box the other day. He cautiously opened the box thinking it may be a bomb. Our guy was present when the box was delivered. Once the box was opened and it appeared safe, Gerry walked over to it and looked in. It was two heads. Two human heads, no one knew where the bodies were. The heads turned out to be one of Gerry's chemists and his assistant, good friends of his."

"Does that put them out of the meth business?"

"No, Gerry has other chemists to work with."

"You know, John, when I think of the Mafia, I think of New York, Rhode Island and Boston. The Canadian Mafia just doesn't seem to fit in my mind's picture," stated Henry.

"Henry, I can tell you one thing about the Canadian Mafia, they sold about four hundred thousand pounds of meat in the form of wieners and burgers to the World's Fair expo concessionaires in 1967. That meat was found to be not fit for human consumption. The Canadian mafia did many things, but that one in particular affected thousands of people."

"As one of your men mentioned earlier, John, we may be getting involved with some vicious people."

"I would assume so. It isn't going to be an easy job. Tell Ernie to be very careful. We will have to have him covered by surveillance every moment that he is out there."

"I will, thanks John. Thanks, men, I will contact you guys when we are up and running."

Everyone wished Henry good luck with the case and he began to leave when he remembered Rabino.

"One thing before I go. Do any of you men know anything about a guy named Jacob Rabino in Quincy?"

One of the men stood up to answer. "Yes, I ran across him during a case I was working. He's a good-sized dealer and I was going to start a case on him."

"We got him also; he wants to work for us as well."

"You'll probably find that he was supplied by Kiefer and did his thing from Quincy," stated Agent John Slater.

"Yes, we were figuring that we could use him for some smaller busts when the time comes should we need something like that'" stated Henry.

"Sounds like a good idea to me. Use his leads as a scare tactic, bust people so that they're worried about the people around them. That type of thing is what you're talking about, right?"

"Exactly, it should all work in well when the time comes."

"Take it easy men, we'll be in touch. Agent Surillo, thanks for coming to this meeting. We will be talking, I'm sure", Henry stated as he left the offices of the DEA.

He got into his car and drove back to his office in Quincy where he completed a report of all the information he gathered and attached it to the DEA reports so that Ernie could go over them and be aware of everything.

Henry read over the files from the DEA and saw that the Canadian drug lords had access to plenty of weapons of all types. That's one reason why Agent Surillo of the ATF was interested in the case.

The next few days went by quietly and Henry was looking forward to getting Ernie up to date on the information that he acquired, as well as beginning the investigation.

Chapter 15

"Eddie"

Monday June 25, 1979

Ernie was up early that morning. He had his breakfast out on the patio where he could watch the lake and the small animals roam the area. He sat there with a cup of coffee after breakfast, getting ready to leave the condo for his office.

"Hey, buddy, that's the Lijoi residence. Do you know them?"

Ernie stood up and looked at his neighbor who didn't recognize him because of the mustache, beard and afro hairdo.

"It's me, Ernie; I changed my look a little."

"Oh, sorry, Ernie, I didn't recognize you with all that hair."

Ernie waved and smiled at the man. He went into his condo to get ready to leave for the day. He kissed Teresa and walked out the door, into the world and life of Eddie Pannoni.

***

Ernie arrived at the office and Henry had all of the reports laid out, the ones he did and the ones from the DEA, for Ernie to read.

"Henry, I'm glad to see you."

"Me too, Ernie, on your desk are all of the reports. Read them over then we'll talk. I'll tell you one thing; we have a bull by the horns here in Armando Kiefer."

"OK, Henry, wow, you're very business this morning."

"No, I'm not. I'm just anxious for you to know what we have. It may change your mind about going into deep cover."

Ernie sat at his desk and read all of the reports then turned to Henry.

"What about the ATF, did you speak with them?"

"Yes, an agent named Paul Surillo, nice guy, was at the meeting."

"This Kiefer is a bad dude if he's involved at this level. I kind of expected that he was a top man, didn't you?"

"No, not really, not that high where he imports from other countries."

"That's OK, it appears that we will have plenty of coverage. Let's give it a shot and see where it takes us."

"You're the main man on this operation, it's your call. I'll go along with whatever you decide, as long as you're aware of all of the facts."

"Then we are agreed. We will move forward."

"Agreed."

"First thing is for me to call Armando. As you know, I can't go into the station at all. I don't want to be seen there. This apartment building is OK. I was thinking of making this the Eddie Pannoni home address instead of the Center Street Boston address that I have on the identification papers."

"That's easy enough, all you have to do is go over to the registry with a letter from the captain and they will issue a new license with whatever address you want."

"Let it go this time. Maybe I'll do it the next time Eddie comes out of his mothballs."

"I'll telephone Armando and see what I can put together, something light and easy to see how he reacts to me. Do you have any suggestions before I call him?"

"No, that's your expertise. You wouldn't attempt to tell me how to test for ballistics would you?"

"No. We've been partners long enough, I trust your judgment."

"Then make the call."

Ernie picked up the phone and dialed Armando's telephone number.

"Hello" answered the voice at the other end.

"Hi Armando, this is Eddie, Eddie Pannoni"

"Who is this? Oh sorry, you woke me up; I understand."

"How are you feeling, Armando?"

"I am ready to do the job and get all of these cranksters."

**(Cranksters are people who use or illegally manufacture Methamphetamine).

"You mean all of the users?"

"Yes they're cranksters. Look Eddie, I have a party to go to tonight. It's a good opportunity to introduce you around as my old boyhood friend."

"Sounds good, but remember, we haven't seen each other for many years. I got into some trouble in New York where I was living for several years and needed to get away."

"Perfect."

"I need to know where the party is, who is running it and who may be there."

"The party is down in Taunton, there will be several dealers there and plenty of broads, crank, horse and blow."**

"You're telling me that there will be meth, heroin and cocaine there?"

**http://www.whitehousedrugpolicy.gov/streetterms

"Yeah, man, the broads love that meth and some of them like the other stuff. Be prepared to see some shit that you may never have witnessed before."

"Where in Taunton?"

"At my buddy's house, Charlie (Red) Wilson, he lives at 53 Court Street in Taunton."

"What time do you usually go to these things?"

"I don't usually walk in until after ten p.m. but we can go earlier."

"Yes, let's do that. I'll pick you up at eight p.m. and we will take it from there."

"I'll be ready."

Ernie hung up the phone. Henry, who was listening in on another line, wrote all of the information down.

"Ernie, we should advise the captain that we're starting tonight, in case he wants to come along and watch with the team."

"Sure, Henry, go ahead, but I doubt that he will want to be there, unless we think we need him."

"What do you think?"

"I think we need a small team, you and maybe one other man, that's all. You know I don't like to have a lot of people around during these things unless I smell problems."

"Yes, I know, but it's for your own protection."

"Yeah, yeah, you're like a mother hen sometimes, Henry" They both laughed.

"Henry, I'll take off now. I'll pick Armando up at eight p.m. and go to the party. If there is any problem at all, flash your lights when I pull up to the house and I will not park I'll drive around the corner."

"OK, but I don't foresee any problems."

"Good, see you tonight"

"Ernie, when you leave the party you'll drive Armando home and go home yourself, correct?"

"Correct. I'll do a report after I get home and we'll discuss my report in the morning"

"Good, I'll be watching you tonight; any problems throw a chair through the window or something"

"OK, see you tonight"

Ernie left the office and headed home. Henry went over to the main police station to advise Captain Richards.

***

That evening at eight o'clock, Ernie pulled up to Armando's home. He was waiting for Ernie, got into the car and they took off.

While in route Ernie advised Armando.

"Look Armando, in the event that there are questions about me, or there are problems with these people accepting me for one reason or another, I don't want you to try to defend me or my position. Let me do the talking and answering of questions. I'm used to being in that position and talking my way through it."

"OK, I'm glad you told me that, because I have never done this before and I don't really know how to react. I know there will be questions. Maybe not too many because I am bringing you in, but there will be some."

"Just be yourself. Introduce me around and I will take it from there."

"OK, Eddie, you got it."

They arrived at the house. Ernie looked around for some sign of an undercover car in case Henry needed to speak with him. The area was quiet and he didn't see any signal. It was time to become Eddie Pannoni.

***

Eddie was dressed in street clothes with his beard, mustache and afro-style hair. Eddie took a pick out of his pocket and fixed his hair. He followed Armando into the party.

They entered a house with large rooms. Ernie could see that the first floor had two living-rooms, a kitchen and dining-room at first glance around. There were several people in the house. Armando told Ernie to follow him into the first living room, where he began introducing Ernie around.

"Hi, Red," said Armando.

"Hi, who's with you? You know this is a closed party."

"Not to this guy, this is Eddie Pannoni, an old buddy of mine from years ago. He's been doing business in New York. He's OK, Red."

"Anyone else, but you and I would be pissed. Since he's a good friend I'll trust your judgment. That means he's a friend of mine. Nice to meet you, Eddie Pannoni," said Red.

Eddie smiled, "Nice to meet you too, Red. I know a guy in New York with the nickname Red, but he is connected."

"Talking about connected, you said your name is Pannoni?" asked Red.

"Yeah, that's the name and all types of goods are the game," replied Eddie

"Yeah, it seems to me that I've heard that statement before. I have a friend that is connected to one of the New York families and he said the same exact thing once," stated Red.

"If that's true and I do not doubt you, then you know that we stop our discussion right here. We never discuss those things outside of the family. Sorry," replied Eddie.

"Armando, you brought in a good man. Maybe I can do some business with him?"

"I hope you can. I trust him and I do business with him."

Red looked at Eddie and Armando, "You guys circulate, enjoy yourselves. Eddie, one day we have to talk. Stop by anytime, you'll always be welcome here. Help yourself to the drug of your choice. The shit is all over the house."

"Thanks, Red, we'll walk around."

As Eddie was walking around a beautiful girl grabbed his arm and asked for a light. She had a marijuana joint hanging from her lips.

Ernie looked at her and saw a well tanned girl about five feet five inches tall, thin with long black hair and blue eyes. He froze for a second because she was so pretty.

"Sorry, I don't have any matches."

"That's OK, you're Eddie, right?"

"Yes, that's my name."

"Red said to take care of you, so if you need anything let me know."

"What's your name?"

"Sorry, I'm high as a kite. I'm Julia."

"Julia what?"

"Julia Lozano, why do you ask about my last name? Most of these guys just want to have sex and forget me."

"I'm not most of these guys, Julia."

"What makes you different?"

"I don't look for sex right away. I want to get to know a girl first, but business always comes first."

"You're just like the rest of them, they all place business first. I guess they have to at the level that they are dealing."

"You should never speak of that to anyone, Julia."

"Why not?"

"Julia, you never know who you're talking to."

"OK, now I have to worry about you being a cop?"

"Yes, Julia, that's right and before the night is over I may arrest you. Is there a bedroom where I can arrest you?"

"Any time Eddie. I can see that I'm going to like you, you're cute."

They both laughed and Eddie continued walking around and drinking his beer. He now had an introduction to everyone in the room. His introduction was hanging on his arm and a beautiful one at that.

Ernie noticed a hallway with doors off of it.

"Julia, what's down the hallway?"

"That's the playrooms, silly. and the bathroom"

"Playrooms?"

"When we have these parties we call the bedrooms playrooms."

Ernie laughed out loud.

"The other bedroom is Red's room and he's the only one that uses it. We can use one of the others later, if you want."

"We'll see how the night goes."

"Hi, Julia, who's your friend?"

"Hi, Pauli, this is Eddie. Eddie, this is Pauli"

"Hi Pauli, what's your last name?"

"Jameson, and you?"

"His name is Eddie Pannoni, he's from New York and he's connected, Pauli," stated Julia.

"Julia, are you having another one of your dreams?" stated Pauli.

"No, Red told me. He's an important guy from New York and he's mine for the night." said Julia.

"Julia, I told you that you should not speak of those things," said Eddie.

"Oh, Pauli's OK."

"That's OK, Eddie. You can't tell this cunt anything that you don't want others to hear."

"Thanks, Pauli, I'm just learning about that."

"You boys are bad, talking about me like that."

"Eddie, who are you here with?"

"Armando, we're old friends, we go way back."

"Oh, I thought he was dead."

"No, he had a close call. Someone wanted him finished, but they missed the mark."

"If you're with him, I believe Julia. If anyone has those kinds of connections around here, he does."

"What's your angle, Eddie? Did Armando bring you in to do the guy that tried to kill him?"

"No, but anything is possible. I got into some shit in New York and I had to leave for a while so I came up here, but I still have people that depend on me for their supplies so I'll be making runs from time to time."

"Do you have a specialty?"

"No, I have cranksters, noses and poppers. I usually sell it all, but my suppliers went down with a group in New York so I have to find some new suppliers."

"You supply meth, cocaine and heroin. You must have a lot of people to supply."

"Yes, I do, and I'll be looking this week."

"What about Armando?"

"Didn't he tell you? He's getting out; he's down to minor dealing. That stabbing did something to him." indicated Eddie.

"He should get out of the business."

"Pauli, it sounds like you and Armando have history, bad history."

"No use in talking about that now. Nice to meet you, Eddie, if I can help you out stop by and see me."

"Thanks, Pauli, I appreciate that offer, but I don't know where you live or how to contact you."

"I'm easy to find, Julia knows me well and how to contact me, she'll tell you. Talking about Julia, have a good time to-night."

"I don't think so; she likes to talk too much."

"Yeah, she means well and she fucks like a rabbit."

"Yeah, I've been there, done that. Can't be too careful with all of the new diseases going around."

"Whatever; have a good time."

"Thanks, Pauli."

"You know, Eddie, you guys have some nerve."

"Why, Julia?"

"Talking about me that way with me standing right here. I'm offended."

"What can I do to make it up to you?"

"Do you have any crank (meth)?"

"Sorry, I'm not set up yet, but when you show me Pauli's place I will be shortly thereafter."

"That's OK, Red has plenty around here. I'll be right back."

Julia left Eddie standing in the living room and went to the kitchen. Five minutes later she returned to Eddie.

"Eddie, I'm getting cranked, wanna fuck?"

"Not right now."

"What's a matter? I'm clean and I'll even blow you if you want?"

"Not right now, I have to get some connections going for my business in New York or else I'll lose my customers to other dealers."

"I'm sure that Red will take care of you. He seems to like you or he wouldn't have asked me to take care of you and introduce you around. Pauli will help you out and I know plenty of others."

"In that case we will have to stay in touch."

"Now that sounds interesting."

"Julia, what's Pauli's address and where does he do his dealing from?"

"He keeps everything in his house. That would be a good score some day, his house."

"You want to rob his house?" asked Eddie.

"Someday maybe," stated Julia.

"Where is his home?"

"He's in Weymouth, up by Quincy. He's got a nice house there and does a fantastic business."

"Do you know where in Weymouth?"

"He's over by the Four River Bridge on Dorothy Drive. I believe it's a green house with white shutters. I've been there several times. He keeps a nice clean house and has his lab in the basement."

"Thank you, that will be a big help."

"Don't forget, I turned you onto him. I deserve a nice tip, you know what I mean?"

"Yeah, we'll take care of you in time, but right now I have to circulate. You know business."

"I'll introduce you around."

Eddie followed Julia to a group of people that were sitting on the couch and talking about their business, the problems and the profits.

"Hi people, I want you all to meet Eddie, he's a friend of Red's and Armando's and now he's friends with Pauli."

"Hi everyone, I'm from New York and getting my shit together here for my business in New York."

"Don't tell me that you don't have suppliers in New York?" one person asked

"No, I wouldn't say that, but we took a major hit and we all have to lay low for a few months. At least that's the word from above."

"So why here?" another person asked

Eddie smiled, "Because I have a friend here that I know I can trust."

"Who is that?" The same person asked.

"Let's see there's Armando, Red and others, we've been friends for a while now, although I haven't been in touch for several years until recently."

A girl asked: "Are you married?"

"Yes, I am, but she's in New York with her family. We're separated at the moment."

"Think you'll get back together?" asked the same girl.

"Hey, Bitch. He's with me," yelled Julia.

"Don't call me a bitch, you fucken whore!"

"Rose, I'll get you for that."

"Julia, all you can get is that donkey you used to fuck in San Antonio."

Eddie grabbed Julia and walked her away from the couch area, stopping the argument.

"Julia what the fuck is wrong with you. You don't own me."

"No, but I'm better then that bitch."

"OK you're better, but let it drop. Now go and play somewhere so that you calm down."

"OK, for you Eddie, for you."

Eddie returned to the couch area.

"Sorry about that, she thinks she owns me."

"She thinks she owns everybody at one time or the other. You smile at her and she wants to fuck your brains out," stated one of the people at the couch.

"That's one way to die," said Eddie.

"She's a card," said another person.

"I don't know your names and I probably won't remember them all at once, I'm a little cranked, but why don't we give it a try?" asked Eddie.

"I'm John, Johnny Orlando."

"I'm Joey (Twister) Calabraisia."

"I'm Rose Deprist."

"Vinnie Testalia."

"Luigi Samora."

"I'm Howie Lawlerest."

"Dale Denham."

"Ryan Kelly."

"Joanna Heinz."

"Roberta Shaw."

One by one they responded.

"I knew it, I'll never remember all those names, but we will all meet again, many times I hope," stated Eddie.

"I certainly hope so," Rose Deprist replied.

"You broads go gaga over every new pair of pants that comes along," said Vinnie Testalia.

Everyone laughed at Vinnie's statement. They turned and looked at Red as he walked over to the area.

"Did everyone meet Eddie?"

They all replied that they had.

"Eddie, there's a few more people that you should meet, but I should be able to supply what you need for your customers in New York."

"I don't know, Red; I have big needs."

"Let's go back to my bedroom and talk."

Eddie followed Red to his bedroom down the hallway, the last door on the right.

"Eddie, be honest with me, what exactly do you need?"

"Red, I'm always honest. I need two keys of cocaine, one key of heroin and two pounds of meth."

"Wow that's quite a bit of shit. I don't have anyone that does that much all at once."

"New York is a City of over seven million people, over fourteen million state-wide, and I only have a very small fraction of the customer ratio."

"I can take care of the meth. You'll have to see Pauli for the heroin and coke. We'll get you fixed up, we'll try and get something going this week. Is that OK for your needs?"

"That will be fine, but I will need a taste first to verify that I'm getting good quality."

"No problem, this week. Stop by one day and we'll do the deed."

"Thanks, Red, I appreciate your help."

They left the room and as they walked down the hallway towards the living room a door opened and Armando walked into the hallway.

"Hey, Eddie, Red."

"Armando, are you being a bad boy?" asked Eddie.

"No, just a satisfied one"

"Red and I have come to somewhat of a business understanding."

"Good, I'm glad."

"Armando, why the fuck are you giving up this fantastic business?"

"Red, do you know I was almost killed a few weeks ago?"

"Yes I'm aware of the problem."

"That's what made me quit. I have enough money, I'll be fine and I'll do some small stuff from time to time."

"Send your customers over to me, I can handle them," said Red

"That's why I brought Eddie here; he was one of my best customers."

"But I thought that you hadn't seen each other for years."

"That's true, but we spoke on the phone from time to time, then about six months ago he began coming to me with his needs. Now I'm out of the business. It's better for me that way."

"OK, I understand."

"Red, we'll see you later, it's been a long day and I need some sleep," stated Eddie.

"Yeah, me too, I'm gonna leave early," said Armando

"What the fuck is wrong with you guys? Most of the broads haven't even gotten here yet."

"Yeah, Red, but it's 11:30, I'm tired, there will be other times."

"OK, if you feel you must leave. Are you leaving too, Armando?"

"Yes, I'm tired; I'm still not completely healed."

"Eddie, stay in touch. We can do those things you mentioned."

"Thanks, Red, I'll see you during the week."

Eddie and Armando left the house. After dropping Armando off at his place, Eddie drove home.

***

Eddie returned to being Ernie Lijoi Sr., a husband, father and homeowner. While en route to his home, he pulled the car over and wrote down as much of the information that he could remember; all of the names, Pauli's address, and more. He knew that the team would grab all of the automobile registration numbers on the street. They would match up the information in the report with the appropriate automobile registration listings the next day.

Chapter 16

Stew

Tuesday June 26, 1979, Morning

Ernie came into the office late and prepared his report for his team members. Henry took the report and began matching up the information with the listings that he had run the night before. He now had the full names and addresses for each of the people in the report. The next step was to get their telephone numbers.

Ernie completed his reports and telephoned Armando.

"Hello"

"Armando, how are you?"

"Fine thanks. Do you want to meet another guy tonight?"

"I'll pick you up at 8pm. Where are we going?"

"I wanted to stop by and introduce you to 'Stew', he's a major dealer and he lives right in Quincy."

"Where in Quincy?"

"Do you know where Forbes Road is? The Sheraton Hotel is right there?"

"Yes, I know it"

"If you go past the hotel there is a street called Partridge Hill Road."

"I'm aware of that street."

"Go down that street and take the second right which is Briarwood Circle. On the left there is a red house with white trim and a large pool in the back yard. That's Stew's house."

"A hard place for surveillance."

"I don't know about that, but you'll like him. He's actually a nice guy."

"OK, Armando, I'll pick you up at eight p.m. and we'll visit your buddy Stew.

"I'll be waiting. Oh, by the way, I heard that he's having some problems with another dealer in Quincy. I just thought I should mention it."

"Thanks, Armando, that's good to know. I'll see you to-night."

That day Ernie decided to ride around town and try his old trick of picking up hitchhikers. Just for the practice.

"Henry, I'm gonna cruise the city for a while. I'll call if I come up with anything"

"I knew you would eventually get back into that, call me and I'll be there for you."

***

Ernie got into his undercover car, a 1978 Ford Thunderbird, white convertible and began cruising. It didn't take long. He saw a girl about twenty-four-years-old with a boy about the same age hitchhiking. He stopped and picked them up.

"Hi, guys, where are you headed?"

"Down the Neck, are you going that way?"

"Come on, I'll give you a ride. I'm just riding around, killing time. My name is Eddie and you?"

"I'm Russell and she's my girlfriend, Beatrice"

"Nice to meet you guys."

"You're just riding around?" asked Russell.

"Yes, actually I'm looking for something for the head, just to hold me over till my guy gets home tonight."

"What do you need?" asked Russell.

"Smoke would be Ok but blow would be even better."

"I got a guy, but I don't have any money," stated Russell

"What are you suggesting?"

Beatrice spoke up, "I'll tell you. If you buy some for us, we'll get something for you"

"That sounds fair, but how much will it cost me to get it from you and what would I be buying?"

"I can get some smoke and if he's holding I can get blow"

"How much do you need for the cocaine?"

"You pay for a gram, it's one hundred dollars, we split it"

"Come on, you want fifty dollars for just making the con-nection or are you including Beatrice in that deal?"

"No, my girl is not included,"

"Don't be so fast, Russell, I like her looks."

"No, she's not included, and I'll take a quarter for the deal," said Russell.

"Now that's fair."

"Let me see the money," stated Russell.

Eddie pulled the car over and took a wad of money out of his pocket to show Russell the one hundred dollars.

Beatrice saw the money and commented: "Now you look real interesting, Eddie."

Once Russell saw the money he said, "OK, I'll direct you."

Russell directed Eddie to a small house in the Hough's Neck area of Quincy, down Sea Street, then a right on Wall Street to number 1184 Macys Street. They came to a white house with grey trim, where Eddie pulled his car into the driveway.

Eddie gave Russell the money and he went into the house. After a few minutes he came out with a large smile on his face.

"I got it, now you have to drive me to where we're going," demanded Russell.

"No problem, give me mine and we're all set. I just have to make a phone call before we go."

"I have to split it. I'll do it while you make your call," said Russell.

"That's fine. Where am I driving you?"

"Not far, over to Richards Street."

"Good, now I have to make the call if I can find a phone."

"Right at the corner," indicated Russell.

"Good."

Eddie pulled up to the Seven–Eleven market on the corner and went inside to telephone the office. There was no answer.

He then telephoned the dispatcher and let him know what was going on. The dispatcher notified Henry via radio and it began.

"Have the cruiser in that area stop him. Tell the cruiser to call me and let me know exactly where they are, then wait for me to get there before he takes any action."

"I already have the cruiser on the way, you'll hear from him in a minute or so," indicated the dispatcher.

Henry got into his cruiser and started out towards Houghs Neck knowing that the call was coming in soon.

"Charlie 4 to November 3."

"November 3 standing by."

"Henry, I have a car stopped that may be of interest to you."

"OK, where are you?"

"I'm at the intersection of Richards and Harvey Streets; I'll wait for you."

"Less than five minutes."

Henry drove to the area of Eddie's car and the cruiser. He got out of his car and walked over to the cruiser, the Charlie car.

"What do you have?" asked Henry.

"What the fuck do I know? I was told by the dispatcher to stop the car and call you."

"OK, go and get their ID's and bring them back."

The officer took all of the information and ran all three names and came up with warrant on a Russell Cross, the man in the car with Eddie.

"Good, that warrant will help. Officer, get them all out of the car, we'll search them and the car."

The officer did as directed by Henry.

While searching Russell, Henry found two packets of cocaine: "What do we have here?"

"That's not mine."

"Then why is it in your pocket?"

"Half of that is his," pointing towards Eddie.

Henry turned to Eddie, winked and asked: "Is that true?"

"If I owned it, I'd have it in my pocket."

Henry arrested Russell on the spot for the traffic warrant and possession of narcotics, he told his girl friend Beatrice to take off.

Eddie said: "If you like, Detective, I can drive her, unless you are arresting me also?"

"No, you can go and take her with you."

Henry took Russell back to the station for booking, then up to BCI (Bureau of Criminal Investigation).

"Mr. Russell Cross, it looks like we caught you holding. You were holding a controlled substance called cocaine. Do you have anything to say for yourself?"

"What is this warrant that you said you have?"

"That's minor, for running a red light and not showing up in court to pay the fine."

"I paid the fine."

"Not according to this paper I have. That's not the worst of your problems, you have the drugs."

"Yes, I know. What can I do to straighten this out?"

"There's not much."

The phone rang: "Wait a minute Russell, let me get this call."

"Hello?"

"Henry, it's Ernie."

"I expected your call."

"The address is 1184 Macys Street, a white house with grey trim. You got the drugs. A few more minutes and I would have been holding as well. Three quarters of it was mine. I paid for it with City Money and he went into the house."

"That's great, thanks. I'll let you know how it goes."

"I hope you don't mind, it's just a little something to keep you busy while we wait for these nightly meets with Armando."

"No, not at all, it's good practice."

Henry hung up the phone.

"Sorry about that, it was a friend advising me on something that is of interest to me. Now where were we?"

"You were saying that there wasn't much that I could do to clear this up."

"I'm afraid not, Russell, unless you want to give up some people and locations."

"I never did anything like that before. Can I ask you a question?"

"Sure."

"Why did that cruiser stop the car I was in?"

"Broken tail light."

"Then why didn't he give us a ticket for the light and let us go?"

"He called and said that he was suspicious for some reason. I came down and took over like it was my case, knee jerk reaction so to speak."

"Oh, ok, I was beginning to think that guy Eddie was a cop."

"He didn't seem like one. I didn't know him, but you never know."

"No, he's not a cop; he was too cool."

"Russell, tell me about the place that you got this cocaine."

"What will you do for me if I do?"

"All I can do is make a recommendation to the district attorney who then recommends to the court."

"What will I get?"

"I can't guarantee it, but you help me and you may get off with a suspended or even less."

"OK, his name is Raymond and he lives at 1184 Macy Street. That's all I really know."

"How much stuff does he have?"

"He deals grass and cocaine. I don't know how much he has, but he has a lot of customers."

Russell indicated that Raymond was a Spanish male, five feet five inches tall, brown hair and eyes.

"Are there or did you see any weapons of any kind?"

"Yes, he had a handgun like yours on the table"

"A 9mm gun like this?" Henry showed Russell his weapon.

"Yes, exactly like that."

"Thank you for that information."

Henry went on to get a description of Raymond, the interior of the house and as much information as possible. He sent Russell back to his cell and began the affidavit for the search warrant of Raymond's house.

Through investigation he found that Raymond's last name was Wheeler. The check for a driver's license showed that he was a Spanish male, five feet five inches tall, brown hair and eyes. All of this information checked out. The information that Ernie gave will be used only for back-up and verification in the affidavit. This would protect his identity.

Once Henry completed the affidavit he went to the court house and spoke with the clerk of courts.

"Hi, Henry, what's up?"

"I have a search warrant paper here."

"OK, let me read it."

It did not take long and the clerk of courts was satisfied.

"This reeks of your partner's work."

"I ain't saying nothing."

"I understand, approved. Go and get him."

Henry left the court and contacted the team to meet them in the Neck about three blocks from the home of Raymond Wheeler.

The team arrived and Henry advised them about what he had. It was agreed that Henry would go in the front with two men and the rest would cover the back and sides of the house. They had three cruisers with one man each to assist with the entry.

As Henry drove up to the driveway he observed Raymond's car parked there. He pulled up behind it and the rest of the cars pulled up in front of the house.

Henry got out of his car and walked over to one of the cruisers that had the large blue bammer in the trunk. Henry went to the rear of the cruiser with the officer to get it. As they opened the trunk and grabbed the bammer, Henry heard a shot, then another shot, then another. Everyone ran for cover behind car doors, trees, car bodies, anywhere they could.

Henry was in back of the cruiser with another officer, he looked at the officer who was calling into the station that they were under fire. Henry reached into the trunk of the cruiser and pulled out the megaphone.

"Raymond, this is the Quincy police, you have not hit any-one yet. It's not too late for you to throw out the gun and walk out with your hands on your head, peacefully, before someone gets hurt."

"Why are you bothering me?"

"I'll be glad to discuss that with you after you come out."

"No, you tell me right now. What the fuck is going on?"

"Raymond, I could bull shit you, but I won't do that. I'll tell you the truth. We have a search warrant for your home."

"What kind of a search warrant?"

"I can't say right now, come out and we'll discuss it."

A shot rang out that hit the cruiser, in the rear quarter. The cruiser that Henry was using for cover, the police had not fired a shot as of this point in time.

"Raymond, if we all take aim at the location where you are standing, you will not survive the multiple shots that will come at you all at once."

"You can't see me."

"Sorry, but we can. Haven't you heard of heat penetration surveillance?"

The officer standing behind Henry tapped him on the shoulder.

"Henry, where the hell did you get that bull shit from?"

"I heard it on a science fiction show, it sounded good and it fits here."

"I guess so."

"Raymond, did you hear what I said?"

"Yes, I heard you."

"Raymond, the house is surrounded and we are watching every move you make."

"Then watch this." yelled Raymond. A six inch round object flew out of the front window of the house and hit the ground on the front lawn in the middle of all of the cars. One of the detectives yelled: "Grenade."

Everyone pulled in behind the car doors and the cars themselves, attempting to get some coverage. The grenade went off and one man began yelling about his foot. He was hit with a piece of metal from the grenade.

While this was going on, Raymond ran out the back door in an attempt to get away. He had his gun in his hand. Two detectives, covering the back door, heard the blast in the front of the house and saw Raymond trying to flee with a gun in his hand, all at the same moment.

"Drop it!" yelled Detective Rule, who was covering with Detective Churn. Raymond leveled the gun towards Detective Rule and both he and Det. Churn opened fire. Raymond was hit in the chest twice, once by each man and went down.

Detective Churn and Rule worked with the narcotics unit at the station on local cases and were borrowed to do this search. It was a common thing for the Special Services Unit to call on the Narcotics Unit for assistance in cases like this.

Everything went quiet and Henry ran to the back to see if assistance was needed, while other men tried to assist the wounded officer.

As he turned the corner, he observed Churn approaching a body which was on the ground and Rule standing back covering Churn. The man was dead. Rule picked up Raymond's gun by sticking a pencil through the trigger guard and placed it in an evidence bag.

"You had to kill him, I suppose?"

"We heard that bomb go off out front and he came running out. We stopped him, he raised his weapon as though to shoot and we popped him."

"I'm not questioning it, guys. I'm sorry you had to shoot him, that's all."

"You're sorry? We have to live with it."

"Yes, I understand. We have a man hit out front. The ambulance should be here soon.. I'll call this in for you. You guys rest for a while, but stay with the body until the ambulance takes him."

"OK, Henry."

Henry went around to the front of the house and informed everyone in front about what had happened.

"It looks like we will be here for quite a while, Henry," stated Detective Wade.

"Yeah, and I'm supposed to cover Ernie tonight."

"Why don't you go ahead home and get some rest, we'll take care of the search and I'll leave the report for you. After all, you don't even have a defendant anymore. We'll gather the evidence to justify the warrant and place it in the evidence locker. You cover Ernie tonight," insisted Wade.

"You're probably right. Just do a good search, make sure you get everything."

Detective Henry Griswold waited for the ambulance and the legal declaration that Raymond was dead by the doctor that came with the ambulance. Henry left the area to get a couple of hours sleep before he had to cover Ernie that night.

Chapter 17

Cocaine & Guns

That Evening at eight p.m., Tuesday June 26, 1979

Detective Ernie Lijoi, under the guise of Eddie Pannoni, a New Yorker hiding out in Massachusetts, drove up to Armando's home where Armando was waiting for him out front. The weather was in the sixties, perfect for working.

"You ready, Armando?"

"As ready as ever, let's get it done."

Armando directed Ernie as he dove to 1920 Briarwood Circle, Quincy, a red house with white trim and a large pool in the back yard, Stew's house. Ernie drove by the house slowly looking to see if there were any of the police undercover cars there covering him. He did not see any signals so he figured there were no messages for him. He and Armando entered the house.

"Hi, Stewart, how have you been?" asked Armando.

"I've been fine, what about you? I heard that you were stuck a few times." stated Stew.

"Yes, who told you that?" asked Armando

"You made all the papers: *'Man found barely alive on Quincy Beach'.*"

"Oh, I thought that maybe someone told you."

"Trying to find info on who did you?"

"Of course I am and if I find out, look out!"

"The only thing I can tell you is that it's well known that you and Pauli, although working together, are not close. You know what I mean?"

"Yes, I'm aware of that; thanks, though."

"If I ever hear anything I'll let you know, don't worry."

"Great."

While Armando and Stew were talking, Eddie made a mental note of Stew's eagerness to help Armando and also noted that Stew was a white male, about thirty-five years of age, five feet nine inches tall, two hundred and thirty pounds, with brown eyes and a slightly balding head of dark black hair and a Vandyke of black hair covering his chin.

"Who's this guy?"

"Stew, meet Eddie, he's from New York. We were friends for many years, then we kind a lost touch with each other. Now he's here trying to connect to some people because of some shit going on in New York."

"Welcome, Eddie. What kind of business are you in?"

"Being from New York I handle everything; guns, meth, coke and heroin. I have a bunch of customers that I have to keep happy and my supplier got busted. I'm looking around for the right person."

"I'm sure we can help you out, Eddie. Come into the kitchen and meet Martin," stated Stew.

They walked across the living room and through a swinging door into the kitchen, a large room with all of the normal appliances against the walls and a table with six chairs in the middle of the floor. There was a man sitting at the table alone, doing a joint which he handed to Stew as he, Armando and Eddie walked into the room.

Stew handed the joint to Armando, who took a hit and then it was handed to Eddie, who stood there while they talked, placed the joint up to his lips and then handed it off. He did not take a hit he only simulated doing so. He acted as though he was holding it in until after he passed the joint. No one noticed that he did not exhale any smoke.

"Marty, you know Armando; Eddie is his friend," Stew introduced Eddie.

Eddie looked at Martin and wanted to remember his looks for his report, he was a white male, thirty-five years of age, six feet tall, one hundred and ninety pounds, blond hair and blue eyes, clean-shaven, yet he had a rough looking face.

"Hi, Armando, Eddie, nice to meet you," replied Martin.

"Me too," said Eddie.

"Where are you from, man?" asked Martin.

"Right here now, but I'm actually from New York."

"Cool, that's one hell of a city, man."

"Yeah, a great city, have you been there?"

"You bet your ass I have and enjoyed it."

"That's nice to hear."

"You here on business, Eddie?" inquired Martin.

"He's looking for new supplier, Marty. His man took a hit," stated Stew.

"Oh, that's interesting, what line are you in?"

"I do it all. In the city that never sleeps, it's all needed, all the time."

"Great, maybe we can do something, we'll talk."

"My pleasure to discuss, that's how I learn who has the best deals."

"Hey, Stew, give me a gram, will you?" asked Martin.

"If you got a hundred," stated Stew.

"Here's your money, you know I wouldn't ask if I wasn't prepared to buy," said Martin as he laughed.

"Hey, Stew give me one too," said Eddie.

Stew looked at Eddie and smiled, then turned and walked over to his kitchen cabinet. He opened the door and reached up to the top shelf to grab two grams from a good-sized glass bowl filled with grams of cocaine. Eddie also saw a handgun sitting on the shelf below.

"What kind of gun it that, Stew?"

"A nine, you like?" Stew handed Eddie the 9 mm handgun.

"Yes, I like a lot. I wish I could get my hands on a few."

"What would you want a few for?"

"I can make a ton on those in New York."

"Oh, I see. I have a connection for these and others that you may like," said Stew.

"I'm sure I will. I have cash to buy them and I have people looking to buy guns all the time. It looks like we can do some business, Stew. This may turn out to be a lucky day for me."

"Yeah, for me too, as long as you buy through me."

"I'd be willing to do that as long as the price isn't ridiculous. I understand that you gotta make a buck."

"I will be respectful," indicated Stew.

"I may want one myself, Stew," Armando said.

"Hey, Armando, you buy a gun from me, I'll treat you right. You know that," stated Eddie.

"We're gonna get along great, I can see that," said Stew, and everyone seemed to agree with that estimation.

"Armando, I would like to get home early and get some sleep. Are you ready to go yet?"

"Yes, I'm ready."

"Stew, thanks for the help and we will talk about the guns at some point. But supplying me with meth and cocaine may be a problem."

"Why do you say that, Eddie?"

"Because I see that you deal in grams. I don't buy less then multiple ounces and I usually do multi-pounds."

"No, Eddie, you got the wrong impression. I can supply as much as you like as long as I have enough advance notice."

"Then what's with the gram packages?"

"That's the small stuff. I have a lot of friends that stop by for a quick set up. Hey, it's an extra buck and they all count."

"I see, good idea, maybe we can do something."

"Eddie, stop by anytime, you're always welcome."

"Thanks, Stew. Armando, you ready?"

"Yeah, take it easy, Stew. I'll see you next week."

"I'm always here, Armando."

***

Eddie had a small buy that could be tested and a strong lead for guns. He felt that the night was very productive. He knew that this type of an investigation was creating a strong court case for the protection of Armando in the event that his identification became as issue down the line.

It was close to 11pm as they drove away from Stew's house. Ernie would make his reports in the morning and then take a better look at Stew and Martin.

"Armando, what the fuck do you want a gun for?"

"I don't, I was trying to help you out."

"I thought so. Let me explain this to you. If you make the buy yourself and the evidence is used, you have to testify in court. If I make the buy, then I testify, not you. That protects you. It's Ok for you to discuss and then bring the situation to me for a final negotiation and purchase, but you should stay out of the deal for your own protection."

"I was trying to help, that's all."

"I understand and I appreciate it, but you must remember what I said about you testifying. I don't want anyone to know who you are when this comes to an end for the protection of you and your family."

"I understand. I'll do as you say."

"Do you want to go home?"

"Why don't we go to the lounge on the beach and have a beer or two? I'll introduce you to some people."

"Sounds good to me, Armando."

***

They drove to the beach and went into the BIG WAVE, a beach bar that Ernie had been in many times over the years, but quietly and without notice, not as Eddie Pannoni.

They entered the bar and approached the bartender who asked what they wanted.

"Two Bud bottles, please."

They stood by the bar and a few people came in and walked over to Armando who immediately introduced Eddie as a friend. Eddie noticed a pool table standing off to one corner and walked over to it. There were two men playing a game. Eddie placed two quarters on the table edge above the coin slide, indicating that the next game was his against the winner of the current game.

Eddie played three games and made sure that he won only one game, in an effort not to show his ability at that moment. He was going to stop playing when a man approached the table.

"Hey, you're a pretty good player. I'll try you next."

"I'm Eddie and you?"

"'Teeth', that's what they call me, but my name is Conklin."

Standing before Eddie was a white male, six feet tall, two hundred and twenty-five pounds, long brown beard, brown hair and brown eyes with a set of 'Teeth' that were large and somewhat crooked. You could see where he got his nickname.

The game Eddie was playing ended. He and 'Teeth' began a game of eight ball. The object of the game is to sink the number eight ball, without scratching.

'Teeth' broke the rack and ran two balls.

Eddie could tell that 'Teeth', was a hustler of sorts from the way 'Teeth' handled the cue stick and softness of his shots. He decided to have some fun with him and let him win. This was not easy since 'Teeth' wanted Eddie to win. Finally, 'Teeth' sank his last ball and then missed the eight ball. Ernie got up to shoot. He had four balls on the table plus the eight ball. He looked at 'Teeth'.

"'Teeth', we have been playing this silly game for a long time. I don't hustle, I just play for the fun of it, but you are trying to hustle this game. Now, what do you want a true game or do you want to try and hustle me?"

"I thought so, Eddie, you are better than you play?"

"I think so."

"OK, clear it and let's do it."

Eddie smiled, bent over and took one shot. He shot at the number four ball which went into the side pocket; the cue ball ricocheted into the number six ball which in turn, sank the hanging eight ball. The game was over with one legal shot.

"Where have you played, Eddie?"

"I was born and raised in Brooklyn, NY, with a pool hall on the corner where I spent most of my childhood. Where have you played?"

"I used to do tournaments years ago, but I gave it up."

"So now you hustle?"

"No, I'm a truck driver, tractor trailers, state to state. Once in a while I see someone like you and think that maybe I can beat him a little."

"That's hustling if you're gonna take my money."

"Oh, I would only have beaten you for a beer or two."

"Shit, that's easy."

Eddie walked over to the bar and ordered three beers. He sent one down to Armando who was talking with some people and took the other two over to the pool table where he handed 'Teeth' one.

"Thanks, Eddie."

"'Teeth', we're playing an honest game here, right?"

"I should hope so. You break, Eddie."

"OK, how about a three game tournament? Two out of three for a beer and the loser pays for the table."

"I'm in."

Eddie broke the rack and ran all the balls including the eight ball.

"Eddie, we have to play some straight pool someday."

""Fine with me, I love playing this game. It's your turn to break."

'Teeth' paid for the next game, racked up the balls and broke the rack while Eddie, the winner of the last game, enjoyed his win by joking with 'Teeth'.

'Teeth' smiled and ran the entire rack plus the eight ball.

"Let's make this last rack a little harder, let's double bank the eight ball."

"That's a good idea or we'll be here all night going back and forth."

It was Eddie's turn and he ran the rack again, but missed the double bank on the eight ball by a fraction of an inch.

"Nice try. It's nice having someone that knows what the hell they're doing on the table in here."

"Thanks. You hold a good stick, also."

'Teeth' ran the table and missed the double bank on the eight.

"I'm very rusty at the banks to begin with, but double banking is another story all together. I suck at it."

"Hey, it makes the game more interesting."

"Yes. it does. Your turn, Eddie"

Eddie bent over the table which was bare except for the eight ball and the cue ball. He looked it over and decided to do a three rail bank which was, in the past, easy for him as a kid. The eight ball was at a perfect spot about two inches from the rail, the cue ball was at the opposite end of the table in the opposite corner.

Ernie took his time and shot the cue. It hit the eight ball just right and the eight ball bounced from the side rail to the top rail to the opposite side rail and right into the side pocket.

"Great shot, it will be a pleasure to buy that beer."

The two men walked over to Armando and ordered the beers while Eddie introduced Armando to 'Teeth'.

"Shit, 'Teeth' and I are old friends" said Armando.

"Glad to hear it. Did you know he's a great pool shooter?" asked Eddie.

"No, I see him playing, but I didn't know that."

"Armando, you and I have played together," indicated 'Teeth'.

"Yes, I know, but I know Eddie is real good at pool. I suck at it," said Armando.

As the men were talking, they heard some loud yelling from the other end of the bar, which interrupted their conversation.

They walked over and saw two drunks arguing and attempting to hit each other with their fists. Someone stepped in and tried to quiet it all down. Another guy stepped in and yelled at the first man that tried to help, telling him to mind his own business.

Before you knew it, the second two were fighting, throwing blows and hitting each other.

"Look at those assholes. I bet they couldn't tell you what they are fighting about," Eddie said.

Armando and 'Teeth' both laughed and agreed with Eddie.

As this was going on, the bartender telephoned for the police and they could hear the sirens of a cruiser pulling up to the front door of the bar.

Armando looked at Eddie. Eddie was afraid that the officers may recognize him, which was what Armando was thinking.

"Let me buy you guys a beer," asked Eddie in an effort to get as far away as possible from the fighting. This fight was sure to draw the police officers very soon.

The men had the beer as the police officers entered the bar. They handled the fighters, arrested two men that were fighting and walked out of the bar without even noticing Eddie.

After they finished the beer, Eddie indicated that he wanted to leave and Armando agreed.

They left the Big Wave Bar and Eddie drove Armando home.

"It's been a good night, Armando. I'll give you a call tomorrow afternoon."

"Make it late in the afternoon."

"I'll talk with you then."

***

Eddie drove off and decided to go to the office. This would be a good time. No one would be around and he could do his report and leave it for Henry in the morning.

While doing his report, he did some preliminary checking on the people that he met this night.

'Teeth' turned out to be Conklin Powers of 642 Franklyn Street, Quincy, while Martin was Martin Zackary of 884 Presidents Drive, Quincy. Stew was Stewart Vigiliano of 1698 Briarwood Circle, Quincy.

The jackets on each of these men indicated that Stew and Martin were associates, but there didn't seem to be any real connection to Conklin ('Teeth') Powers.

Ernie completed his reports, left them for Henry and locked up the office. He arrived home at 2am.

Teresa was asleep so he quietly got ready for bed and went to sleep.

Chapter 18

Invitations

Wednesday June 27, 1979

Ernie got up late. After being out until 2am, he was a little drowsy. Teresa asked if he wanted breakfast or lunch. She made breakfast for him with coffee and he sat out on the porch, but the large fish were not chasing the bait fish, the small animals were finished with their early searches of the area. The lake was quiet and peaceful, the sky was clear and the air was warm, at least seventy degrees.

The phone rang. Teresa answered and yelled for Ernie, saying that it was Henry on the phone.

"Hi, Henry, what's up?"

"I got your reports and they're great. I think we should bring in the ATF, what do you think?"

"Why don't we wait on that until I have a better picture of the guns?"

"That's fine. Armando called saying that you are supposed to call him and he has something that you'll want to know."

"OK, sorry about that. I got home about 2am and I'm not use to that so I slept all morning."

"No problem. Believe me; I know what that's like. Give him a call as soon as you can."

"I will. Is there anything else that you need?"

"What do you have going for today?"

"I was thinking of skipping Armando, unless he has something I can use and dropping in at a few places on my own."

"Just give him the night off and let me know where to meet you so that I can provide cover."

"It will be a shake and bake. Shake hands and heat them up for a deal down the road and additional gun information. I'll call you later."

"OK, I'll be here for whatever you need."

"Oh, what did they find at the Raymond Wheeler search warrant?"

"I'm sorry to say that we were forced to kill him. He tried to get us and we got him. As far as the warrant goes, we got him good. Three grenades, four ounces of meth and an ounce of cocaine besides some grass here and there in the house"

"Did we get any cash or handguns?"

"Yes a .44 cal six shooter, he must have thought he was a cowboy, plus we got seventy-six thousand in cash. We filed the papers with the court and placed everything into evidence."

"Good job, thanks, I'll call you later."

Ernie hung up the phone and then dialed the telephone for Armando.

"Hello."

"Armando, sorry I didn't call as I said I would, I got tied up."

"That's OK. I wanted to let you know that there is a party on Saturday night that may interest you. Do you mind working on the weekend?"

"Armando, the only thing more important to me then getting the drugs off the street is my family, so yes I will work on the weekends and any other day that I am needed."

"Good, then I have this party at Bronco's house on Saturday night if you want to come. His real name is Richard Medeiros and he is a supplier of meth and cocaine."

"I don't know him."

"I know you don't, but he's a large dealer and he'll have Johnny (Whiskers) Zales and Enrique Risotino there as well as many other people."

"That could be dangerous if Risotino recognizes me."

"I would be surprised if he did. Shit, I didn't recognized you after you grew that beard."

"OK, let's do it, I'll pick you up at eight p.m. as usual. Where does this guy Bronco live and what does he look like?"

"He's about five feet eightinches tall and weighs about one hundred sixty pounds, has black hair and dark brown eyes and wears a mustache. He lives at 1455 Everett Street in Quincy. It should be a good time."

"OK, I'll pick you up at eight o'clock and we'll go to the party."

Ernie hung up the phone and went back to the porch where Teresa was sitting enjoying a cup of coffee.

"Here, let me freshen that coffee for you."

"Thanks, Teresa. I will be out late tonight again and maybe a lot for quite a while."

"What do you mean by quite a while?"

"I don't know where this case will take me and I'm not sure how far I can get with it. I may get into guns as well and I may wind up as far away as the Canadian border. This is a wide open case right now."

"Ernie, I can put up with a lot, but I have to know that you're safe, that's all I ask."

"I'll be safe, don't worry."

"Those are your favorite words to me, 'don't worry' I can't help worrying."

"I understand, but I'm safe right now, Henry is covering everything I do."

"I guess there is nothing that I can do, but worry."

"I have to get going so we'll talk about this later."

"OK, give me a kiss goodbye."

"Don't I always?"

"I know I just don't feel right today. I don't know what's bothering me."

Ernie gave Teresa a kiss goodbye and left the condominium, got into the unmarked car and drove off to Quincy.

***

He stopped to telephone Henry at the office.

"Henry, its Ernie"

"That didn't take long."

"No, I had to get out of the house. Teresa was starting to take off on her quest to keep me safe."

"Shit, you can't blame her for worrying."

"No, I don't, I appreciate it, but I really can't listen to it right now. We have too much boiling in the pot as it is."

"Yeah, I understand. What do you have planned?"

"I was thinking, why don't you take the day and relax? I'll just stop by a few places and strengthen the friendships I've been developing."

"That's fine with me. You never need that much coverage anyway. Sometimes it can be a detriment instead of an asset."

"That's right; I'll leave a report or call you in the morning."

"OK, if you need me I'll be home after two p.m."

"Oh, by the way, I am going to a party at the home of Richard (Bronco) Medeiros who was described to me as being about five feet eight inches tall, about one hundred sixty pounds, he has black hair and dark brown eyes and he wears a black mustache. He lives at 1455 Everett Street in Quincy. He deals out of that address."

"Very good, I'll be there. What time?"

"I should get there around 8:30pm, but you should know that Enrique Risotino will be there, among others."

"I don't think you should go to that party. What if he recognizes you?"

"Don't worry, he's high all the time he will not know who the hell I am."

"OK, it's your call, but I vote against going."

"Saturday night, bring some extra help, just in case."

"You can bet your ass. I will have both the Special Services Unit and the Narcotics Division there that night."

"Henry, let's not get carried away."

"Ernie, let me worry about that end."

Ernie chuckled, "OK, Henry, you got it."

"Is there anything else that I should know?"

"No, that's it for now."

"OK, you know how to contact me."

"Thanks, Henry"

Ernie hung up the phone and took off in the car.

His first stop would be the home of Stewart Vigiliano, 1920 Briarwood Circle, Quincy. He pulled up to the front of the house and observed a large black dog, chained to the garage area with the garage door opened.

Ernie pulled his car into the driveway and stopped. The dog began barking and trying to get loose so that he could attack Ernie who was safe as long as he was sitting in the car.

He blew the car horn to attract attention from inside the house. Someone looked out the window and then Stew walked out and over to Ernie's car.

"Hey, Eddie, what's up?"

"The sky, man, the sky."

"Come on in."

Eddie didn't move from the car; the dog was still barking.

"What about him?" Eddie pointed towards the dog.

Stew turned and walked over to the dog and slapped him, "Shut the fuck up, you bastard."

He then turned and walked back to Eddie, "Come on, he won't bother you."

Eddie got out of the car and walked into the house with Stew.

"What do you need, Eddie?"

"Nothing, I stopped by to say hi, and talk about the guns. You intrigued me with that talk about a gun connection. I got more people wanting guns in New York then I can handle."

"I have to talk to my guy, but I think we can get almost anything you need. Want a beer?"

"Sure, I'll take one. Can he do machine guns?"

"Machine guns? Nobody does those old fashion machine guns. He does things like the M11-9mm Submachine Gun and the MAC 10-9mm and then he does all the handguns, 38's and 9mm, etc."

"Yeah, that's what I'm talking about, but what about quantity? How many can he do at a time?"

"I wouldn't worry about that. He owns his own business, so he has all you could need and if he doesn't he can get them"

They heard the dog barking and then the front door open. Stew signaled Eddie not to speak of it now as Martin Zackary walked into the house.

"Stew, you gotta do something about that mutt, he drives everyone crazy."

"Someday I'm gonna put a bullet in his head and bury the bastard. He's a eating machine and drives me crazy," stated Stew as he walked out to stop the dog from barking.

"Hi, Eddie, how are you doing?"

"Great, Marty, and you?"

"I need some blow, I ran out last night," stated Marty.

"Where do you live, Marty?" asked Eddie

"I thought I told you. Maybe not, I'm on Ivy Lane, number 992 Ivy. Stop by anytime, I'm busy as hell at night, especially on the weekends."

"Yeah, I may do that as long as I'm welcome."

"Shit, any friend of Stew's is a friend of mine, you're welcome anytime."

Stew walked back into the kitchen.

"What do you need, Marty?"

"I'll take two ounces of blow and two of meth for the week coming up."

"Marty, do you cut that shit before you sell it?"

"Are you kidding me? I cut the fuck out of it; these assholes can't take any more than maybe (10%) ten percent purity. Of course for you I would hold back on the cut, Eddie."

"Thanks, but I think I'll buy from Stew like you do and if I'm in a pinch I'll take from you."

"Don't feel that way, It's just business."

"Yes, I understand, I run a business myself; a little different, but I do fine."

"Look guys, I have to get going. I'll stop by and see you about our little discussion tomorrow, Stew. Marty, maybe I'll stop by your place to see your action on Friday night."

"Any time, I'm always around. Best to make it after eight p.m., and then you'll see my followers as I call them."

Eddie left the house and took off. He drove to a telephone booth and called Armando. He remembered something that he read in Henry's report that the federal agent mentioned and wanted to clarify it in his own mind.

"Armando, can I pick you up, we need to talk for a few minutes? We'll go for coffee."

"Sure, I'm just relaxing, watching TV."

Eddie drove over to Armando's home and Armando was waiting out front. They drove to a coffee shop in another town, which was a short drive from where Armando's home was located.

They walked in and ordered coffee.

"Armando, the DEA and the ATF apparently know who you are. I'm not telling you anything you don't already know."

"That's true; I know that they have heard of me."

"Why would they be interested in you?"

"Eddie, I told you that I was going to be honest with you so I'll tell you. They probably heard of me in relation to my Canadian connections."

"Can you explain that? I have to know everything, Armando, if you want me on your side."

"Yeah, you're right; I was bringing in the methamphetamine from a Canadian chemist who was producing it. Then the drug war started up there and I finally gave up and left."

"You know that the DEA is not going to leave you alone. They will want you to work with them after you are finished here."

"Yes, I understand that and I kind of expected it."

"Then we are in agreement. You will finish up with me and then go with them on the Canadian case, if there is a case going at that time."

"I'm willing to do all that I can to stop what I started, this debauchery of "Meth and Myth."

"That's good, because if you don't show an interest in working with them, you will be facing federal charges in time."

Armando's face turned white, "I didn't know that they had any real evidence against me."

"It would appear that they know more than you think. That's all I have to say on that subject at this point in time."

"What should I do?"

"You should not worry about it. You do a good job with me and I will talk to them for you and make some arrangements so that you can do some things with them if it is needed."

"Thanks Eddie, I appreciate that."

"That's OK, just focus on this job for now; we'll put the rest together in time."

"Again, thanks"

"By the way, Armando, did you have any partners from Massachusetts in the Canadian connection?"

"Yeah, I had a guy. I hate to roll over on him unless I really have to."

"Is he from this area?"

"Yes, he's a business man here in town. He helped me out when I was down and out. I don't want to do him."

"We'll let that sit for now, but we will have to discuss it at some point."

"OK, let me think about that."

"Fine, finished with your coffee?"

"Yeah."

"I'll drive you home."

Eddie drove Armando back home.

His next stop would be the Big Wave Bar for a few games of pool and some 'meet and greet' with the people in the bar. He parked and entered the bar. He approached the bartender and ordered a beer.

Eddie leaned against the bar and looked out into the crowd. Sitting at a table with Pauli Jameson was Enrique Risotino.

A chill ran down Eddie's back. He wondered if Risotino would remember who he was, then he heard Pauli yell out, "Hey, Eddie."

Eddie looked at Pauli who was waving for Eddie to come over and join him and his friends.

Eddie walked over and was introduced around the table to a Jimmy and then to Ricky, who was Enrique Risotino. Eddie (Ernie) and Henry had searched his home.

"Hi, Jimmy, Ricky, nice to meet you guys."

"What's your name, Eddie?" asked Ricky.

"Yes, that's my name and goodies are my game," said Eddie.

"Man, you look a little familiar to me, have we met?" asked Ricky Risotino

"No, I don't think so. I'm from New York. Have you been there?"

"Yes, but that's not it, I guess I'm wrong. Maybe you look like someone I know; you Italians all look alike anyway."

"I get that shit all the time. Once a guy stopped me in the street in New York and said that he knew me from his childhood. I figured him for a cop and told him to go fuck himself."

Everyone at the table laughed and the whole question was forgotten. They sat and talked about, girls, drugs, business and other things for a couple of hours.

About ten o'clock they all decided to leave the bar when Ricky said not to forget that Bronco was having a party Saturday night.

"Bronco, I don't think I met him," Eddie stated.

"That's Ok, you'll be with us, see you there," said Pauli.

"Where does he live?" asked Eddie

"I forgot you're new around here. He lives at #1455 Everett Street in Quincy," said Ricky.

Eddie left the area along with the other three men and headed home. He decided to stop and telephone Henry.

"Hi, Henry."

"You OK, Ernie?"

"Yeah, I'm OK; you'll never believe what happened."

"Tell me, man."

Ernie went on to tell Henry about meeting Enrique Risotino and that Risotino has a nickname of Ricky.

"He didn't recognize you at all?"

"He recognized something, but I talked my way around it. I'm free and clear now. He even invited me to the party on Saturday night. Now I don't need Armando anymore. We'll have to discuss that."

"OK, are you heading home now?"

"I'll stop by the office, first to do a preliminary report for you. I'll talk with you tomorrow"

"Tomorrow."

Ernie hung up the phone and drove to the office where he prepared a report for Henry. The report included his discussion with Stew about the guns and with Marty about his business, as well as the meeting at the Big Wave bar with Ricky, Pauli and Jimmy.

He finished his report and went home for the night.

Chapter 19

The Game

Friday June 29, 1979

Ernie spent the day with Teresa. They did some shopping then visited Teresa's mother and enjoyed each other's company for the entire day.

After supper, Ernie got ready to leave. He telephoned Henry and advised him as to his plans for the night. He had telephoned Armando earlier that day to tell him that he would not be needed that night. Armando was curious about what Ernie was doing, but Ernie did not specify his plans.

At about eight p.m., Ernie drove up to the home of Martin Zackary at 992 Ivy Lane, Quincy.

As he approached the building he could see that it was an apartment house with three floors and at least sixteen units in the building. He walked into the main entrance and didn't even have to look for the apartment.

There were six kids that walked in the back entrance as Ernie walked into the front entrance. He could see where they were going, up the stairs to the second floor. He followed and watched from a distance. They walked down the hallway to unit number eight and knocked on the door. The door opened and Martin greeted his guests.

Ernie walked down the hallway to unit eight and knocked. Martin Zackary answered the door and greeted Eddie.

"Eddie, come on in, have a seat. Want a beer?"

"Sure Marty, why not?"

"Whatever you need, man, just mention it and you got it. These kids don't know what the fuck is going on they just want to get high."

"You're probably right."

"You can bet I am. Watch the next guy that comes in."

A knock at the door, Martin answered.

"Hey, kids, come on in. What do you need?"

"Some cocaine."

"OK, kid, if you can pick the right one, you get it for free." Martin held out two packets, one with cocaine and one with cutting material which was similar, except that the cutting powder glistened much more than cocaine.

The boy, who was with his girlfriend and another boy, looked at the two packets and picked the one that glistened more; he picked the wrong one.

"Wrong, you owe me double, kid."

"You didn't say that I had to pay double."

Martin looked at Eddie, "See what I mean? They don't know shit."

"OK, kid, here, this is the right one. Give me the fifty and get the fuck outta here."

"Yeah, I guess you're right, they don't know enough, not yet. The day will come though," stated Eddie.

"You bet your ass I'm right. They all come here and they are all idiots."

"Man, they're kids. What the fuck do you expect? How old are they?"

"Late teens, anyway."

"Yeah, that's all those kids were", stated Eddie.

"Eddie, do you need anything?"

"This shit that you sell those kids? Are you crazy?"

"No, you get the good stuff. Take a walk with me."

Martin went into the other room. He asked a woman that was watching TV in that room to mind the store for a moment. He gestured for Eddie to follow him; they left the apartment.

They walked up one flight of stairs to the third floor where Martin opened the door to apartment fourteen. When they walked in Eddie could see that the apartment was set up like a cutting room with tables, scales, papers for wrapping the drugs and a box of drug paraphernalia. In one corner was a safe.

"This is a nice set up, Marty"

"You bet your ass it is. Turn around while I open the safe."

Eddie turned and Martin opened the safe, then he told Eddie it was OK to face him.

"What do you need, Eddie?"

"I'll take an eight ball (1/8 oz) for now, as long as it is not all cut to shit."

"No, I'll weigh it out for you right here."

Martin took a half-pound bag of cocaine and weighed up an eighth of an ounce for Eddie.

Eddie paid him and Martin locked up the cocaine in the safe, then left and locked the apartment. They went back down to the apartment on the second floor where all of the action was. As they came down the stairs and as they approached Martin's apartment, they could see about seven kids in the doorway. They were all looking for drugs. Martin went ahead of Eddie and took over the distribution of the drugs and collection of the payments.

Eddie walked in a little behind Martin who introduced his wife and partner to Eddie.

"Eddie, meet Priscilla, my wife and partner in everything."

"Hi, Priscilla, so you're the brains behind this man."

Priscilla laughed as she replied, "I guess so."

Eddie had seen enough. He saw at least twelve kids in less than an hour. He needed to end this unofficial drugstore. He said his goodbye's and left the apartment.

"Eddie, anytime you want, feel free to stop by, you're always welcome."

"Thank you, Marty, I will be back."

Ernie headed back to the office to write this up for Henry. This report would create a lot of surveillance work. Ernie then left the office and went home.

~*~

Saturday June 30, 1979

Ernie got out of bed late, had breakfast and telephoned Henry to make sure that he had the information on Martin Zackary who was running his own little drugstore for kids.

"Henry?"

"Yeah, Ernie, I have this report you left. I think we should put a team on that tonight. We'll take down a couple of cars and then hit the place. When we arrest him we will be sure to place him in a cell close to the ones we bust so that he will put the responsibility for the search on them."

"I will be going to that party at Bronco's house. I should have no problem with that party."

"We'll have a team on you as well, just in case."

"OK, Henry. You know that this guy Martin is not gonna stop even though we bust him."

"Yes, I know, but at least we will put a dent in his business for now. Then when we take down your case we will do him again and that should put him away for a while."

"The only problem we have is that no one knows about that third floor apartment so see what you can do to keep me out of that."

"Yes, I was thinking about that and maybe we should leave that apartment alone."

"No, you know what you can do? Go through his apartment, do the whole search and then check his keys. Find an outstanding key that does not fit his door. Then check every door in the building until you come up with the second apartment. You know how to play the game."

"That's a great idea and it places everything on his stupidity."

"Correct, if it works."

"I'll do it. Stay in touch, Ernie."

"I will."

Ernie hung up the phone and turned to Teresa, who was sitting having coffee and listening to the conversation.

"So, you're going to a party?"

Ernie laughed, "You heard that entire conversation and all you got out of it was that I am going to a party tonight?"

"No I understood the rest, you guys are tricky."

"We have to protect people and by people I mean me right now."

"I understand."

Ernie and Teresa went out shopping for the day, had lunch, drove down to the park and they went for a two-mile walk around the walking path which borders the lake.

After supper Ernie left the house for Quincy.

***

It was 7pm when Eddie walked into the Big Wave bar, looked around and saw 'Teeth' shooting pool alone. He walked over to the pool table.

"Hey, Eddie, how about a game of pool?"

"Sure, why not, 'Teeth'."

The two men played and drew a crowd of people around the table, watching and commenting on how well they played the game.

"Look at these guys play," said one patron.

"Remind me not to play against them," said another.

"Hey, 'Teeth', I didn't know you were that good."

"I never get a chance to play anybody like Eddie around here. I never take advantage of you guys, you know that."

"Yeah, we know, but from now on you are gonna have to spot us some balls."

"Yeah, yeah, Carlos, you always want an edge."

The banter went on and on. They were all talking and kidding around. The best thing was that Eddie was accepted in his own right by all without Armando. This was good for Armando.

"Hey, Eddie, you are gonna have to spot us too"

"No problem, guys, I just enjoy the game; I'm not trying to take advantage of anyone. I guarantee at least a two-ball spot to any of you."

The game ended and Eddie walked over to the bar with 'Teeth'. They ordered some beer's and talked for a while.

"'Teeth', I think I will call it a night."

"Yeah, me too, Eddie."

The two men walked out together. When they were outside Eddie spoke with 'Teeth' for moment before he left the area.

"'Teeth', who is that loud mouth, is that Carlos?"

"He's a bad dude. Eddie, be careful of him. He's a collector and hit man for the top drug people around here."

"Thanks, 'Teeth', I was curious since he seemed to be so loud. Everyone seemed to stop speaking when he spoke."

"Nobody wants to cross him, that's why."

"Good to know. I'll see you when I see you."

"Eddie, maybe we should get together sometime and play at my house I have a pool table and we would have no interruptions."

"That's great to hear, 'Teeth'. Let me know where and when, I'll be there."

"OK, we'll talk the next time I see you here at the Wave."

The two men split up and went their own way.

***

It was almost eight o'clock, time to pick up Armando and head over to the home of Richard (Bronco) Medeiros for the party.

Chapter 20

Broncos' Party

Eddie picked up Armando at eight o'clock that evening. They arrived at 1455 Everett Street in Quincy. Ernie looked the entire area over to see if there was any car blinking its lights. If there was a signal like that, Ernie would drive away to another street. That type of signal meant that Henry or one of the team members wanted to speak with him. There was no such sign. He parked the car and they entered the house.

As he entered, there were at least twenty people milling around. Ernie was surprised to see the man that 'Teeth' called Carlos, from the Big Wave, talking with some people.

Eddie walked over to the crowd with Armando and Carlos greeted him.

"Eddie the shark."

"Not really, just learning the game."

"Yeah, you guys should have seen him and 'Teeth' on that pool table. Eddie was a wiz, they both play great."

Just then Armando spoke with a white male, five feet eight inches tall who weighed about one hundred and sixty pounds, with black hair, dark brown eyes and a mustache.

"Eddie, meet Bronco."

"Oh, you're the man that I have been hearing about."

"What do you mean, are people speaking about me?"

"No, I was at the Big Wave and Ricky and some friends mentioned you and this party. They told me to come on down. They said that I would be welcome and it would be a blast."

"Oh, I understand. If you're a friend of Ricky's you're OK and you're welcome to stop in anytime."

"Thanks, Bronco, that's nice to know."

"What business are you in, Eddie?"

Armando got the hint when Eddie looked at him and tilted his head. Armando found another group to speak with while Eddie spoke with Bronco.

"Bronco, I'm kind of in a business that you may not like."

"Shit, I can't think of any kind of business that I can't accept with one exception, a rapist. That's the worst kind of maggot."

"I agree with you, but you see, I buy product and transport it to my people in New York."

"Product, do you mean drugs?"

"Yes. If you like I will leave."

"Hey, guys, guess what? Eddie here is a drug dealer, the lousy bastard," stated Bronco with a hearty laugh.

"I'll leave, Bronco, there's no reason for that kind of ridicule."

"Don't be an asshole, everybody here is a drug dealer."

"Sorry, you mean I am at home here?"

"You're at home, friend. What's your specialty?"

"You know New York. I need everything for that place."

"What do you call everything?"

"Where I have my business, I have to deal in everything; meth, cocaine and heroin. I give a gift to my dealers of grass once a year. That's basically my whole job."

"You're with the right people. You can get what you need right here."

"That would surprise me because I buy in quantity. I have a lot of customers."

"What are we talking about for quantity?"

"Multiple pounds in the meth; cocaine and heroin I use multiple kilos and once a year I buy about a hundred pounds of grass."

"You know, I like that grass idea, it shows that you care and you like your people. I may use that."

"Be my guest. It also keeps the customers coming back, knowing that they have a nice gift coming."

"Look, Eddie, I can get you all you need. I only supply top people. I would have to check you out, but as long as you are clean, we can do business."

"I'm not clean, man. I have a record and a warrant in New York."

"That's what I call clean."

"Oh, I see, then I will pass muster."

"Eddie, enjoy yourself tonight and stop by next week and we will talk some more."

Bronco walked off and left the room while Eddie turned and walked over to Armando and Carlos, who were discussing a young lady that was sitting in a corner quietly feeding a baby.

"Eddie, look at that bitch, RJ," stated Armando.

"What does 'RJ' mean?" asked Eddie.

"Rotten blow job," stated Carlos and all three men began laughing.

"What's wrong with her feeding her baby?" asked Eddie.

"That's what we're talking about. Where did the baby come from?" asked Carlos.

"What the fuck are you guys talking about?"

"She was at the last party a couple of weeks ago and she wasn't pregnant and she didn't have a baby," said Armando.

"That is curious. Maybe she had the baby and you guys didn't know about it, although the baby does look like a newborn infant," stated Eddie.

"Yeah, maybe we just didn't know about it," said Carlos.

"That's always a possibility," stated Armando.

Eddie looked over at RJ and noted that she had blond hair with brown eyes, was about five feet four inches tall and weighed around one hundred and ten pounds.

"Hey, Eddie, I hear good things about you from the scuttlebutt around here."

"Carlos, I hear good things about you also."

"Maybe we can do some business sometime, Eddie. Give me a call if you feel that you may need my services."

"Sure, but what exactly are your services."

"Man, someone must have mentioned that I'm a collector and I do a good job collecting. I really enjoy my work."

"That's what I thought, but I have collectors in New York that work for me."

"Oh, I'm sure you do, but you never know when you may need an interference run or support in this area sometime. I do many things. If you can verbalize it, I can get it done."

"Now there's a man after my own heart," Eddie said.

Carlos laughed and put his arm around Eddie. "We are gonna get along great."

The three men spoke for a while and then Eddie decided that he would start up a conversation with RJ, the girl holding the baby. He wanted to see what he could find out. He walked away from Armando and Carlos and sat down in a chair next to her.

"Hello, young lady, nice baby that you have there."

"Not tonight, man. I have to take care of this baby."

"What's not tonight?" as RJ looked up from the baby at Eddie.

"Oh, who are you?"

"I'm Eddie; I noticed the baby and thought that he was a cutie."

"Yeah he is, isn't he? I thought you were someone else, wanting to screw around tonight."

"I don't mind screwing around, but you have the baby."

"Not you, numbness. I thought you were another person."

"Yes, I understand."

"Leave me the fuck alone so I can take care of this baby."

"I'll be happy to, but shouldn't you take him home, instead of staying around here with all this smoke and marijuana in the air around here?"

"He'll get use to it. Don't worry"

"I'm not worried, he's not my baby. When did you have him?"

"What the fuck? Hey, Bronco, get rid of this guy, I think he's writing a book."

Bronco walked over and asked Eddie what happened.

"Nothing, I was just curious about the baby, normal stuff about his age and such, he looks like a brand new infant. I was trying to be friendly and she went off on me."

"Yeah, she can get that way," stated Bronco.

"Rosina, RJ, he's a friend. Knock off your asinine attitude."

"Well then, leave me alone. I got this kid I gotta do something with."

"Well, then take the kid and get the fuck out a here."

"If I were loading up with a pound of meth you wouldn't treat me this way."

"Look, you want to buy, OK. If you want to cause trouble, I don't need it."

RJ got out of the chair with the baby in her arms and walked off in a huff. After about twenty minutes of being shunned by everyone there, she left the house.

Armando walked over to Eddie. "Hey, Eddie, what the fuck. I could have told you that she was a nut. She'd as quickly cut your heart out as look as you."

"Yeah, I can tell that she's not easy to get along with."

"Screw her, let's go and talk with Carlos."

As they walked across the house to the room where Carlos was with a young lady, Eddie told Armando that he would have to fill him in on this Carlos character.

"I don't want to say much now, but his name is Carlos Ruiz, check him out. You'll be impressed, I'm sure."

"I will."

As they walked toward Carlos and the young lady Eddie made a mental note that he was five feet eleven inches tall, two hundred and twenty-five pounds, dark black hair and dark brown eyes. He was clean-shaven and when he spoke he did not have an accent of any kind. Eddie would check this Carlos out when he went back to the office.

As they approached Carlos and his girl, a female grabbed Eddie's arm.

"Are you trying to get away from me, Eddie?"

"Rose, I'm sorry, I didn't even see you,"

"Of course not, why should you notice me, I'm an ugly pig,"

"You are a beautiful girl and I appreciate the attention that you give me, but I have had business on my mind, that's all."

"Rose, do you know RJ?"

"Yeah, I know that crazy bitch. Watch out for her, she's a nut."

"Do you know her real name?"

"Yeah, similar to mine, she's Rosina, Rosina Jessup I believe. Why do you want to know?"

"She was a little rough on me earlier; I want to fuck her head up."

"As long as you don't fuck her head."

"Rose, I think you are a nut sometimes." They both laughed.

"You know, Eddie, I have some wonderful exercises to help relieve that tension from all that business worry. I have a good head for that, so to speak."

Rose wanted to introduce Eddie to some close friends and directed him over to two men.

"Eddie, meet Tet, Vinnie Testalia and this big lug is Sam, Sam Roller. They're good friends of mine."

"You know, Rose, there is no reason for you to tell people our last name, the first name is enough," stated Vinnie.

"Sorry guys, but you're gonna want to be nice to Eddie."

"Why is that?" asked Sam

"For two reasons; one, if you want me, you will have to go through him, the other is that he is a very big dealer from New York."

"You, we ain't worried about, but, Eddie, what type of specialty and quantity do you control?" asked Sam.

"I do it all, but we shouldn't speak of that in mixed company. Sam, didn't we meet at Red's house?"

"Yes, we did, I was high as a kite, you're right. I have one question, what brings you here? I can hear your accent so I believe you're from NY," Sam said.

"My connections got hit badly. I'm looking for new ones and I had some friends here that said they may be able to help," Eddie replied.

"OK, you seem to come highly recommended with Rose on your side. She's a talker, but never about business. She's a good friend," stated Vinnie.

"Thanks, men."

Eddie and Rose were speaking with Enrique Risotino, who also offered to help out Eddie with his needed supplies, when Sam Roller walked up to them.

"Eddie, you and I should talk, give me a call when you get a chance. I can handle anything," said Sam as he handed Eddie a card with his contact information on it.

"Sure, Sam, I'll call you in about a week or two if that OK."

"Anytime, I think I may be able to help you out."

As Sam and Eddie were talking, Rose was whispering in Eddie's ear something silly and sexual.

"Rose knock it off, I'm trying to talk with Sam."

"Go fuck yourself," Rose stamped off.

"Our first fight," said Eddie. Sam and Risotino laughed

"You're better off staying away from that vacuum cleaner."

"She's not all that bad. She has her moments."

"Guys, I have to run, I have a date later and she will be pissed if I'm late again."

"At midnight?" asked Risotino

"Yeah, she works and I promised to have a late dinner with her."

As Eddie began to walk away, a man introduced himself as "JZ".

"Hi, I'm JZ, how's everything going?"

The men standing there replied that all was good.

"Eddie, I got some good information on you and good vibes. Give me a call or stop by, we can do something."

"I will, JZ, thanks for the offer."

"I'll walk you to the door," stated Risotino

Eddie went over and thanked Bronco for the invite. Bronco told him to come by anytime and they could talk. Eddie stated that he would do that.

Eddie and Risotino walked toward the front door.

"Eddie, these guys have good connections, but you can get the best stuff through me. Keep that in mind."

"You probably cut the shit out of it. I buy from you and you'll get me killed by my own customers."

"No, no, I only take a small percentage of the payment for handling fees and I never cut my stock."

"OK, I'll contact you. You got a card?"

"Yeah, here, call anytime."

"I will definitely call you next week for a taste and then we can do business."

"That sounds like a deal."

Armando, who was talking to a woman, remained at the party with her.

Eddie left the party got in his car and was too tired to write up the reports that night so he went home and would do the reports over the week end. Eddie would take the next day off and relax, maybe go fishing.

Chapter 20

The Baby

Sunday July 1, 1979

Teresa got out of bed at her normal time and tried not to bother Ernie, who was still sleeping. She went into the kitchen and made some coffee and then a bowl of cereal for herself. She went out on the porch to have breakfast and read the newspaper.

Nothing special seemed to be going on in the world except a lot of talk about some young lady who did freestyle skiing in Belmont Massachusetts. On page four was a small caption that read, ***"Women Found Dead, Baby Missing."***

Teresa read the story about a pregnant young girl who was found on Saturday night and had been dead at least thirty hours. An unnamed source at the police department stated that the autopsy showed that her blood was loaded with the drug methamphetamine. It was believed that she entered an old abandoned building to purchase drugs. She was pregnant and while ingesting some drugs became involved in an altercation of some sort with an unknown party. This altercation resulted in her beginning labor. Because of the excessive drugs in her blood, she then had a massive heart attack and died. However, some unknown party helped the baby to finish its birth and now, the baby was missing.

Teresa was very upset because of that story and was worried about the baby.

Ernie got out of bed, grabbed a cup of coffee and joined Teresa on the porch.

"Ernie, now this is something that you guys should work on. Read this about that poor baby. The mother was a junky, but that baby, I can't stop thinking about it and hoping that it is OK I hope someone took some kindness on it and is at least taking care of it."

"What are you talking about? Let me read that story."

Ernie got out of his chair and picked up the phone.

"Henry?"

"Yeah, I was sleeping, man."

"Sorry, but do you have this morning's newspaper around there?"

"It's probably down by the mailbox, why?"

"Go and get it right away, go to page four, the story about the pregnant girl. Read it and call me back."

"OK, give me a couple of minutes."

"Ernie, do you know something about that girl?"

"I think that I may know where the baby is."

"Is it OK?"

"I saw a girl last night with a baby that was no more than a couple of days old. I spoke with her and she was a bitch, but she was only interested in taking care of the baby."

"Well, that's good, maybe the baby is safe."

"Read the paper and get back to me." Ernie turned to Teresa.

"Teresa, she's a drug dealer and a user, so it could be safe for one minute then the next she will not give a shit about it. The drugs take over and they're stronger than the mother's instinct that you girls have."

They spoke for a while and then the phone rang.

"That must be Henry, I'll get it."

"Hello."

"It's me. I read the story, but it's a Boston case, not ours, unless you have some info for them?"

"Have you ever heard of a girl named RJ?"

"Yeah, she was a peripheral, very small case when we did something a while back, why?"

"I think I do have something. Meet me at the office."

"Hey, can't this wait till Monday?"

"No, I think I know where that baby is."

"I'll get dressed and go right in. Give me a half hour."

Ernie did the same. He got dressed, got in the car and left for the office.

***

Henry stopped at the main police station first to pull the file on RJ. When he arrived at the office and while waiting for Ernie, he read all of the information that he could find.

"Hi, Ernie."

"Henry, what's that you're reading?"

"I stopped and pulled the RJ file. She is a small to medium dealer, lives here in Quincy, but right near the river, close to the Boston line. What's more interesting is her associates. Over a period of time, the cruisers have been submitting reports about seeing her. She has been seen with guys like Risotino, who is a decent sized dealer"

"That's great, her associations fit the case. I was with her last night and she has a newborn baby. The other people at the party were wondering where she got the baby. No one had any idea that she had been pregnant. One guy said she wasn't pregnant last week."

"With that information, your report and the existing file, we may have enough for a warrant. We will search for the baby and then, if it's not hers, we'll take her and lock her ass up until she tells us what happened."

"That's fine, but you can't be involved, Ernie."

"I don't give a shit about that, you can handle it. I'm concerned about the baby. She's a junky and God knows what could happen. Although I have to tell you, Henry, she was very attentive to the baby when I spoke with her."

"Yeah, but you know junkies. She could flip at any second. Don't worry, I'll take care of it," Henry stated as he began working on the paperwork.

"Henry, call Boston and find out what you can while I call Armando. I have an idea. If I can arrange it, I will be in the house when you hit the place. We can go from there. Arrest me and place me close to her so that I can talk to her after we're arrested."

"Good idea. If she doesn't talk to me, she may talk to you when you're in the same boat."

"That's right, let's give it a try," directed Ernie.

"Give me a couple of hours to get everything together and then I will hit her house."

"I'm gonna help. I'll start the affidavit while you put the info together. While you're at the court house getting approval, I'll go over to the house."

"I was hoping that you would suggest that, Ernie, thanks."

The two men worked together for two hours, placing all of the information into the affidavit that was needed to get into the house. They finished it in record time.

"I think this one is gonna be close," Henry stated.

"Yeah, I'm hoping that the clerk will take into consideration that this is a baby and give us a bit of a break. On the other hand, he may feel that we have enough."

Henry telephoned the Boston Police Department and spoke with the investigative unit. He was informed him that the medical examiners report stated, "Had someone called for help, this girl would have been saved along with the missing baby."

When Henry was finished with the call he told Ernie what he was told.

Ernie did not say a word; he just shook his head in disapproval of the entire situation.

Ernie telephoned Armando.

"Armando this is very important. Do you know RJ very well?" Ernie asked.

"I should, I went out with her for a while."

"OK, what can you tell me about her?"

"She's a drug dealer, not enormous, but a dealer and she is as crazy as a loon."

"What have you seen her do that was crazy, as you call it?"

"For one thing, she threatened to kill more than one person while I was present."

"Have you ever seen her sell to the youth of the city?"

"She sells in those old broken down tenements in Boston and to anyone that has the money."

"OK, Armando thanks, I'll get back to you later."

"I know what you're thinking" stated Armando

"What's that?"

"I read the paper this morning, you think that baby she had is the one that's missing, don't you?"

"Exactly."

"I think you are one hundred percent correct."

"Thanks, that may help."

"I hope the baby is all right, good luck with that."

"How about you and I going over there in a little while?"

"Sure, just come and get me."

"OK, say in an hour?"

"I'll be waiting."

Ernie hung up the phone and turned to Henry.

"That's my guarantee into the house, Henry. I'll be in there when you hit the place."

"OK, why don't we add what he gave us? He's a reliable informant so we can hide him behind that façade. I'll go to get the warrant and two other men to assist."

"OK, I'll go pick up Armando and meet you there."

***

Ernie and Armando drove to the home of Rosina ("RJ") Jessup located at 1998 Prospect Street off of Billings Street, Quincy.

"Eddie, this RJ is a weird broad. She can love you one minute and hate you the next without reason or logic of any kind."

"That's good to know, Armando, thanks."

"Look, make sure you don't have anything on your person. My men are gonna hit the place and I don't want you arrested. I'll have whatever I can buy from her. I want them to be able to let you go," Ernie instructed Armando.

"I never hold anything anymore, I'm clean and I'm gonna stay that way," Armando replied.

"Actually, I know that, but I felt that I had to say what I did."

"No problem. There's the house now."

They walked up the walkway and knocked on the door. No answer.

Eddie rang the bell. No answer.

"Shit, I bet she's out with the baby," said Eddie.

"She could be in Boston dealing her poison," replied Armando.

As they were talking the door opened and standing in the door way was RJ.

"Do you guys know what to do with this giant diaper? All this kid does is shit and eat."

"Is that the baby crying that we hear? I know what to do for that baby."

"What, what do we do?"

"First thing we do is pick it up. Is it a boy or a girl?"

"It's a girl, how the fuck does that matter?"

"Where the fuck did you get her?"

"Some cunt came to my spot in town to buy some drugs. I sold her a gram of meth. She began to act crazy like something was wrong and fell down, then she said her baby was coming and she passed out on me."

"So you let the baby come and you took it?" Armando asked.

"Yes, I just did what I had to. I have to find someone to take her."

"Why didn't you call the cops, maybe they could have saved the girl?" asked Eddie.

"I don't know, I got scared, so I wrapped the baby in my sweater and left. I figured when she woke up she would get in touch with me and I'd give her the baby back."

"Didn't you read the papers?"

"No, why?"

"A dead girl was found and her baby was missing."

"Oh fuck, now they'll blame me."

There was a knock at the door.

"Police Detective Griswold, open the door please."

Eddie walked over to the door and opened it. Speaking loudly so that RJ could hear, he asked, "What can I do for you, Detective?"

"Are you the owner of the house?"

"No sir, the owner is inside with her baby."

"I have a search warrant for this house," Henry stated and entered the house with the other officers.

He went directly to the baby and took custody of her baby.

"Are you Miss. Rosina (RJ) Jessup?"

"Yes, I am."

"You're under arrest for distribution of illegal narcotics and aiding in the murder of a Miss Rolanda Romero. Any additional charges will be placed on you by the District Attorney. Do you understand those charges?"

"Yes, I do, but it was not like you think. I didn't murder her."

As Henry was arresting RJ and taking custody of the baby. The other officers were searching Eddie and Armando for weapons and or narcotics; nothing was found.

"Detective, the baby needs some food or formula, can you take care of that?" asked Eddie.

"Don't worry, the juvenile authorities are on the way and they will do all they can for her, starting with a stop at the hospital for the baby to be checked out. Now you two men sit down and be quiet."

"Yes, sir."

The juvenile authorities showed up, took the baby from Henry and signed for her on the search warrant return.

Before speaking with Eddie, Henry asked the cruiser officers to transport the prisoner back to the station and book her under his name.

"Eddie, where does she keep her drugs?" asked Henry.

"I have no idea. Armando do you know?"

"Yes, I do. I used to live here with her. If you go down the cellar and count overhead three beams, you'll see a small box on the third beam. That's her drugs. Then she has some in the attic, but I have never seen the exact location."

Henry and three other men split up and went to the designated areas. They found the drugs that Armando spoke of and confiscated them, placing the information on the return.

After that they did a quick check of the entire house and attic. They found some very small quantities of marijuana and cocaine.

"Eddie, how do you want to work this?"

"You can let us go; I have more than we need from her. She told me everything about the death of the woman. I'll do a report and bring it in tomorrow morning. You got her for the murder. She just let the girl die. There may have been some panic involved, but that's for the jury to decide. How much drugs did you find?" asked Eddie.

Henry answered, "We got four ounces of cocaine and it looks uncut, some grass and a few pills."

"Then you're covered all the way around."

"Yeah, you guys don't have to hang around," stated Henry.

"I'll take Armando home and head home myself."

"Ernie you better stop by the office and do a quick report with just the highlights, in case you don't get in early enough for court."

"I intend to do that. I'll drop off Armando and then go over to the office."

"OK, as soon as I am finished with the booking and interview process of RJ at the station house, I'll meet you at the office."

***

When Ernie arrived at the office he began doing the preliminary report for Henry's case against RJ. He was finishing up when the phone rang.

"Hello, this is the pizza house." Ernie wanted to see who it was before he identified himself.

"Hi, is Ernie there?"

"Teresa, yes it's me."

"I never know what to expect if I call your office, now it's a pizza place."

"Yeah, it doesn't matter, whatever comes to mind when we answer the phone."

"I was curious about that baby, can you tell me anything?"

"Yes, the baby is fine. A little hungry, but that will be taken care of right away."

"Oh, wonderful, I'm so glad. I was worried about that baby."

"Hey, what are you saying, you want to use that motherly instinct?"

"We could have another child, we're both healthy."

"Let's talk later. I'll be home in a little while, about an hour and a half."

"OK, what do you want for lunch?"

"Honey, right now I am very busy and I don't care what we have for lunch."

Ernie finished up and left the report for Henry to use on Monday morning when the case came up at the preliminary hearing. He left the office for home.

Chapter 22

Gunman

Monday July 2, 1979

Ernie had gone to bed early Sunday night and woke up very early Monday morning. He went to the window overlooking the lake and observed a mist in the air. He knew that this would burn off as soon as the sun got high enough in the sky. Probably by ten o'clock at the latest.

He went into the kitchen, made some coffee, sat down to do his report and turned the television on so that he could hear the weather, which was expected to be in the low eighties. After he finished the reports, he returned to the bedroom and laid down hoping to fall asleep.

Teresa woke up and could see that Ernie was awake.

"Would you like some breakfast?"

"I may as well, I can't sleep."

Teresa went into the kitchen and saw that the coffee pot had already been turned on.

"Ernie, you've been up already?"

""Yes, I did my report on that baby case."

"No wonder you can't sleep anymore, you had coffee."

"Yeah, I did, I'll have another cup with breakfast. Want to eat on the porch?"

"Sure, that sounds good, here's your coffee."

Ernie went out to the porch and sat down. He enjoyed the early mornings, watching the little animals that were out searching for food.

Teresa brought out the breakfast and they sat and enjoyed the view as they spoke about the squirrels, chipmunks and the fish rising for bait fish that were jumping out of the water to get away from being eaten.

Teresa asked about the baby case. Ernie explained all that happened and Teresa felt bad for the baby and the two girls.

Ernie decided to spend the morning doing some small chores around the house that Teresa had been asking about. He fixed the leak under the sink, went out to the garage and changed the oil in the car, checked the air in the tires and then he helped Teresa to wash the windows.

They had fun working together and by the time they were done they both needed a shower because they got more water and suds on themselves then on the windows.

Ernie decided to leave the house and go into Quincy where he would visit with some of the people that were associated with RJ.

***

Ernie drove to the home of Enrique Risotino at #12 Federal Street in Quincy, parked his car and walked up the driveway.

"Eddie, I saw you parking your car, come on in."

"Hi, Ricky, thought I would stop by, as you suggested, at the party."

"What are your needs, buddy?"

"Do you have an eighth ounce for me?"

"Sure, but what do you want meth or cocaine?"

"Meth, of course; as a matter of fact, give me some blow too, let's say a gram to mix in."

"Done, man, those are small buys. I thought you bought quantity."

"I do, but I have to check out your stock, don't I? You don't expect me to come in cold and buy a key or a pound, do you?"

"Yeah, you're right, you'll love this shit. Is there anything else I can do for you?"

"Not unless you can get me a gun."

"The cops took mine; I have to buy another one. Are you looking to buy right now?" asked Ricky.

"Yes, I have plenty of cash, why do you ask?"

"How about you drive and we go see my main man, maybe he can take care of us?"

"I'm in. By the way, did you hear what happened to RJ?" asked Eddie.

"Nothing would surprise me with that broad."

"I was there when the cops came in. They took the baby and arrested her for murder."

"I knew that wasn't her baby. There is definitely something wrong with that bitch."

"I guess so. It was a good thing that I wasn't holding or I would have been arrested too."

"You were lucky. Did they take your name and information?"

"Yes, they did, and they bought the story that I was just visiting from New York and met her the other night for the first time. She confirmed it when they spoke to her in another room."

"Well, fuck her. Let's get going."

Eddie drove and Ricky directed him to 7433 Chapman Street in Weymouth a small town just south of Quincy.

"Eddie, you'll like this guy, he's a real nice person, easy to get along with and loves to play pool."

"So do I."

"That's why I said you'll like him."

They knocked on the door and 'Teeth' (Conklin ('Teeth') Powers) opened it.

"'Teeth', this is who you were talking about, Ricky?"

"Yeah, you two know each other?"

"We played pool at the Big Wave together, several times," stated 'Teeth'.

"You know, now that you mention it, I did see you two together in there. My mind is slipping, I think."

They entered the house, into a large living room.

"Come on down the cellar."

Ricky and Eddie followed 'Teeth' down into the cellar where they saw a full-sized pool table, nine feet by four feet, in the middle of the room. The rest of the cellar was all nicely done with wood walls and chairs and tables all round the pool table area. the floor was tile. In the pool room area, on the walls, were racks with cues. The table balls were racked and ready to play.

"Shall we, Eddie?" asked 'Teeth'.

"What about Ricky?"

"We'll play nine-ball and he can have a cue."

"I'm in; how about you, Ricky?"

"Sure, I'll play."

The bell rang and 'Teeth' went up to the first floor to answer the door. After a couple of minutes he returned, followed by Martin (Marty) Zackary whom Eddie had met at Stews home on the twenty-sixth of June.

"Hi, Marty," stated Eddie.

'Teeth' said, "Now we can play eight ball, we have a fourth."

"Ernie, you take Ricky and I'll take Marty. Let's see how it goes."

"That's fine with me. I can only play a few games, then I have to get going," Eddie said.

"'Teeth', the reason we stopped by was that I need a nine," Ricky announced.

'Teeth', bent over the table, getting ready to break the rack when Ricky asked to purchase a nine millimeter handgun. He stood up straight and looked at Eddie, then Marty.

"Eddie, you're from New York, right?"

"Yeah."

"You have the accent so you must be legit. Marty I know for years, he's OK. So you're just being as asshole, Rick. I've told you many times that we do not discuss that type of stuff in public," stated 'Teeth' with an angry voice.

"I know, but Eddie was looking for one," stated Ricky.

"Eddie, what's your story?" asked 'Teeth'.

"Hey, I agree with you, I would have pulled you aside and spoke with you about it quietly."

"That's right, but I didn't realize that you were in the business," stated 'Teeth'.

"Because I don't believe in speaking in public, the same as you, how would you know anymore then I tell you and that's next to nothing. You have the right idea. Your friends fuck you up," stated Eddie.

"Yeah, you're right. Guys, I don't want discussion in public like this, always speak to me alone or privately."

Everyone in the room agreed that they'd conform to his wishes.

A few minutes later, Eddie was leaning against the wall watching the others shoot when 'Teeth' walked over.

"Listen, if you need a nine, I can sell you one, but if it's for a single job I'll rent it to you, then you won't have to lay out so much money."

"Now that's interesting, but I need one for myself and I have about fifty guys in New York and Brooklyn that will want to purchase some guns. Can you cover them?"

"Man, I didn't know that. We definitely can do business. I can get almost anything you want or need, including quantity."

"How much will it cost me for one nine millimeter today?"

"Don't tell these guy, but for you it will be four hundred dollars."

"Done, I'll take it and we can talk about whatever else I need later. I'll stop back alone, so that we can talk."

"That's good, give me the money and I'll wrap up the weapon for you."

Eddie counted out the correct dollar amount and handed it to 'Teeth'.

"Hey, you guys playing or you gonna stay in that corner talking all day?" yelled Ricky.

Eddie picked up the cue, looked at 'Teeth' and winked. 'Teeth' hung up his cue. He turned back to the table; he knew that Eddie's wink meant that he was going to clean the table.

Eddie ran all the balls on the table and told everyone that he had to leave. He had business to attend to.

"Ricky, are you coming with me or staying?"

"You're my ride, man. I came in with you."

"OK, let's get going."

Eddie looked at 'Teeth' and 'Teeth' said that he would be right back. He went around a corner and could be heard opening something on the other side of the wall. He returned with a paper bag and handed it to Eddie.

"Hey, what about me? I need one," asked Ricky.

"Rick, I'm out at the moment, but I'll re-up in a day or two, then you can have what you need."

"OK, you ready, Eddie?"

"Let's get going."

"Take it easy, Marty. 'Teeth', I'll stop by again, as we discussed."

"I'll be looking forward to it, Eddie."

***

Eddie and Ricky left the house and Eddie dropped Ricky at his home. During the ride, Ricky was upset that 'Teeth' sold the last gun to Eddie.

"Ricky, that's because you were crazy enough to talk about it out loud."

"Yeah, I guess so, but we've been friends a long time, he should have sold it to me before you."

"He was just trying to give you a message. He sold to me because I was quiet about it."

"Yeah, I guess so. You want to come in?"

"No, I have to run, another time, maybe."

***

Eddie left Ricky's home and began to drive to the office, but decided that he would stop by at JZ's house and attempt to make a buy.

He drove to 2400 Midland Ave, the Baker Hill area of Boston, which was an apartment house of at least five stories. He parked the car, went into the entrance way and rang the bell.

"Who is it?" came over the speaker.

"It's me, Eddie, you mentioned for me to stop by."

"Yeah, yeah, Eddie, is Armando with you?"

"No, I'm alone. I prefer to do business alone."

"Come on up, apartment nine."

Eddie entered the building and climbed up the two flights and went to the door with the number nine on it. He knocked on the dark brown metal door.

"Eddie, I'm glad to see you. I can use a hand, if you don't mind."

"What do you need, man?"

"I got this motherfucken asshole that owes me five thousand. I am gonna collect."

"Why don't you call Carlos? He handles that sort of stuff."

"You know something, you're right, I didn't even think about him. I'm so used to doing things myself. How much does he get?"

"I have no idea. Do you have his number?"

"Yeah, I got it."

"Be sure to tell him that you don't want the guy injured, you just want your money," stated Eddie.

"OK, I'll do that," replied JZ.

JZ telephoned Carlos and told him the problem. He also told Carlos not to hurt the guy, just get the cash due. Carlos agreed to collect the money for five hundred dollars and told JZ to stay home with someone for at least three hours. Eddie would be his witness. Carlos was asking questions and JZ replied with an address that Eddie could not hear very well. He thought he heard Lathrop Street, but was not sure and a name of Lawrence.

"Eddie, will you stick around for a few hours as my witness?"

Eddie wanted to leave and try to stop what was going to happen, but he didn't know who the victim was or where he was. The best thing was to stay with JZ and find out as much as he could about the case.

"It will be my pleasure, JZ."

***

CARLOS

Carlos had the name and address from JZ and he didn't waste any time. He took pleasure in hurting people.

He picked up one of his men named Jesus. They drove to 785 Lothrop Street in Boston and knocked on the door. A male came to the door.

"What do you want? I ain't giving to any charities right now."

"Sir, are you Lawrence?"

"Yes, who are you?"

Carlos reached over and grabbed Lawrence by the collar. "I'm your worst nightmare, asshole." He threw Lawrence back into his house and followed as he went backwards. Lawrence hit the floor.

"You owe me money; I get it now or you get some busted fingers. If I have to wait, I'll bust two fingers every hour until I am paid. When you give me the money it will be over. If you don't pay me, I'll move to your arms, then shoulders, but by then I'll probably just put a bullet in your brain. That would be fun, don't you think?"

"Not for me. I don't owe you any money."

"I get five thousand or I start. Don't be an asshole."

"I don't even know you, how can I owe you money?"

"You know my employer. I represent him."

"Oh, I owe JZ five thousand dollars. He sent you?"

"Now you understand."

"Fuck him, he fucked me and gave me some bad shit. I ain't paying him."

Carlos looked at Jesus. Jesus grabbed Lawrence's arms while Carlos took hold of one of his fingers. "This will be painful."

"You're full of shit, you ain't gonna do that."

With those words, Carlos grabbed the first finger and bent it so far back so fast that Jesus could hear the bone break right out of the joint.

Carlos watched Lawrence's face as he screamed in pain. Carlos laughed and took pleasure in the screams of Lawrence.

"You motherfucker, I'll kill you for that, you're a dead man," hollered Lawrence, once he stopped screaming.

Carlos shook his head and grabbed another finger and broke that one.

The screams began again, louder and longer.

"Be quiet, you're gonna bother the neighbors."

Jesus looked at Carlos, "I think he needs a little diversionary pain so he doesn't feel those fingers so badly."

"Yes, you right." Carlos stepped on the arch of Lawrence's right foot. The screams got worse.

"Now I ask you, sir, where is the five thousand?"

It took about fifteen minutes before Lawrence could answer Carlos.

"Man, I'd rather give you two guys a few grand than pay that asshole."

"Good thing we're not cops, that would be a bribe."

"I'm serious, two grand for you."

Carlos lifted the third finger and placed a small amount of pressure on it.

"Stop, stop, don't do it again. I'll pay you."

"Now you are being reasonable."

"I have to get the money. It's down in the safe."

"Where is the safe, Lawrence?"

"Downstairs in the basement, you'll have to help me get there."

"Shall we go down?"

Carlos and Jesus took Lawrence by the arms. They dragged him, more then helped him, down the stairs.

"Over there in the corner is my safe."

Jesus stepped over to one side and had his hand on his gun ready to shoot if it became necessary. Carlos stood directly behind Lawrence watching every move that Lawrence made.

"Step back. I don't want you two pricks seeing my combination."

Carlos did as requested, but still tried to keep an eye on exactly what Lawrence was doing.

Lawrence was down on his good foot, opened the door reached in and pulled out a gun, He fired at Carlos, hitting him in the right arm. Jesus fired at Lawrence, hitting him in the back twice and killing him.

"Why, that asshole," Carlos stated as he walked over to the body and kicked it.

"Now we have to clean up", said Jesus

"Yes, go upstairs and see if you can find a few rags and some bleach to clean up and soak up the blood. Look for something to bandage my arm, it hurts like hell."

While Jesus was getting some equipment and rags to clean up, Carlos went into the safe and took all of the money, which amounted to over thirty five thousand dollars. He placed it in his pockets.

They worked on Carlos arm and got that under control. The bleeding was minor, so was the injury.

The two men cleaned up the cellar, wrapped the body in some plastic that they had in the car and began covering their tracks on the first floor by wiping everything they touched and touching everything with some bleach.

"You know Jesus, this wiping everything isn't gonna work. Let's torch the place. Back the car up to the door and we'll put the body in the trunk. We'll dump it in South Boston by the tracks."

"OK, boss."

They did all the work required and set the fire. There was no sign of the flames as they drove off. But about twenty minutes later they could hear the sirens from fire trucks in route to the fire.

They left the body in the trunk while they went to collect from JZ.

***

Carlos walked into the house and told JZ that they had a small problem.

"What kind of a problem?"

"Hi, Eddie, how are you?"

"I'm doing fine. I'm the witness that "JZ" was here directing the play."

Carlos and Jesus laughed, "We had to cap him."

"Oh, fuck, what happened?"

"He refused to pay so I broke a few fingers. Then he agreed. We went down, opened the safe and he pulled out a gun with his good hand. He shot me in the arm and Jesus shot him in the back twice. Very simple, they will never find him. His house is a big blaze right now"

"You torched the house?"

"Yeah, we had to cover our tracks and prints."

"OK, did you get my money, at least?"

"Yes, we collected the entire five thousand."

"That's good, what do I owe you?"

"Normally, this type of a thing is a lot more expensive, but he had a few thousand in the safe and we can call that money as payment for the job we did."

"That's fine with me," replied JZ.

"Carlos, can I get you guys a pick-me-up or a drink?"

"No, we're all set. We still have to dump this prick."

"Where the fuck is he?"

"He's in the trunk. You wanna look at him?"

"No thanks, you go ahead and do whatever you have to do."

"OK, we'll speak later. Eddie, nice seeing you again. We are always available for you guys."

"Thanks, Carlos, but I don't know how to get in touch with you," stated Eddie.

"Here's my phone number, call anytime."

Carlos and Jesus left the house.

***

"Can you believe that, Eddie?"

"I guess we have to believe it. Turn on the local news and see if there is anything about the fire."

The local news channel had a news truck at the fire and mentioned that it was the home of a Lawrence Dupree. It appeared that no one was home at the time of the fire. Once they got the fire under control they would take a better look at the causes and possibilities of its origin.

"There's your answer, Carlos was not giving us any bull," stated Eddie.

"I guess not. He's pretty good at his job. I may use him again."

"Yeah, I may have more to do with him also, now that I know his game. Look, it's time for me to get going. Can I grab a couple of grams?" stated Eddie.

JZ went into the kitchen then stopped. "No, I have some better stuff downstairs, I'll be right up."

He went down the stairs to the cellar and returned quickly with an eight ball and handed it to Eddie.

"I only wanted a couple of grams, not an eight ball. I don't have enough cash for that on me."

"Take it as my gift. Thanks for the help," stated "JZ".

"Thank you, "JZ", I have to get going. I'll talk with you later and set something up," stated Eddie.

"Anytime Eddie, anytime and thanks again."

***

Eddie left the house and went directly to the office to write up what he did and what he found out. The report requested that warrants be issued against Carlos, Jesus and Johnny (JZ) Zales for premeditated murder. Henry would work on that once he read the reports.

Captain Donald Richards walked into the office as Ernie was finishing up with the report.

"Hi, Don, you better read this report right away."

"I've been reading all of your reports. You're getting into these people in a way that only you can. That accent of yours must put you over the top with them."

The captain sat down and read the report. Ernie could see his face getting red. Eddie knew why he was getting red; we were unable to stop the murder and save the guy's life.

"It's a sin that we were unable to stop this murder."

"Sorry, Captain, I had no control at all."

"I understand, but we will get these guys. When the time comes, they'll do life without parole, I'll press for that."

"Captain, please be sure that Henry sees that, in case he runs into Carlos or Jesus and ask him to run their records. Let's see what we are really facing with those two, although I have a pretty good idea right now."

"He's on his way in now to brief me on the cases. I'll give it to him. Is there anything else you need?"

"Yes, some cash, I made several buys, including the gun. Because of the gun buy, I think we should bring in the ATF and turn that portion over to them with us in control."

"OK, let me open the safe."

The captain went back to the safe in the back room and took some money which he gave to Ernie.

"Ernie, sign here for the cash."

"OK, how much am I signing for?"

"Four thousand."

"Thanks Captain, I think we are getting close to some buy busts and maybe even closing down this portion."

"What about this Risotino? I can't believe that he didn't recognize you."

"He's high as a kite most of the time and he probably doesn't even remember he was busted."

"You know he called here the other day?"

"No, I didn't know. What did he say?"

"He spoke with Henry, who probably hasn't had a chance to tell you. Wait for him to get here, you'll love this."

***

Henry walked into the office, "Ernie, I called your house"

"You did? What did Teresa say?"

"That you left, that's all. I have some news."

"So do I. You first."

"Risotino called and he has somebody that he wants to give us in exchange for some help with his case."

"Who might that be?"

"Oh, just some major dealer from New York named Eddie, who has warrants on him in New York."

"That's funny. We'll have a nice talk with him one day."

"We'll do that. I have some info for you; read these reports and give me a call later, Henry."

"Will do."

"I'm outta here, people. I'd like to spend a night with my wife at dinner," said Ernie.

"Go, it's still early," stated the captain.

"I'll call first."

He telephoned Teresa and told her that he would be home shortly. "Did you eat dinner yet?"

"I'll wait for you to eat."

"OK, I'll be there shortly."

As Ernie walked out the door, he spoke with the captain. "Captain, Wednesday is the 4th and Thursday I am going to take a look at New Hampshire and Vermont. So I'll take tomorrow off as long as you don't mind."

"Ernie, you guys work weekends and whenever I need you. How could I complain about one day?"

"Thanks, I'll talk with you Thursday, Henry."

"See you then, Ernie."

Chapter 23

Out of State

Wednesday July 4, 1979

Ernie and Teresa got up early and had breakfast on the porch. People from the town were already placing chairs all along the beach front for a view of the fireworks which were held every July 4th on the lake. The condominium property was opened for all to attend.

They sat there having breakfast and coffee speaking to some of the people as they walked by and telling others that they could not place chairs in front of the windows to Ernie's condo, because his chairs would be placed there. Everyone was friendly and understood. There was plenty of room for everyone.

Teresa looked at Ernie and asked him to please explain why this case was taking so much of his time.

"Here we go again. You're gonna get upset about my work and try to get me to take a desk job, right?"

"No, I didn't say that, but now that you mention it, I do worry about what you're doing and how safe you are."

"Teresa, believe me I am perfectly safe. I have plenty of coverage when I need it. Henry is always looking out for me. He's like a mother hen."

"Thank God for Henry. I know you wouldn't worry at all, it's not in your nature to worry."

"No, that's not entirely true, but you must understand that if I dwell on the possible dangers then I defeat my purpose and I may as well not be out there."

"Yes, I understand, I do worry though. I watch the news waiting to hear something about you and when the phone rings I jump. I'm almost afraid to answer it."

"Teresa, all I can say is that you shouldn't do that to yourself. Look at it this way, suppose something did happen to me?

By the time you hear, it's over and the healing has already begun. So why worry?"

"You're over simplifying what is a very worrisome situation, Ernie."

"Maybe, but I hate to think about you worrying all the time."

"OK, let's enjoy the day and let this go for a while, but I want to know one thing."

"What's that?"

"When do you expect this to be over?"

"It's hard to tell right now, but remember, some good came out of this already."

"You're talking about the baby?"

"Yes, I am, now let's forget it for a while."

"OK, I'll try not to be so concerned."

"To be honest, it's nice to know that you care enough."

"Oh, you know I care."

"Yes, I do."

The rest of the day went perfectly. They enjoyed a cookout with the neighbors and that evening everyone enjoyed the fireworks which ended around eleven.

***

Thursday July 5, 1979

Ernie got up late. He went out to the porch to watch his little friends, the animals, but the commotion from the fireworks the night before must have scared them. There was not an animal in sight.

He had his breakfast and telephoned Henry. He told him what he had planned for the day. Henry told Ernie that he ran the name Carlos Ruiz in the teletype. He found Jesus as an associate to Carlos and stated that they were both known for extremely serious crimes. They had not been caught since they were young men in their twenties. Henry asked him to be careful of these guys.

"Don't worry Henry, you're worse than my wife, she drives me nuts sometime, but I appreciate the concern from both of you."

"I know you'd do the same if I were in your shoes."

"You're right; I'll call you when I get back."

He then telephoned Armando.

"You awake yet?"

"Yes, I'm awake."

"I'll be working alone today."

"You're getting so well known on the street as Eddie, I have people telling me about you. That's actually funny."

"Yes, I know they are calling the hot line. They think that if they turn me in, they will get some special treatment in the future."

"OK, if you need me, Eddie, I should be here."

The call ended and Ernie telephoned Julia Lozano, the girl that chased him at the first party.

"Hi Julia, what's up?"

"Who's this?"

"Sorry, it's Eddie."

"Oh, Eddie, why did it take you so long to call, you wanna come over?"

"I was thinking about taking a nice drive up to Vermont. Take the highway up, then take the side roads back. What do you think?"

"That sounds like it would be fun."

"It should be; do you wanna come with me?"

"Yes, I would love it. Pick me up."

"OK, I'll be there in a half hour. I have a call to make first."

"I'll be here"

Ernie then hung up from Julia and telephoned Sam Roller, who was believed to be a very large supplier of meth in Vermont. Eddie met him at one of the parties.

"Hello."

"Sam, it's Eddie."

"Eddie Compensatori?"

"No, Eddie from Bronco's party the other night. You told me to call you."

"Yes, yes I remember. What's up, Eddie?"

"Not much. But I promised Julia that I would take her for a ride up north and then I thought of you for a stop and some discussion."

"Great, do you have the address?"

"I have the card with your phone number and P.O. box address, but that's all."

"I live in the town of Franklyn. You take Rt. 89 all the way until you come to Rt. 202 which turns into Rue De la Riviera. The farm is number 7595. How long will it take you?"

"I don't know. I never did a run up there before."

"It should take you about two hours. Give me a call if you run into trouble."

"I will; see you in a couple of hours."

Ernie went and picked up Julia and they were off to Vermont.

***

Julia enjoyed the trip, but she suddenly leaned over toward Eddie and tried to grab him by the crotch while he was driving.

"Julia, I'm driving, I can't be involved with that and drive at the same time."

"I can lick it for you and keep it nice and limber. I love to play with it."

"I know, but let's wait until the time is right."

"OK, I won't try again, not until you ask."

"Deal."

The rest of the ride went very nicely. They stopped at a couple of overlooks to see the sites and went for lunch at an out of the way Pizza Hut which surprised them both seeing that way out in the country.

They finally arrived at the home of Sam Roller, parked and walked up the driveway to the front door.

The door opened and Sam was standing there welcoming them to his farm.

"Guess what Eddie, Keith stopped by and he's here now. This is great, I love company. Hey, Julia, I didn't know that you knew Eddie."

"Oh, yes, I know him a long time. He's not very cooperative with me, though," said Julia.

"Eddie you gotta treat her right," claimed Sam.

"Yeah, but she's too hungry all the time," said Eddie.

"Not anymore, you prick," said Julia.

Eddie and Sam laughed. They all went inside and Eddie saw Keith sitting in the living room. When Eddie and Julia walked in, he stood up to shake hands with both of them.

"Keith, you must be another Frenchman?" asked Eddie

"Yes, Lenard is my name and meth is my game."

"Oh, good business, what kind of territory do you have?"

"I cover most of New Hampshire, why do you ask?" questioned Keith.

"I thought that Johnny Zales, or JZ, as he's called, handled New Hampshire."

"He has the southern portion, but we both do business there," Keith said.

"That's a lot closer than way up here in Vermont."

"Yes, it is. Give me a call anytime, Eddie, here's my card."

"Thanks, I may do that."

"Hey, Keith, you visit me and steal my customers. What kind of a guest are you?" asked Sam.

"I wouldn't do that to you Sam, but you never know when Eddie may need a load."

"Sam, I don't have a lot of time can we talk privately for a few minutes?"

"Sure, come in here."

"Julia, stay with Keith and hands off. I noticed you looking at him."

"Oh, you leave me alone."

Eddie and Sam went into the other room where Eddie spoke of testing the meth that Sam sells.

"How much do you want to test?"

"I'll take a gram. That should be enough."

Sam opened a draw in a desk and reached in. He pulled out a bag with about a quarter-ounce in it and handed it to Eddie.

"That's too much, I don't need that much."

"No problem. If I read you right, that's just a pinhead compared to what you're gonna buy."

"You're right there. If this is OK we can start talking multiple pounds."

"That's good; I can handle all you need."

"What do I owe you?"

"Give me a hundred and call it a gift."

"That's a nice gift, here's the hundred."

Eddie and Sam returned to the others in the living room and Eddie told Julia that they had to leave.

"Are you sure you don't want to stay and have a bite to eat with us?" asked Sam.

"No, Sam, we ate on the way up. I want to get back before dark. I have some business meetings tonight."

"OK, great seeing you, next time plan to stay a day or two."

"We'll do that."

Julia got up, fixed her clothes and waited for Eddie to say his goodbyes and then they left the house.

***

On the ride back Julia wanted to stay the night in Vermont.

"Didn't you hear me back there?"

"No, what did you say?"

"We could have stayed at Sam's house for the night, but I have some business back in Boston."

"Am I coming with you?"

"No, sorry, I'll drop you off at home. We had a nice day and got to know each other a little."

"I guess."

Eddie drove on the highway back towards Boston.

"How come you're on the highway? I thought we were going to go back through the back roads and take it slow and easy."

"Yeah, but I didn't realize how far it was to Sam's and now I have to rush or I'll be late for my meeting."

"Oh, OK then, I'll take a nap."

Eddie was relieved that she was taking a nap. Now he would have some peace and no one grabbing at him. He drove directly to Boston and she never woke up.

***

"Julia, you're home"

"Oh, wow! That was fast, what did you do, fly?"

"No, I took my time, but I have a meeting. I'll call you later or tomorrow."

"OK, don't forget to call. Eddie, you should know that I like you."

"I like you too"

She got out of the car and Eddie drove off. He went directly to a telephone booth and called Henry.

"Henry?"

"Yeah, Eddie, is everything all right?"

"Yes, it is. It's better than all right. I got another buy from Sam Roller and an invitation from a guy named Keith Lenard of New Hampshire. He claims to be the top supplier in New Hampshire."

"That's great. It's time to bring in the Feds, don't you think?"

"Yes, Henry I agree. Why don't you speak with them and I can take them into Vermont and New Hampshire then they can go from there and I believe they can go all the way to Canada, at least it may be possible."

"They will be happy to oblige, but they will want to speak with you at some point."

"That's no problem; set it up and we can talk if they like."

"Will do."

"Henry, I'm gonna stop by Richard (Bronco) Medeiros house and grab a small buy to get into him good."

"Do you want cover?"

"I don't think so. I'll be in and out. If anything goes wrong, I'll call you."

"OK, be careful."

"Talk with you tonight or tomorrow."

"OK."

***

Ernie hung up the phone and drove over to Broncos house, 1455 Everett Street in Quincy.

Bronco was out trimming his bushes when Eddie pulled up.

"Hey, Eddie."

"Bronco, what's up?"

"Doing some work around the yard."

"What's the chance of talking for a while?"

"Sure, come on in."

The two men entered the house and sat on the couch in the living room.

"What's up, Eddie?"

"Look, I'll come right down to it. Is 'Teeth' your gun supplier?"

"How did you know that?"

"I was with someone who said that they wanted to get a gun and asked me to come along. We wound up at 'Teeth''s house."

"Did he sell to you?"

"Yeah, I knew him from the Big Wave. I don't want any animosity between us."

"No, no problem. It's better this way. I'll take care of the drugs and he'll take the guns."

"Good, as long as you don't feel slighted."

"No not at all, that's not my specialty; I would have been the middle man for a few bucks, but I really don't have any connection except him, for guns. Now meth and cocaine, I can sell you all day long."

"Great, talking about that, how about a small taste?"

"Blow or speed?"

"I'll try both. Give me a gram of each. That should be enough to test it out and check for purity."

"Check for purity?"

"Yeah, I have to make sure I am getting the most for my money, don't I?"

With a smile, Bronco answered, "Yeah, I guess so. You won't get any better than the stuff I have."

"If that's so, and I don't doubt you, I'll be back for a large supply."

"That sound good, wait here a minute while I get it for you."

Bronco went down the hallway to his bedroom, entered and came out after less than a minute and returned to Eddie.

"Here you go this is the meth and this is the blow" Bronco handed Eddie four packets, two of meth and two of cocaine.

"Thanks, Bronco. How much do I owe you?"

"One of each is for testing, those are a gift and the other one of each is for you. So pay me for them, two hundred dollars."

"Now that's a deal. I can see that you are a good businessman."

"Hey, I try. Want a cold drink or anything? No broads here today."

"No thanks, Bronco. I have to get going. I have a date with a gorgeous broad."

"OK, stop by anytime."

***

Eddie left the house and went to a phone booth. He telephoned Teresa and told her that he would be home early.

"Do you want some dinner?"

"Yes, I could eat. It's been a long day, I'm tired."

"OK, I'll make you a steak and then you can get some sleep."

"Thanks, Teresa."

Chapter 24

The Feds

Friday July 6, 1979

Ernie and Teresa had breakfast together and discussed taking a trip to Maine over the coming weekend.

"I'll go into work and take off a little early. As soon as I get home we can leave."

"Good, I'll get everything ready"

"OK, I'll call you later, when I'm on my way home."

Ernie telephoned Henry and told him that he was coming into the office to do his reports on the buys that he made after he left the office the day before. Henry agreed to meet him there.

***

It had been raining all morning. At times the rain was so heavy that you could not see the road. Ernie stopped along the road for safety sake until the rain slowed down.

When Ernie arrived at the office he got soaked running from the car to the entry hall in the office building. Henry was already there and made a pot of coffee.

"That's a great idea, making the coffee. I was thinking the same thing."

"Yeah, I figured we both could use a cup with all this rain. It makes it feel so dreary and colder than it actually is."

Ernie began to do his report and Henry telephoned the federal agencies. He spoke with Agent John Slater, who was very interested in the case. He asked if it would be possible for Ernie and Henry to meet them later that day and update them on what could be done and what they would do to assist.

"Ernie, they want to meet this afternoon."

"Can we do it this morning? I want to take off a little early and spend the weekend in Maine with Teresa. Also, ask him if he can contact the ATF, Agent Paul Surillo for the meet."

It appeared that the morning meeting was OK. Henry asked Agent Slater to contact Agent Paul Surillo of the ATF and ask him to be present at the meeting because of the gun connection. The meeting was set for ten o'clock that morning.

"We can be there in a few minutes, Henry, if we hurry."

"Let's get outta here."

The two men drove to the federal building and went through the normal process of turning in their weapons and were directed to a meeting room where there were several men waiting for them to arrive.

"Hello, everyone, I'm Detective Ernie Lijoi and this is Detective Henry Griswold, my partner."

"Ernie, you never change," said Agent John Slater.

"He hasn't changed since I worked with him a while back, but now I have some grey hair, not him," stated Agent Paul Surillo.

"John and Paul, it's great seeing you guys. You're gonna love what I have for a case, but I gotta tell you now, we need cash. Mostly flash rolls, but we have to have it."

"Have a seat guys and a cup of coffee and tell us about the case. But first let me introduce the other people here. That's Bryan, Greg, Linda and Jack. The whole team is here for your case. How do you like your coffee?"

"Nice to meet you guys. I hope this interests all of you."

"How do you guys like your coffee?" asked John, a second time.

"Black," replied Ernie and Henry replied that he liked his with milk and sugar.

"Give us the breakdown," said Paul Surillo.

Ernie and Henry began explaining about the drug buys, the guns, the murders of Lawrence Dupree and RJ, the trip to Vermont and the meeting with Sam Roller, where Ernie met Keith Lenard, the New Hampshire supplier of methamphetamine.

"I also have the reports that we have been writing. If you decide to join us, we'll give you copies. You can make copies for the whole team."

"Why would you say, "IF"? We are definitely in. We'll work out a plan and get together to discuss it. John and I will be in your office on Monday around noon. Is that OK?" asked Paul.

"That's fine; here are the reports, make copies. Henry, do you have anything to add."

"No, I think you covered it all. We'll see you guys on Monday."

***

Ernie and Henry returned to the office. Henry drove off to the headquarters so that he could advise the captain about the meeting with the Feds. Ernie drove home.

Henry told the captain that it appeared they would be starting with the Feds on Monday.

"No doubt, they will want to be cut into the New Hampshire and Vermont people."

"I agree, and they are willing to assist us in the local cases."

"OK, keep me advised and let me know what is happening. I have another situation I want to discuss with you and Ernie."

"What is it?"

"That Risotino that keeps calling and wants to turn in Ernie as Eddie, what do you guys think of using him for a while? I can put him with another team."

"Let me discuss it with Ernie, we already have a buy into him and he's primed for a good size load down the line."

"You guy's discuss it and get back to me."

"OK, Captain. I'll speak with Ernie before the weekend. I'll give him the gist of it now via telephone and he can think about it over the weekend."

"Good idea, he knows these people better than anyone. Have a good weekend, Henry."

"Thanks, Captain."

***

Henry telephoned Ernie who had just walked in the door at his home. He advised him as to the captain's idea and told Ernie to think about it over the weekend.

"That may be a good idea. Risotino could legitimize me even more by having me arrested. On the other hand, I don't really need any more help on the street. They all accept me. Let me think about it. We'll discuss it on Monday."

"Have a nice weekend."

"You too, Henry. Hey, Henry, you know you are welcome to come up to the camp, if you like."

"I know, you've mentioned it before and one day I will, but I have too many personal things to get done."

"OK, see you Monday."

Ernie hung up the phone and turned to Teresa. She was placing a couple of packed bags by the front door, to be loaded into the car.

"Are you ready?"

"I am," with a smile as she replied.

"What do you want me to do?"

"Just load the car. I'll get a couple of bottles of water for the trip. Are we stopping for lunch?"

"Sure, why not, is there any place special that you want to stop?"

"No, same old places I guess. Except that I would like to stop at LL-Bean in Freeport if you don't mind?"

"No, they have some flies that I want to look at."

They finished packing the car, locked up the condominium and headed for the camp in Maine.

***

At LL-Bean, Teresa purchased a couple of blouses and pair of slacks while Ernie searched for the flies he wanted. He had been given an old fly rod and had an old fly reel. All he needed was some flies and he'd be in business for the weekend. He would have to practice and learn the 10-2 process of casting out the fly.

They went to lunch and then drove the final part of the trip to arrive at the camp just after dark.

"I'll unload the car tomorrow morning. Let's go inside."

Ernie started a fire in the stove to take the chill out of the cabin. It would be out by morning and the place would stay warm for the next day or two.

Teresa began putting things away and then cleaning up the kitchen area while Ernie turned on the TV and sat down to watch a show.

***

In the morning, Ernie left the house very early. He was excited about trying out the fly rod. He took the small 12 foot boat.

He went out to a feeding area that he knew about on the lake. He began trying to cast the fly rod and it was not going bad. He watched fish chasing the fly, but they were unable to grab it. This told him that he was retrieving the fly too fast. He slowed the retrieve down and he had his first fish on a fly rod. He released the fish and tried again, his confidence was high.

On the next cast, the line was somehow wrapped all around him and the boat. All he could think of was that cartoon about the guy fishing with a fly line, getting wrapped in the line and hooking himself.

Ernie laughed because this is exactly what happened to him. *Too much confidence*, he thought to himself.

That night he took Teresa out for dinner at a local restaurant and they had a great time dancing to the 60's music.

The rest of the weekend was spent getting experience with the fly rod. By Sunday morning he was casting like a pro, but he and Teresa would be heading home that afternoon.

~*~

Monday July 9, 1979

Ernie arrived at the office very early. He wanted to refresh his memory on the various aspects of the case by reading the reports over. He opened the window and smelled the dry warm air. A beautiful day was ahead of him. He placed a screen in the window to keep the bugs out and returned to his desk.

The reading of the reports would help him to remember areas of the case that he may have forgotten to mention at the meeting with the federal agents and give him an idea of who he already had buys from and who he could place orders with for large buys.

About an hour and a half later, Henry walked into the office.

"Ernie, what are you doing? Refreshing your memory?"

"Yeah, and thinking about Risotino."

"Any ideas on that?"

"I don't know if that would be a good thing or if we should save him for another deep cover case at a later date. What do you think, Henry?"

"I agree with your thought. It would be better to take him down again and then use him if he has anything of any value. Another case on his shoulders would place him in a position of having to do a good job for us."

"Let the captain know that we are in agreement on Risotino. We'll take it from there."

"I'll do that."

***

The two men read all of the reports and waited for the federal agents to arrive.

While they waited and discussed the case Ernie telephoned Armando.

"Armando?"

"Yes, Eddie?"

"Yeah, look, we have most of this case completed and we're looking at a close in a couple of weeks. Armando, don't worry, you'll be helped with your case."

"Eddie, I think you should know that JZ was talking about you and how you are his witness when some guy, I don't know him, said that he thinks you're a cop."

"Where and when did this happen?"

"At the Big Wave last Saturday night."

"Have you seen this guy there before?"

"Yes, I have, but only lately. He's not a regular."

"OK, why don't I meet you there tonight and if he's there, you point him out to me?"

"OK, I'll be there from eight o'clock on. What are you gonna do?"

"Let me worry about that, you just point him out."

"OK, I'll see you there."

Ernie hung up the phone.

"Henry, I need some coverage tonight."

"No problem. What's up?"

"Some asshole is telling people that I'm a cop."

"That's not good, what are you gonna do?"

"I'll confront that asshole and make him look like an idiot."

"OK, we'll be there covering you. If there is any trouble, we'll have four guys hanging around the area."

"That should be plenty."

***

As Ernie and Henry were discussing the coverage of the bar for that night, the door to the office opened.

"Hi John, Paul."

"Hi. guys, what do you think we should do? Go over the case here or go for some coffee?" asked John Slater of the DEA

"We have plenty of coffee here. I'll make a new pot," replied Henry.

Henry went into the other room and put the coffee on. It only took a few minutes, he returned with four cups of coffee.

"Ernie and Henry, we will be glad to do whatever you need us to do; however, we want something too," stated John.

"We'll appreciate any help that you give us, but what do you want?" asked Henry.

"We want Ernie to cut me into the Vermont and New Hampshire people," replied John

"I don't mind, but why are you so interested in those guys?" asked Ernie.

"Those guys are part of an organization that includes a group from Canada. We have heard that they call themselves the Musketeers. We have been hearing a lot about them and want to get involved with the Canadians to bring the whole operation down. We also want this guy Armando when you're finished with him, if he'll work with us."

Henry looked at Ernie when the name Musketeers came up.

"I believe that my main informant, Armando Kiefer, was one of the original musketeers. While I was out with him one night, someone referred to him as a Musketeer and during discussions he seemed to know a lot about them."

"That's Armando Kiefer, right?" asked John.

"Yes, that's him," answered Henry.

"Yeah, he was one, but word is that he withdrew after somebody tried to kill him," stated John.

"That is also true about the attempted murder," replied Ernie.

"So what do you think, Ernie?" asked John.

"For one, I can cut Paul into "Teeth" and he can show a bunch of cash to make a large buy of guns from 'Teeth'. Secondly, I can cut you guys into the Vermont and New Hampshire people and then I can introduce you to Armando. He will be the key. If he is willing to work with you, then the entire case should go nice and easy. However, I don't want you to close any of those places down until I close down the Massachusetts part of the operation. We may not even need Armando. I have a back door that we can look at. We'll have to see how it goes."

"When do you think you may shut down this operation?" asked Paul.

"I feel as though it will take about another month, maybe a little less," replied Ernie.

"Ernie, do you think it may be better if you take all of the people in your end of the investigation down? We may be able to turn some of them to be used later," stated Paul.

"That is another option and it would free me up to work with you guys up north," replied Ernie.

"That's right, it would be like old times, working together again," said Paul.

"Let's think about that. It's your decision, your's and Henry's that is. Whatever you decide we will go along with and help you in any way possible," replied John.

"Then you guys should know that if things don't go right tonight, we may be forced to shut down the operation here in Massachusetts," said Ernie.

"What's going on tonight?" asked John.

"Some asshole is telling people that Eddie Pannoni is a cop," stated Henry.

"What do you guys plan to do tonight?" asked John and Paul almost simultaneously.

"I am gonna confront the guy and see what the hell is going on and how much of a danger there is to the operation. It could be an asshole shooting off his mouth and not knowing what he's talking about," stated Ernie.

"Where is this confrontation going to take place?" asked Paul.

Ernie replied that he was planning on meeting the guy at the Big Wave Lounge down at the beach. Both John and Paul offered their assistance and said that they would be there.

Ernie told them not to worry that he had plenty of coverage and would get back to them as soon as he and Henry made a decision about which route to take regarding the investigation.

"Don't worry guys, we will be in touch. At the very least, I will take you into Vermont and New Hampshire, no matter what happens."

"Great, Ernie, give us a call tomorrow or Henry, you call us. Let us know how things go tonight. We can make plans from there."

***

Pauli and John left the office. Ernie finished reading the reports and decided to try and get some rest before he had to meet Armando that night at the bar.

"Henry, I'm going to go home and get some rest before I meet Armando. Do you need any help setting up the guys for tonight?"

"No, Ernie, you go ahead. I want you well rested in case this breaks out into something more than a verbal disagreement."

"Thanks, Henry, I'll be there at eight p.m." stated Ernie. He walked out of the office and drove home.

***

Ernie arrived home and Teresa was vacuuming the condominium. She didn't hear Ernie walk into the unit. He yelled to her and she jumped.

"Oh, you startled me. What are you doing home so early?"

"If you like I'll leave."

"No silly, I'm glad you're here. I want to speak with you about this case. I'm curious about when it will be finished. I would like us to spend some time together away from all those people that you have to work with, maybe go to visit your family in New York."

"That sounds like a good idea, Teresa, but it will have to wait for a while."

"What is a while? You know you're never here. I am alone all of the time. I don't want to put undue pressure on you, but I am a little worried. You seem to be enjoying this sleazy part of the job too much."

"No, I don't. I just have to play the role; you know, tough and ready for action."

"Ernie, you're dealing with people that have no conscience. They steal from each other and even kidnap children from each other. If they find out that you're a detective they will have no problem killing you."

"Teresa, what do you want, for me to live forever?"

"Ernie, don't make a joke out of a serious situation."

"I'm not, but what do you want me to do? If I start worrying it becomes more dangerous to me."

"Yes, I know, you explained all that. OK, please be careful and end this thing soon."

"I will do the best I can Teresa, the best I can."

"You know, all I have are these walls to talk to and I don't want them talking back. I do worry about you. I know you say don't worry, but that's easier to say then to do."

"I know. I'll do my best to end it soon. Right now I have to get a couple of hours sleep."

Ernie went to their bedroom and fell off to sleep.

Chapter 25

The Big Wave

Monday July 9, 1979 at eight p.m.

At 8pm sharp Ernie walked into the Big Wave Lounge. He could hear the waves pounding the surf across the street at Wollaston Beach in Quincy. Once inside, he looked around and saw Armando standing at the bar. Armando looked back and shook his head to the negative. This signal meant the guy calling Eddie Pannoni a cop was not there. They would wait for a while to see if he would show up.

About an hour later, Armando looked at Eddie who was playing pool and nodded his head, signaling that the man Eddie was looking for was coming through the door. Eddie did not recognize this man. This person walked in and sat at a table with two other people, neither of whom Eddie recognized.

Eddie finished his pool game and approached Armando.

"Armando, get him into a conversation about me. I'll walk over with you."

"Hey, buddy, didn't I meet you the other night in here?"

"Yeah, I think you did, but I don't remember your name."

"Me, I'm Armando, I don't remember yours either."

"I'm Milo, that should be easy to remember."

"Yeah, that's right. Milo. Where are you from, man?"

"I'm from Southey down by the Triple-O's."

"Oh yeah, the Irish Mafia hang out at the Triple-O's bar. I haven't thought about that place for a long time."

"I come in here for the broads and the band. I like to dance."

Eddie, who was standing behind Armando listening, but facing another direction turned and joined in the conversation.

"Hey, Milo, did you mention that you like 'The Renotes'?" asked Eddie

"Yeah, man, they're great," replied Milo.

"I enjoy them too. By the way someone mentioned that you know a guy named Eddie Pannoni and you said he's a cop?" Eddie asked.

"Yeah, I know him from way back, he's a cop alright, be careful of him."

"What does he look like? It would be nice to have a heads up?"

"Oh, he's about six foot tall with brown hair and brown eyes."

"Thanks for that information. By the way do you have anything for the head?" Eddie asked Milo.

"I got about a half-ounce of blow in the car. How much do you want?" stated Milo.

Eddie stood there checking his pockets. "Sorry, I must have left my money home. I'll catch you another time."

"Yeah, anytime By the way, what's your name? I must have forgotten it from the other night."

By this time there were several people standing around Milo's table and when he asked that question they all began to laugh.

They were waiting to see what would happen when Eddie confronted Milo. It was obvious at that point that Milo did not recognize Eddie. Milo described Eddie Pannoni as being 6 feet tall. Eddie was only five feet eight inches tall. The other people waited to see if Eddie would beat the hell out of Milo and throw him out of the Big Wave or not.

"Me, asshole, I'm Eddie Pannoni."

Milo turned white as a ghost and didn't say a word.

Eddie looked around at the people standing there. He had met most of them at the parties and in the bar.

"Do you all see this asshole who said I was a cop? He said I was six feet tall. He obviously didn't know me. We were talking for quite a while and he had to ask me for my name. People, he's just an asshole, I wouldn't have anything to do with a piece of shit like this."

Eddie turned his back and began walking away from Milo.

Eddie got two steps away from Milo when he felt a burning sensation in his the upper right shoulder and a push by someone or something at the same time. The burning got bad and he went down. He turned his head and could see Milo standing over him with a knife in his hand.

With his left hand, Eddie reached for a gun he had in his back, tucked into his belt, but Milo kicked the gun from his hand.

Eddie saw two other detectives, dressed in street clothes, pushing through the crowd. He got up and with his left hand he hit Milo so hard that Milo went over the table and dropped the knife.

Suddenly, Milo wasn't so ambitious. He got up, looked at Eddie, turned and ran out the door.

***

The two detectives, Jack Wade and Gerry Gibson, followed Milo out. Eddie had given them a signal. He didn't want the detectives to get involved with his wounds. They recognized what he was saying and doing. They went after Milo and the drugs he stated that he had in his car. Ernie would add the charges of the assault and battery by means of a dangerous weapon later, after he was finished at the hospital.

As soon as the detectives got outside they contacted the other team, Rick Bradshaw and Carl Robinson. They explained what had happened inside the Big Wave with Detective Ernie Lijoi. They asked the other team to meet Ernie at the hospital, but to be cautious because Eddie (Ernie) may be with people from the lounge.

The other team agreed and Henry chimed in, saying that he was going to the hospital also. Henry asked Jack to call a cruiser if he and Gerry needed help with Milo.

Milo was booked and charged with assault by means of a dangerous weapon. During booking they found out that Milo was a Michael Muzzy of South Boston and had a criminal record for dealing.

Ernie went up to the hospital, parked his car and walked in through a back door, alone, so that he could be treated without anyone seeing him. Henry was already there waiting for him.

"Thanks for coming down, Henry, but I think I'll be OK."

The doctor came into the room. Ernie was sitting in a chair. The doctor looked at his back and told Ernie to get up on the gurney.

"You're going to ruin that chair with all that blood. On your stomach, please"

"Doc, until now the adrenalin was running, but I'm beginning to feel a little sick to my stomach and woozy." With those words, Ernie passed out from the loss of blood.

A nurse walked into the room, "Detective Griswold, there's a man out front asking for Detective Lijoi. What should I say?"

"Who is it?"

"I think he said his name is Kiefer," stated the nurse.

"Oh, yes, tell him to wait. I'll be right out."

The doctor turned to Henry and told him, "You may as well go and speak with him, Detective. Your partner will be fine in time. I'll be working on him for a little while and it's better if you're not here."

Henry went out to the waiting room and signaled Armando to follow him to a small room at the end of the hall.

"Is Eddie OK? That Milo opened him up pretty good. Eddie didn't want anyone else to get into it or I would have helped him."

"Yes, he's that way, I've seen him do that before."

"Will he be OK? He took a bad hit."

"The doctor seems to think that he'll be fine in time. Let's give him a couple of days and then he will get back to you."

"OK, let me know if he's not gonna be OK."

"I'll do that Armando, and I'll tell him that you were here."

Henry returned to the room where Ernie was being worked on.

"What do you think, Doc?"

"I think he'll be fine by tomorrow morning. He'll need some healing time."

"So you're gonna keep him overnight?"

"Yes, unless he hollers that he wants to go home. I would like to have him stay the night for observation."

"OK, I'll call his wife."

***

"Hi, Teresa."

"Henry, he's not here, I'm sorry."

"No, I want to speak with you."

"What happened, Henry?"

"Don't worry, Ernie is OK."

"Everybody tells me not to worry. What happened?"

"He has a small injury, but he waited too long to get to the hospital so he lost a lot of blood. They're taking care of him as we speak and he will be home in the morning."

Teresa began to have tears. Henry could hear it in her voice.

"Where are you? In Quincy? I'll be right there. It will take me a half hour."

"Teresa, have I ever lied to you?"

Henry heard a shallow "no" reply, a "no" that expected more and worse information.

"He will be fine, I just left the doctor. He will sleep all night and I'll drive him home in the morning."

"Henry, please do not lie to me about this. He's very important to me. He's my life."

"Teresa, I would never lie to you, I would be there to drive you to the hospital if it was a worse injury then I am saying."

"So, he'll be alright?"

"He'll be home tomorrow and need a couple of days to recover. Some of that chicken soup you make will really help him."

"OK, Henry, I'll expect to see him in the morning, no later than noon."

"I will call you as soon as I see him in the morning and let you talk to him."

"Thank you, Henry."

***

Henry hung up the phone and walked over to check on Ernie who the doctor said was doing fine and would sleep the rest of the night.

Henry thanked the doctor and left the room.

As he began to leave the hospital, the other men started showing up. Henry advised them of the situation and told everyone to go home for the night. Ernie would sleep all night.

***

The next day Ernie went home to face the music. He felt like a kid again when he lied to his parents, after he climbed a telephone pole that his Mom told him was too dangerous for him because the spikes were too far apart.

~*~

Brooklyn 1955

Ernie was going out to play that morning, he was twelve years old. Where the boys were playing was near a small building of only two stories. The kids had a bad habit of hitting the ball in the direction of that small building and on occasion would hit the ball so high that it would land on the roof.

One day, Ernie was in the outfield and one of the boys hit the ball up and onto the roof of the building. It was Ernie's job to retrieve the ball.

He ran over to the building and looked up at the pole. He threw his glove down on the ground and began climbing. He made it to the top, got onto the roof, which was a little wet from a recent rain and found the ball. He started down from the roof and there was a stretch of about two feet from the roof to the top spike. He reached over with his foot and he made the start down. About half way down, he was reaching with his right foot to get down to the next spike when his left foot slipped off of the spike above.

Ernie felt a scraping in his right leg, but paid no attention to it until he was safely down on the ground and by then he totally forgot about it.

He played the game in the outfield and the other fielder came over to talk for a moment. As they were speaking to each other the other fielder, whose name was Ralph, looked down at the ground.

"Hey Ernie, what's that red stuff all over your sneaker?"

Ernie pulled up his Wrangler pants and saw a large, deep gash in his leg from the spike that had scraped him.

"Hell, what do I do now?"

"You better run home."

"My mom is gonna kill me, I wasn't supposed to climb the pole."

Ernie walked home and while en route, the old men sitting in front of the Italian club stopped him, noticing the blood all over his sneaker.

"Ernest, come over here. What's a happened with your leg?"

"I cut it on that spike on the pole. My mom told me not to climb that pole, but I did anyway."

The men took Ernie inside the club and bandaged the cut to stop the bleeding.

"You sit for a few minutes. We'll get your mother."

Two of the men left and went around the corner to the sixteen-unit building that Ernie lived in and notified his Mom. She went to the club with them and never hollered at Ernie about the incident again. She just checked the wound every day.

Ernie was amazed that he did not get in trouble.

~*~

BACK AT HOME, 1979

Ernie arrived at his home and thought that Teresa would be very upset about his stab wound.

She asked what happened. Ernie told her the story and she only looked at him. She checked the bandages. She changed them twice a day every day and each day made sure that Ernie had everything he needed. All day long she would constantly check on him.

He was amazed that she didn't start hollering about him doing a job that may kill him and not being as careful as he should be.

Chapter 26

Return

Monday July 16, 1979

Ernie was up early. He had plenty of rest and decided to return to work. He went into the kitchen and made himself a bowl of cereal with fruit and took it out to the porch.

He sat down with his coffee and cereal. He was looking out over the lake and the grounds when Teresa came out with a cup of coffee.

"How do you feel this morning, Ernie?"

"I feel great. I'm going into the office today."

"Are you crazy? Your arm is in a sling and you want to go to work? Am I that hard to be around?"

"Don't be silly. I have a lot of work to do. I have things that must be done."

"Your arm is in a sling. You should stay home until you get the full use of it back."

"Teresa, that will take some therapy and I can't waste that much time. I've made promises to certain people and I must finish this job."

Teresa folded her arms and looked at Ernie, "I am very upset about this. You should stay home."

"OK, I'll tell you what I'll do, if I begin feeling any discomfort, I will come right home. How's that?"

"Well, it's something, but you should not even go."

"Sorry Honey, I have to go in. If I feel bad I'll come home."

"OK, I guess if that's all I can get you to do, then that's it. You are a stubborn man, Ernie."

"Yes, I'm afraid so, but you know that."

"Yes, I know it all too well."

***

Ernie left for the office. During the ride he noticed a slight mist that coated his car window as he drove along and wondered if the weather would clear up.

He arrived and parked the car. As he walked to the office building he did not feel or sense any rain in the air and noticed that the air was warm and the sun was shining.

He unlocked the door to the office. Ernie was the first one in that morning. He opened the window and placed the ten inch screen in the window. This gave the rooms some clean fresh air.

His desk was very close to the window. He sat down and began reading the reports that had been made while he was out with his injury. They were mostly surveillance reports of the people that he and the team were working on.

***

The men began to enter the office. They all walked over to Ernie, shook his hand and welcomed him back. Some of them were asking what he had planned. He wanted to wait and speak with Henry before he made a decision on what should be the next move.

Henry walked in and noticed Ernie sitting behind his desk.

"What the hell are you doing here?"

"Well, I ain't dead."

"Ernie, are you sure that you should even be here?"

"Hey, guys, did you hear Henry? He's worse than my wife, who I had to argue with to come in here this morning and make all kinds of promises."

"I'm only concerned for your health, that's all."

"I know, Henry. and I appreciate it. I'm just messing with you."

"Have you decided what the next move should be?" asked Henry.

"No, I wanted to discuss it with you first."

"Do you have any ideas?"

"Yes, I think I should introduce the feds in New Hampshire and Vermont for a starter."

"OK, what else?"

"I should flash this shoulder around. It's good stuff if we use it right."

"Any other ideas?"

"Then I think we should shut this thing down before someone else gets killed."

"I am in total agreement with that plan. I need a break too," stated Henry.

"That's good, now we have to see if the feds will agree."

"By the way, while you were out we served a search warrant at the home of Martin Zackary and cleaned him out. He doesn't know when to stop. He now has had two warrants served at that same location. He wants to talk and said that he could give us a very large dealer from New York."

"Did he use the expression, 'You bet your ass?"

"No, I was aware of that from your reports. When he asked if he was looking at jail time I said, "You bet your ass." He looked at me like I was crazy. Then he started offering us you in exchange for some good words to the court."

"Did you get much?"

"Yeah, he has some business. Twelve people walked in as we searched and a couple of them actually asked for drugs. The phone kept ringing, I answered it and told them to come on up. It was a mad house."

"Good, I'll try and get another buy out of him before we shut down."

As the two men were speaking and checking information, the office door opened and in walked the two federal agents, John Slater and Paul Surillo.

"Great you're both here," said John.

"How's your shoulder, Ernie?" asked Paul.

"I'll be fine, just can't use the arm for a while. What brings you two devils here?"

"We were hoping to get some sort of a final plan down so that we can get things rolling on our end," replied John.

"You're in luck," stated Henry as he explained the basic plan that he and Ernie had just finished putting together. The federal agents liked the basic plan and did not want to make any changes.

"We were going to call you guys a little later," stated Henry

"Then we are all set?"

"Yes, when do you want to go up north?"

"Today is Monday; how about Wednesday morning? We will be here with the teams that we need at eight o'clock and leave as soon as you arrive at the office."

"John, it may be better if the teams go ahead of us and set up before we get there."

"OK, you're probably right. We'll do it that way. I'll meet you here Wednesday morning at eight."

"Great, we'll run it by the captain and I am sure that he will approve."

"If you run into any problems that change the situation, let us know as soon as you can."

"Will do."

***

It was just after noon time when the feds left the office. Eddie got ready to head over to the Big Wave. Henry went to visit with the captain and advise him about what was going on.

Henry arrived at the captain's office. He told the captain that Ernie was back to work and also stated that he was against Ernie coming back so soon after being stabbed.

"You don't have to worry about Ernie. His wife Teresa wouldn't let him out of the house if he wasn't well enough to do the job."

"He kids around about that, but I thought it was only a joke."

"You know her well enough to know that she can get Ernie to do anything she wants. She cares a lot for him and he for her."

"Yes, I know. I guess he can handle it."

"Sure he can. Anyway, he has you to count on for help if he needs it and you can get an entire army of men, if needed."

"Yeah I guess you're right. So you're OK with the way we want to handle it?"

"Yes, the basics are there. Ernie and you have been doing this a long time. I have confidence in your opinions. I may need some input from you two men on another case that one of my other teams have. That is, if I'm not satisfied with their solution. They don't have the experience that you men have."

"Anytime, Captain, we are always willing to help, you know that."

"Yes, I do. I'll let you know."

Henry left the captain and went to the Big Wave to cover Ernie in the event that he needed some backup.

***

In the meantime, Ernie went to the Big Wave. He stood in the entrance way for a while and looked over the entire bar area. He saw Red at a table with Marty and Pauli and 'Teeth' at the pool table.

Red waved, wanting Eddie to join his table and 'Teeth' waved at Eddie to join him. Eddie looked at 'Teeth'. With his good arm he pointed to his bad arm indicating that he could not shoot pool. He went over to join Red's table and sat down.

"Wow, it's amazing that you survived the blow by that asshole," stated Red.

"Yes, he got me good. I should have never turned my back to him."

"You know, Eddie, he had everybody worried until you confronted him that night," said Pauli.

"I was there. You were amazing with a knife in your back; you still took over the situation. He ran like a scared rabbit and no one has seen him since," said Marty.

"Yeah, the prick should be in jail. He put me way behind in my business affairs," said Eddie.

"What do you mean?"

"I usually make a run, every so often, to New York and when I go, I'm usually loaded with shit for my people. Because of this incident, I don't have what I need. I expect to run down in a couple of weeks, they will be expecting me."

"What is it that you will need?"

"I need grass, heroin, cocaine and plenty of meth."

"Shit, that's no problem," stated Marty.

The three men looked at each other, smiled and then each of the men threw a small packet on the table, one with heroin, one with cocaine and one with meth.

"Try those and let us know what you need," stated Marty.

"Thanks, men, you guys are life savers. I have to go up north for a week or so and when I get back we'll put a deal together. I assume that you guys can do pounds and keys for me?"

"Eddie, as long as you have the cash we can do a truckload," stated Red.

"Great, but I don't need a truckload. By the way, who can get me the grass?"

"When you're ready, we'll take you over to our little farm, it's not far."

"That's wonderful, now I don't have to worry at all. I hate to look a gift horse in the mouth, but why are you guys being so nice?"

"Hey, after what happened to you right here in this lounge last week, we know we don't have to worry about you." answered Red.

"OK, I was just wondering. Believe me, I really appreciate the assistance that you men are giving me in my work."

"We will be making a buck on the deal also," said Marty

"I think I'll go over and play some pool with 'Teeth'."

"How are you gonna do that with your arm in a sling?" asked Pauli

"One handed, I'll play one handed."

"I gotta see this," said Red and every one of them got up and walked over to the pool table.

Eddie walked up to the bar and told the bartender to send over a beer for each of them. By the time Eddie walked over to the pool table after paying for the beers, they all had a fresh beer in their hands.

"'Teeth', Eddie wants to play you one handed," stated Marty.

"That's a good idea, now maybe I can beat him easier," said 'Teeth', laughing.

"'Teeth', you can try. Actually, I play about the same game. It should be interesting playing with one arm. As a kid we used to play with one arm for fun. I bought the first round expecting to be beaten."

~*~

Brooklyn 1954

Ernie was spending the day at the pool room playing pool on the nine foot tables against a friend named Tony. They played only using one arm, meaning that they did not use the bridge arm or left arm if you were right-handed.

It was about nine p.m. and the pool room was crowded, all four tables were being used and several boys were hanging around watching the games.

There was a commotion outside and as one of the boys walked over to the door to open it. a red headed man fell in. As he hit the floor with his face, everyone gathered around him to look. They saw a long thick knife, like a bowie knife, sticking out of his back.

The owner of the pool hall pushed people aside to get in and try and help the injured party, who turned out to be one of the local boys from an older group of neighborhood boys. Everyone later found out that he had been stabbed by a couple of guys from another gang in another section of Brooklyn.

The boy that got stabbed was with the Washington Avenue crowd, the boys that stabbed him were from the Vanderbilt Avenue crowd. They were all from Brooklyn, but different sections of the city.

The boy was taken to the hospital and survived. All hell broke out in Brooklyn that night. The hospitals were crowded with bleeding people.

~*~

Back at the Big Wave:

'Teeth' broke the first rack and ran a few balls, not worrying about Eddie's shooting of the game.

It was Eddies turn; he laid his cue on the table and stroked it with one arm, then took his shot and made it.

"It's like I never used my left arm, 'Teeth'. It's gonna be fun to beat you with one arm."

Eddie ran all of the balls except the (8) eight ball which was a tough shot that he missed because he did not use a bridge.

"Too bad, Eddie," said 'Teeth' as he ran the rest of the table including the eight ball.

"OK, I expected to lose that one."

'Teeth' racked for another game and Eddie broke.

They played about eight games and broke out even.

"I've had enough," said 'Teeth'.

"What's the matter, a one-arm man too tough for you?" Eddie said with a laugh and in a joking manner.

'Teeth' looked around at the guys, who were all laughing. "OK, Eddie we have to play on my table again. This table has a bit of a roll to the right."

"Yeah, I noticed that myself, 'Teeth'," Eddie answered with a chuckle.

"Guys, I have to get going. I'll talk with all of you in about a week."

They all said goodbye to Eddie and each man told him to call or stop by anytime for whatever he may need.

***

Eddie went to the office to type out a preliminary report, which he would finish in the morning, on what happened and about the drugs that he was given. He left it for Henry to read in the morning and locked up the three packages of drugs; meth, cocaine and heroin.

Tomorrow he would drive up north with the federal agents and start the end of the case rolling so that he could move on to Mr. Enrique (Ricky) Risotino, who had been calling the office, showing sincerity about working with the men to bring down some dealers and suppliers in the Cape Code area of Massachusetts.

The simple fact that Risotino seemed to be close enough to the Cape Cod people made him an interesting subject for further investigation. Cape Cod is a common location for offloading boats of illicit drugs that come into the United States from the Islands and Columbia.

For now, Ernie had to concentrate on the case at hand; Vermont, New Hampshire and cleaning up the Massachusetts cases that he and Henry started.

Ernie headed home to dinner with Teresa and a good night's rest.

Chapter 27

North Country

Tuesday July 17, 1979

Ernie arrived at the office very early. He was finishing the reports from the day before, about the drugs he was given by the three men in the Big Wave, when Henry walked in. Ernie asked him to contact John and Paul and see if they could come down to the office.

"Sure, I'll call them now. Are you gonna go today?"

"Yes, everyone else is primed for large buys. They are waiting for me to call and order. Buying the guns will not be a problem. I'll bring Paul and let him order a good supply. In Vermont and New Hampshire, I'll introduce the feds. They can make the buys, set them up and order the big load. Then we'll take everyone down at the same time. I hope it all works."

"What about this guy Carlos Ruiz, Ernie?"

"We have him for murder. We have to make sure that everyone is super careful because there are several guns in almost every house and some of these people will not hesitate to use them, like Ruiz and his partner, Jesus."

"I'll start the ball rolling. I'll call the feds and while you're up north, I'll work with the district attorney and start the affidavits for searches and arrests. We must have about twenty-five different ones to get done."

"Thanks, Henry, that'll save a lot of time."

"Hey, that's what I'm here for, to do my part."

"OK, I thanked you what more do you want?" Ernie said with a smile.

"A little respect around here, I need a little respect."

Ernie looked at Henry like he was crazy, "Are you serious, Henry? We all respect you."

"Oh, I guess you didn't watch that TV show last night. Some guy went around demanding respect in a very funny way. I was just trying to joke the way he did. Sorry, I didn't mean to worry you."

"Oh, OK, you had me going for a minute."

***

Henry went into the other room to make all of his calls while Ernie tried to set up some sort of a plan to do his ordering for the close and get the feds into a position where they could close down at the same time.

"Oh, Henry", Ernie yelled into the other room

"Yeah?"

"You didn't read this report yet. Do you remember hearing bits and pieces about a marijuana farm in town somewhere?"

"Yes, someone referred to it, but we got busy with this case and didn't follow through."

"I think we are going to get the farm. They offered to take me there."

"Give me that report so that I can read it. John is on his way with Paul."

"Thanks, I'll have a cup of coffee and relax a few minutes."

"Yes, do that. How's your shoulder?"

"It's beginning to ache a little. I'll rest inside on the couch."

Ernie fell into a light sleep while waiting for the feds to show up.

***

"Hey Ernie wake up. You ready?"

Ernie looked up and saw John standing over him.

"Wow, I feel as though I just closed my eyes."

"That was an hour ago," stated Henry.

"Are you sure that you're OK to make this run?" asked Paul

"I'm fine, let's get going."

"Henry, we'll be back late so I'll catch up with you tomorrow and fill you in."

"Paul and John, we would appreciate a copy of your reports for our files if that's OK with you guys," stated Henry.

"We'll check that out, but it shouldn't be a problem."

***

Ernie, John and Paul started out for Vermont. Ernie was driving.

"Where are you going, Ernie?" asked John.

"I want to make one stop for Paul at 'Teeth''s home, so that he can make an order for the close."

"Thanks, Ernie" said Paul.

They pulled up to 'Teeth''s house and 'Teeth' met them at the door.

"Eddie, I didn't know what this was; I thought it was a raid till I saw you."

"No raid, I'm leaving for New York next week and I wanted to place an order with you. I figured that you may need some time to put it all together. You should meet these two guys. They are my New York distributors. John does most of the drugs and Paul handles the gun end of the business. You don't mind dealing with them for me on the guns, do you?"

"No not as long as you're vouching for them."

"Thanks, 'Teeth'."

"Paul, what exactly do we need in New York?" asked Eddie

"I can sell twenty 9mm overnight and there are people looking for even more powerful weapons."

"You guys better come down to my cellar."

As they followed 'Teeth' down they entered the main room of the cellar which had a loading station for loading bullets, and about fifty guns mounted on the walls.

As Ernie looked around the room he noticed a gun case with a glass front. Inside that case were some antique guns from the 1800's. All three men, John, Ernie and Paul made a mental note of that point.

"'Teeth', I need at least the twenty 9mm and we can do more business from there," stated Paul.

"When do you need them?" asked 'Teeth'

"In about a week, I can give you a call next week," replied Ernie.

"That's good, I'll have them here for you by next Wednesday and you can pick them up after that."

"One question," stated Paul.

"You want to know how much I will ask for the guns?"

"That's right," replied Ernie.

"Since you're buying so many at once, I'll only charge you four hundred dollars each."

"No, no, that's too much; I'll give you three hundred dollars each."

"I'll go down to three hundred and fifty, but that's my best offer."

Paul and Ernie looked at each other and Ernie replied, "OK, we'll do that deal."

"I'll call you on Wednesday, 'Teeth'," said Ernie.

"I'll be waiting to hear from you," said 'Teeth'.

***

Ernie, John and Paul left the house and started for Vermont.

As they were driving and talking, Ernie made a statement about the dealers.

"The underlying, driving force for these men is greed. That's what puts them all out of business," stated Ernie.

"Yes, that's true. Thank God for greed or we would have a harder time working these people," said John.

Three hours later they arrived at the home of Sam Roller, the Vermont distributor who took a liking to Ernie and to the girl Ernie showed up with the last time he visited. They parked the car and walked up the walkway to the front door.

Ernie knocked and yelled for Sam.

"Who is it?"

"It's me, Eddie."

"Who are those motherfuckers with you, man?"

"They are my partners; I wanted you to meet them."

"Eddie, you know I don't like to meet strangers. I hear that you are a cop, Eddie."

"Man, that guy saying that shit was a nut. He stabbed me for calling him out. You can see that my shoulder is bandaged and my arm is in a sling."

"I have a shotgun pointed at the door. One bad move and I will bury all three of you guys where no one will find you, not in these mountains."

"I guess I will not be making any false moves."

Paul and John pulled their guns and Ernie signaled for them to put them away. He could handle this guy.

"Sam, you know Bronco, don't you?"

"Yeah, I know him, why?"

"Give him a call while I wait out here and ask him about what happened to me."

"I'll do it, but if he gives me bad news I'll start shooting."

The entire place went quiet for about four minutes, a very long four minutes while Sam contacted Bronco.

The door opened: "Come on in. I'm sorry about that, but I have to be careful. I ain't going back to that jail, I'd rather be dead."

"That's OK, I don't like to have a gun held on me, but in this case it's understandable."

"What can I do for you, Eddie?"

"The first thing that you can do is call Keith in New Hampshire so that I don't run into this problem with him. I swear, I'm gonna bury that motherfucker if I ever catch up with him."

"Who, Keith?" asked Sam.

"No, that asshole that called me a cop."

"I don't blame you. Bronco told me what happened. I would have buried him right there."

"Don't worry; he'll get his, everything in good time."

"I'll call Keith."

Sam went into the other room and telephoned Keith and Ernie was cleared of the suspicions. This would also let his partners, John and Paul into the fold with these men.

"Eddie where is that cunt you were with? I really like her."

"You mean Julia?"

"Yeah, I was with her once and she is unforgettable, especially when you use a little meth."

"Yes, she is unforgettable, I can't shake the bitch. Every time I see her she latches on to me like a leech."

"Eddie, I never met a better leech then her."

"You can have her if you want her."

"Bring her up here and I'll take over from there."

"If she'll come with me, I'll bring her, the next time I come up."

"Great, what do you guys need?"

"Sam, these two men are my distributors; this is John and he is Paul. I figured that you should know them for future buys," stated Ernie.

"I really don't like dealing with people that I don't know," said Sam.

"I have it set up so that they can call you directly. I would do the pickup unless I'm busy, then they will pick up the orders," said Eddie.

"I see. Is that because of the long distance that is involved?" asked Sam.

"Yes, partially and it's for convenience sake as well," said Eddie.

"As long as they represent you, I'm OK with it. What do you need?" replied Sam.

"Next week, we will be doing a run and we'll need four kilos of blow (cocaine). After that we'll need up to four kilos every couple of months," stated Eddie.

"You realize that we are talking about one hundred and forty thousand dollars?" asked Sam.

"No, we are not. We're talking a profit of over a million on the street with the shit you have," stated John.

They all laughed and Sam stated, "Maybe I should raise the price for the blow?"

"Sam, you're getting top dollar and you know it, now how about the meth? What can you do for us?"

"How much do you want?"

"We could move two pounds over the same period."

"No problem. As long as you have the cash, I have the flash."

"OK, then it's a deal, four and two, by the end of next week and we pick it up here."

"I will be ready for you."

"I may send John, if that's OK?"

"Yeah, sure, no problem, I'll see you then. Would you guys like some lunch or something to drink?"

"No thanks, we have to get on the road; I have a lot to set up for next week. These deals that we do are between us and only us understand, Sam?"

"It ain't nobody's business, but ours. I wouldn't be where I am if I was a blabbermouth."

"Thanks, Sam. You never know who can be telling people our business and causing a problem for us. Look at that asshole that said I was a cop," Eddie stated as he walked out of the house.

"Yes, you're one hundred percent correct." stated Sam.

***

Eddie, John and Paul left the house and started out for New Hampshire and the home of Keith Lenard.

They went to Vermont first, because that was the farthest drive. The New Hampshire stop was on the way back to Massachusetts.

John noticed a sandwich shop as they drove over the New Hampshire border. They stopped, had a sandwich, used the facilities and left for Keith's house.

"I haven't been here yet, so I don't know what to expect, how he lives or anything. He seemed like a responsible person when I met him at Sam's house."

"Do you have the address or a phone number?"

"Good thing you mentioned that. I have his address from the record checks, but all he gave me is a phone number. We'll stop at the first phone booth we see and I'll call him."

***

"Hello?"

"Hi, Keith, this is Eddie we met at Sam's house in Vermont."

"Yeah, Eddie, Sam just called about you and what happened in Quincy."

"I'm glad he did, everybody was getting hinky. I couldn't do any business."

"What actually happened?"

Eddie went on to explain what happened with Milo at the Big Wave and Keith was satisfied with the explanation.

"Look, I'm traveling through New Hampshire and I have my New York partners with me. We are attempting to set up some special deals for next week. I have really fallen behind in my business, because of being stabbed. It would be nice if you met my partners while we are here in case they have to do a pickup."

"Sure, sure, come on over."

"I don't know where you are or live."

"OK, here's what you do. Follow Rt. #89 south to Rt. #2 which is Memorial Drive. Stay on that to National Life Drive and take a right. Stay with that street to Abbey Road and I am at #7465 Abbey Road in Dewey Hill. How many guys are with you?"

"Two, why?"

"Good. I have four broads here, we can have a party."

"We'll talk when we get there. I have another meeting in Boston late this afternoon."

"OK, take your time. If you have a problem give me a call."

"Will do"

Ernie hung up the phone and joined John and Paul in the car.

"He's got a bunch of broads there and wants to have a party."

"We can always use the excuse that we have a meeting somewhere," said Paul.

"I already planted the seed for that excuse. We'll play it by ear."

***

The three men followed the directions that Eddie was given by Keith Lenard.

"I checked out his criminal record and it indicated that Keith was a tall, thin man, six feet and one inch, with dirty blond hair and dark brown eyes. His criminal record further indicated that he dressed very neatly, usually was careful about what he said and when he said it. It further stated that he was a known distributor of illicit narcotics and was believed to be involved with importers from Canada," indicated Ernie.

"No mention of guns, Ernie?"

"Oh, yes, it said that there was a possibility that he was involved with the murders of several of the Devil's Angels gang members and with a group that you guys mentioned. The Musketeers and another group called the 'Clean Bloods', a biker group."

"Yes we are well aware of all of these groups that you mentioned. We have been receiving reports from Canada on the information that they have along those lines. That may be a way in at some point in the future", indicated John.

"Let's see what happens. As I said, all we can do is play it by ear."

The three detectives continued driving. It would be a long drive.

Chapter 28

Keith & Gerry

Tuesday July 17, 1979: That Afternoon

After traveling across Vermont and across parts of New Hampshire they finally reached the home of Keith Lenard.

They turned onto a roadway that had a sign out front stating, "The Lenard's, #7465 Abbey Road."

The long driveway was lined with trees. They came to an opening, a large field with grass and yard ornaments of different types. In the middle of the area was a large brown house with white trim. It had to be at least fifteen rooms.

There were three cars parked out front and Ernie pulled up and parked in line with the others.

They exited the vehicle and walked up to the front door, rang the bell and waited.

The door opened; Keith was standing there.

"Hi, Eddie, come on in."

"Keith, I want you to meet my partners, John and Paul."

"A pleasure to meet you guys, how about a drink?"

"I'll have a beer," stated Eddie.

"Yeah, that sounds good," indicated Paul.

"I can't go without," said John.

"Grab a seat guys, introduce yourselves to the girls, I told them that you were coming."

They walked into a living room. They observed three shotguns and three rifles mounted on racks on the wall. The furniture was nice and clean and the entire area was well kept.

In the living room there were four girls sitting and drinking and on the coffee table were several lines of white powder.

Eddie had seen these girls at the different parties in Massachusetts. One of them was Julia whose eyes lit up when Eddie walked into the room.

"Hey, Julia, girls, doing a little meth?"

"Oh, Eddie, I'm so glad you're here" stated Julia.

"Why is that?"

"I've missed you and I heard about the stabbing. I am so sorry. He must have been a nut of some kind."

"I guess you could say that. I've had some time to think about that guy and I believe he was simply looking to make friends and thought that calling some guy a cop would help his chances, which it did for a while, until I had the opportunity to confront him."

"Are you OK, Eddie?"

"Yeah, I'll be fine."

"Eddie, I have an idea. Would you like to go upstairs to the bedroom and play for a while?"

"Yes, I would, but I don't have time. Anyway you're a guest of Keith's. Shouldn't he have first preference?" answered Eddie.

"Oh, the other girls can take care of him and your friends too, right girls?" said Julia.

"A few more lines and we'll be ready to take on the entire town," stated the blond blue-eyed doll.

There were a total of four girls, Julia, Maria – a Spanish looking girl – Roberta and Rose, who Eddie had met at other parties.

Eddie introduced John and Maria grabbed his arm. Then Eddie introduced Paul and Roberta walked over to him and grabbed his arm. Julia took hold of Eddie and was not going to let go of him.

"Girls, we don't have time for this," stated Eddie.

"That's right, Eddie, we have a meeting in Boston in three hours."

Keith walked into the room with the beers, "No, you ain't taking on the town, not here. I like it very quiet and I don't tell anyone what I do. Not in this town" He overheard the girls talking.

"Now, there's a smart man," stated John.

"Yeah, John, I try to stay low key here."

"That's the only way to do things, my friend," stated Paul, with John and Eddie agreeing.

"Eddie, can you men spend some time and help me out with these lovely ladies?"

"We're in a bit of a rush, Keith."

"By the way, Eddie, we could use some help, we're getting low on man power. Do you have any men that you can send up to Canada to help us out?" asked Keith

Eddie looked at Paul and John; he then turned back to Keith.

"Keith, what the fuck are you talking about?"

"Come into the study. Girls, you stay here and enjoy yourself."

They followed Keith into the study and waited for him to speak.

"Don't you guys know what's going on between this area, Vermont and Canada?"

"What the fuck would we know, we're from New York. These areas are all new to us," said Paul.

"Yes, that's right. I'll explain. There is a war going on in Canada that is beginning to spill over into Vermont and New Hampshire."

"What's this war all about?" asked John.

"The mafia wants control of the methamphetamine. The Musketeers built up a multimillion dollar business. The mafia wants to take it over. One of the brothers of a Musketeer was murdered. He was shot to death by the French Mafia while doing a pickup. Basically that's the story. Now we need help."

"Are you one of those Musketeers?" asked John.

"No, there are only three and one of them left the fold. He couldn't take the action."

"Do you know who that is, because I had a friend that used to speak of Canada a lot." asked Eddie

"Yeah, I his name was Armando, I don't know his last name; he was a good guy."

"Who are his partners?" asked Eddie

"There is no need for you to know that at this point. If you feel that you may be able to give them some assistance, then I'll introduce you."

"Right now, we don't have any people to spare, but in a few weeks we may be willing to help you out. We have to finish up our New York business for the month and catch up on the business that we lost when I was stabbed."

"I understand. You get your shit together and then we can talk some more."

"Good, that will work for us; remember we're not saying no to helping out."

"Yes, I understand. Is there a specific reason that you stopped in?"

"Yes, your specialty is meth, right?"

"I can get anything, but yes, I specialize in meth."

"We will need twenty pounds of meth by next week. Is that correct, John?"

"Yes, that should take care of us for a short time."

"Can you help us out with that much, Keith?"

"Yes, I can have it here by next Tuesday or Wednesday. Call me before you make the trip to pick it up."

"Good, we will do that. If you have no objections, Paul or John will do the pickup while I do some other pickups closer to home," Eddie said.

"As long as they have the cash, we can do business."

"How much do you want for twenty pounds?" asked Paul.

"I will only charge you twenty five hundred per pound and that's giving you one hell of a deal."

"OK, so then we will have fifty thousand dollars in cash for you," stated John.

"That's a pretty good deal, especially since it's not cut at all. Once you cut it up and move it you have a million dollars," stated Keith.

"It's not cut at all?" asked Eddie.

"That's right. This is primo stuff, right from the chemist."

"That's great. We will be in touch with you next week. Keith, please do not discuss this deal with anyone. We must be very careful. We have a long way to travel with this shit," stated Eddie.

"Do you think I am nuts? I want to keep you guys coming back to me for more."

"As long as this deal goes well, you can count on a similar order every three months," stated John.

"That's fantastic and I will do all that I can to satisfy your needs."

"Now that we have business straightened out, what about those broads in there?" asked Eddie

"What do you mean, Eddie? Let's have a ball, they are all set and primed," stated Keith.

"Yes, I agree and I wanted to speak to Keith about those guns and possibly some dynamite," said Paul.

"Sure, stick around a while."

The three men agreed to stay for a little while. The main reason was to give Paul a chance to discuss some gun deals with Keith.

"Keith, we have several people that are always looking for guns in New York. They are hard to come by down there. Where do you get yours?"

"One of the sources is a guy named 'Teeth' in Massachusetts and the other is a guy named Gerry in Canada. I can set you up with them if you like, after we do our deal" stated Keith.

"I know 'Teeth' and I already made a deal with him for some of what we need, but I didn't want to get everything at once. I didn't even ask him about the dynamite that the guy in upstate New York wants," stated Eddie.

Ernie realized that he had interfered in Paul's move to try and get explosives. He looked at Paul in a way to say, "Sorry, I screwed up."

Paul shook his shoulders as if to say, "No problem."

The three men hung around for a while and let the women chase them until they finally had enough.

"Keith, we have to get going", stated Eddie.

"Hey, Eddie, don't you like girls?" asked Julia.

"Yes, I love girls, Julia, why?"

"I don't know, you never want to let me get close enough to do anything."

"After I get back from New York, we will have some time together."

"I'll hold you to that", stated Julia.

"OK."

The three men left the house and started back to Quincy.

"Ernie, you blew that one."

"Yeah, sorry about that, but when he mentioned 'Teeth', I thought that it would help but it didn't."

"No problem, now we know what we can get out of him down the road. This Keith is a key person to convert to our side once this is over."

The drive back to Quincy took a couple of hours and they discussed all of their options for the upcoming close of the operation.

"You see what I mean about guns? They all have plenty of them and will use them at the drop of a hat."

"Yes, we will have to advise everyone about them."

***

Ernie dropped John and Paul at their car and he drove home to his wife Teresa.

He arrived home late. As soon as he walked into the condo Teresa wanted to make him something to eat.

"You look tired, Ernie."

"I am. We drove through half of New England today."

"Who was with you?"

"I was with some federal agents. We're getting ready to close down the operation."

"Am I glad to hear that, is your arm hurting?"

"No just a little muscle pain. I am probably going to need some therapy when this case is over."

"You need therapy for getting involved in this case," she laughed.

Ernie joined her laughter. "You're probably right about that."

"Do you want to watch some TV or just go to bed?"

"I think I'll just go to bed, I'm very tired."

"OK, you go ahead. I'll be in as soon as I clean the kitchen. Do you need any help with your sling?"

"No thanks, Teresa, I think I can handle it."

Chapter 29

The Meet

Wednesday July 18, 1979

Ernie got out of bed and was ready to begin closing of the operation. He had a tremendous amount of information rolling around in his head. He wanted to be sure that he ran it correctly. He didn't want to see anyone get hurt during the raids. It would take two or three working days to get everything ready.

He went out to the porch with a cup of coffee and was deep in thought when Teresa walked out.

"You look very preoccupied Ernie, what's wrong?"

"No, nothing, I am a little concerned about the work I have ahead of me for this case."

"Concerned about the work? You've never been concerned about work in your life. You look at everything as though it is easy and will only take a few minutes. You always say that, 'It will only take a few minutes', next thing I know it is four hours later, you finish and you're happy. Don't say you're concerned about the work. What's really going on?"

"It's not so much concerned about the work as it is getting everything the way we need it to be. It will be OK, I'm sure."

"If I know you, and I do, nothing will be missed and it will all go smoothly."

"Yes, smoothly, that would be nice."

"For the first time, I am not worried about you at all. I'm very happy that this is ending."

"About that, completing this case may not be the end, it may be the beginning."

"What are you talking about, Ernie?" Teresa said in an unhappy voice.

"This case is going to open a lot of doors that have not been opened before and it may be up to me to go through them."

"Why is it always you? You are the one that gets shot, stabbed and almost killed. Are you stupid or smart? I'm not sure anymore."

"Don't feel that way. You know I love my job. I feel as though I am contributing in a small way."

"It may be small to you, but I have to stand by your bed, fix your wounds and cry alone because I don't want you to see me."

"It's just a possibility and it won't happen for at least a couple of months, if anything at all comes of this."

"Don't tell me that, you're planting the seed now for the full blow later."

"That may be so, Teresa, but don't worry about it now. I have to get into the office and work on the affidavits. Give me a kiss goodbye."

Teresa, kissed Ernie and he left the condominium.

***

On his way to the office he thought about Teresa and how calm she had been through this entire case and other cases that he worked.

He was concerned that the next case would probably be more involved than this case since it may include the Canadian French Mafia, The 'Clean Bloods', The Devil's Angels and the Musketeers. These were all very serious and very treacherous groups that would do anything to stay out of jail.

He couldn't think about that now, he had to complete the task at hand, closing down the current operation.

He arrived at the office and Henry was already working on the affidavit for the arrests and search warrants.

"Ernie, you read the affidavits as I draft them. We can correct them wherever you think it is needed later."

"Sure, Henry. Should we run these by the District Attorney before we take them over to the court?"

"No, I spoke with the D.A., we'll be OK, you write them as well as the D.A. does or at least very close."

"I think I'll contact the feds and the captain and see when we can get together and have a meeting to cover our needs for this operation."

"Try for tomorrow, I was thinking that we would take Friday off and start fresh on Monday," stated Henry.

"That sounds like a great idea to me. Maybe I can get some fishing in, visit my shack in Maine. Would you like to come up with us, you and your family, that is?" asked Ernie

"Yes, that sounds like a great idea. Thanks for the invite. I had better check with the better half before I commit to that."

"OK, let me know."

Ernie picked up the telephone and spoke with the captain. He decided that the next day was good for him, but he wanted Ernie to check with the fed's before he set a time for the meeting.

He telephoned Agent John Slater of the DEA and had a conversation with him regarding the case.

"John, can you and Paul make a meeting for tomorrow? This meeting would be to set up time factors, arrange for manpower and coordinate the entire operation."

"What time do you want us there?"

"What's good for you?"

"We have a thing in the afternoon so how about early morning? We'll be there at eight o'clock if that's OK with you?"

"See you at eight a.m., I'll have the coffee ready when you get here."

Ernie hung up the phone. "Henry, eight o'clock tomorrow morning, I'll tell the captain."

"OK"

Ernie telephoned the captain who stated that he would be present for the meeting.

"Ernie is there anyone else that we should have at this meeting?"

"I think the whole team should be there, Captain. We can set everyone up with their individual jobs at the same time, barring anything that may change before the actual shut down of the operation."

***

The rest of the day, Henry and Ernie were busy working on the evidence gathered, affidavits which encompassed illicit narcotics violations, gun violations, several murders, various conspiracies, over a dozen search warrants and putting everything together in a readable and understandable order for the courts and the D.A.

This was the part of the job that neither Henry nor Ernie liked doing. It encompassed a tremendous amount of detail. This work, although not enjoyed, was a necessity, the most important necessity being to complete the job in a logical and comprehensible manner.

They finished out the day and were looking forward to the meeting the next day.

~*~

Thursday July 19, 1979

Ernie left the condo early. Teresa was still sleeping. He grabbed a quick cup of coffee, a couple of pieces of toast and went out the door. He wanted to be in the office early to make the coffee as promised.

During the drive to the office he noticed that there was still a slight mist in the air, but not as bad as it was the day before.

He walked into the office and was the first one there. He filled the coffee pot, turned it on and pulled the milk, cream and sugar out to be placed on the desk. He was ready.

Ernie sat at his desk and looked over the information in the reports. He wanted to see how many men would be needed for the raids, the best time to begin the raids and what type of weapons would be needed to help defend the men involved.

As he was writing different points down, Henry walked in.

"Henry, you're here early."

"I guess I want to get this day over early. I'm looking forward to some peaceful relaxation at your place in Maine."

"Oh, good, then you guys are coming up?"

"Yes, as long as the invitation is still open."

"Always for you, do you know how to get there or do you want to drive up with us?"

"Yes, I remember pretty well, but write down the directions for me anyway, in case I screw up."

"You got it"

Ernie drew a map with every turn and directions in writing below the map and gave it to Henry. As he finished the map

John, Paul and the captain walked in and a few minutes later the other teams in the unit followed.

Everyone knew each other from other investigations that they had all worked together with Ernie as the deep cover man.

"Captain, if you don't mind, I will start the meeting", said Ernie

"Not at all Ernie, its Henry's and your investigation so you guys take the lead"

"Thanks. You guys all know each other so we don't have to go through that introduction thing."

Everyone looked at Ernie, quietly waiting for the information that needed to be discussed and hashed out.

"Henry and I are finishing up with the affidavits and they should be completed on Tuesday at the latest. On Wednesday we will start the confirmation of orders."

"How many places do we have?" asked Detective Jack Wade

"We will be under twenty by the time we are finished and that includes the two that the Federal Agents will close down. One in Vermont and the other in New Hampshire." answered Henry.

"What time will we be closing this thing down?" asked Detective Gerry Gibson.

"That's one of the things we have to discuss; I was thinking that we could close them all down at the same time. The best time should be at six o'clock in the morning" answered Ernie.

"What about personal property, houses and cars," asked Detective Rick Bradshaw.

"I have been reviewing the reports and I don't think we will take any of the cars or houses right now. Let's leave that to the D.A. to make a final decision. There's no rush on those items."

"Ernie, don't forget the weapons."

"Yes, I was getting to that, Henry. In every house that I was in there were plenty of guns hanging on the walls. We will have to be careful of that. Some of these locations do not have a way of getting to them without being observed before you get there so be very careful."

"Talking about weapons, I have to show up with my team at 'Teeth's house for the pickup. Once we make the arrest, where do I book him," asked Paul.

"Yes, do you want me with you, Paul?" asked Ernie.

"If you like, but we can handle it," said Paul.

"OK, you take the prisoners to the main headquarters garage. The captain will have it all set up with tables the same way that we've done it before. As far as my being with you, we'll play that by ear."

"What about logistics? Where are we meeting, what time, what day? You said we hit at six a.m. so we have to meet much earlier than that," stated John Slater of the DEA.

"I will leave that to the captain. I believe he has some information on that subject. Before I turn this over to him, does anyone have any questions or suggestions?"

No one replied to the question, they were all experienced detectives and knew enough not to ask for the subjects names. They would be told when the time came

Captain Richards rose from his seat and took the floor. He told everyone that there would be about (20) twenty teams consisting of six men each and three backup teams.

"We'll all meet at the Emergency Services Command Center on Sea Street at four a.m. In the event that there are any changes, you will be contacted."

"Captain, will there be any coffee or anything like that?" asked Detective Carl Robinson.

"That's just like you, Carl, always worried about your stomach."

Everyone began laughing and Carl looked down at the floor, then looked up and said, "Well, we have to have breakfast."

"Yes, you're right, Carl. I'm just messing with you. We'll have coffee and donuts courtesy of the D.A.'s office."

"Are there any questions?" asked Henry.

There was no answer from the group.

Ernie said, "OK, men, you have all that you need right now. We'll set up the teams and coordinate with the feds. Each warrant for searches and arrests will have warnings indicating what to look out for such as guns, hiding places, etc."

Captain Richards indicated, "Look, men, you're going after top people here. This can be very hazardous, so everyone be careful. I know that I don't have to say this, but I will anyway. Make yourselves available to Ernie and Henry in the event that they need your help."

The men broke up and stood around talking to Ernie and Henry about the case. There were no congratulations, it was too premature. They all left the office in numbers of one and two men at a time, except Ernie, Henry and the captain.

"Captain is there anything that you need done?" asked Ernie.

"No, you guys know what you need to do."

"We were planning on going up to Maine tonight. Sort of a get together before the action starts."

"Good idea. I'll see you both on Monday."

"Thanks, Captain."

Ernie and Henry finished up with the men, the reports and created a check list for Monday morning on things to do.

***

That night they all met in Maine at the broken-down camp that Ernie and his wife owned.

"Ernie, I love this place, it is right out of some old 1930's cowboy movies," Henry stated.

"Yes, we were talking about building a new house on this footprint, but I hate to do it; I'd have to worry about carrying sand in the house on my feet and things like that."

The weekend was busy with fishing, sleeping on the front lawn, riding around the lake in the twelve foot boat and enjoying life.

By Sunday they were all relaxed and ready to return to Massachusetts.

Chapter 30

Ready & Go

Monday July 23, 1979

Ernie and Henry arrived at the office at about the same time. They discussed the plan and what would be the best way to begin. They made a few decisions and Ernie left the office.

The first stop would be at the home of Martin Zackary at 992 Ivy Lane, Quincy. Marty was the dealer that supplied the kids in town with the meth that they wanted and in some cases needed.

He entered the apartment building, walk up to the second floor, apartment #8 and knocked on the door several times.

"Who the fuck is there?" he heard from the other side of the door.

"Marty, it's me, Eddie."

Marty opened the door with a gun in his hand and looked at Eddie. "Hey motherfucker I heard that you were talking to the cops. I got hit right after you left here. You'll never rat on anyone else."

Eddie acted a little perturbed by this same old comment, "Marty, you know me better than that. Where do you think I got this bad arm from?"

"Come in, Eddie, but don't make any false moves."

Marty got on the phone and Eddie could hear Marty say to the party at the other end of the line, "No shit, I almost capped the bastard." He hung up the phone and walked over to Eddie and put his arms around him.

"I'm sorry, Eddie, all I knew was that asshole was calling you a cop and I got hit. It all fit together."

"I don't appreciate being met like that, but I understand."

"What do you need?"

"I want another eight ball and I will need two pounds for Wednesday. Can you do a load like that?"

He turned and opened a draw and handed Eddie the eight ball.

"You can pay me for the whole transaction when the package is ready."

"How much do you want for the entire package?"

"For you, because I fucked up like that, give me seven grand."

Eddie knew that that was too much money, but decided to take the offer anyway.

"OK, I'll be here Wednesday about seven in the morning. I'll be leaving for New York right after I leave here."

"No problem, I'll see you then."

"One more thing Marty, can you show me the marijuana field that you guys have set up?"

"How much do you need, Eddie?"

"I only need ten pounds. I have a few customers for that shit."

"Sure, come with me."

Marty and Eddie left the apartment and Marty drove to a field in the Blue Hills a section of the State Park. They parked and Marty directed Eddie through the thick bushes and trees of the forest area until they came to a field. Eddie looked and could not believe his eyes. Standing in front of him were about 200 marijuana plants ranging from 8 to 10 feet tall.

"Where do you dry it out and press the bricks?"

"In the apartment on the third floor in my building, that's why there were so many tables and shelves when you were there."

They left the farm and returned to Marty's apartment.

Eddie didn't go up to the third floor apartment. He put in an order with Marty for Wednesday. Eddie left the apartment and drove over to the next location.

Between Monday and Tuesday he contacted each and every dealer to make sure that they were ready with the packages that he needed for his New York trip.

On Tuesday morning he went by the home of Carlos and the home of Jesus to confirm that they still lived in the same location.

On Tuesday afternoon he brought the final residential information to the office on Carlos and Jesus. This final information would be the last paragraphs on the affidavits for the warrants.

***

"Shall we go and see the clerk of courts, Henry?"

"Should you go, Ernie?"

"No, you're right. I don't want to be seen at the court house with you. Not now."

"I'll take them and sign for the warrants. No problem," said Henry.

"Thanks, I'll contact the feds and make arrangements with Paul and John. I'll see if Paul wants me to confirm the gun order or if he wants to do it. After I am finished, I'll go home and get ready for tomorrow. Call me as soon as the warrants are issued."

"Will do."

Henry took the pile of paperwork and went to the court while Ernie did his follow ups, after which he went home. The next day would be a long and busy day.

While driving home he was going over every aspect of the case in his head. He was trying to be sure that he did not miss anything. By the time he arrived at home he felt confident that between Henry and him, they had covered everything.

~*~

Wednesday July 25, 1979 at 2am

Ernie got out of bed and stayed in the shower extra long, trying to wake up, got dressed and went into the kitchen where Teresa was already out of bed, making breakfast and coffee for Ernie before he left for work.

"This is the big day, Ernie?"

"Yes, I guess you should know, you've been through it enough."

"Be careful, please and call me as soon as the day is over."

"OK, Teresa, I'll call you as soon as we book the last man or woman."

Ernie left the house for the meeting with the men. Many of these men didn't know exactly what they were showing up for. Ernie didn't know what he had to look forward to on that day. The day he would forever call, "The day of dreams."

***

Ernie walked into the hall, immediately went over to the coffee table, had a coffee and a couple of donuts. The rest of the men began showing up.

On the front table were stacks of paperwork, the search warrants, the arrest warrants and instructions where applicable, small pictures of the houses and the people that each warrant applied to.

On the board behind the table were the team layouts and pictures of most of the people being sought during this raid.

Most of these men had been through this before and were used to this procedure. Everyone was looking forward to doing the job and taking some of these people off of the street for good.

At 4:50 a.m. the captain called the meeting to order.

"Some of you men have farther to travel then others so let's get this meeting started. I would like to hit every location at six a.m. sharp. You men know the drill. You have all been through this before. Everyone, synchronize your watches, I have 04:55 hours."

Every man in the place set their watches exactly at the time indicated, 4:55 a.m.

"I believe that most of you know Detective Ernie Lijoi and Detective Henry Griswold. Ernie, Henry, do you have anything new that you need to add to what we have?" asked the captain.

"Yes Captain I would like to add that I was in the home of Martin Zackary at 992 Ivy Lane, Quincy on Tuesday and he answered the door with a gun in his hand. He was going to kill me because he thought that I was a cop. Please, whoever has that location take some extra care," answered Ernie.

"Who has what location?" The question came from the audience.

"I'll answer that in a minute. Anything else, Ernie?" asked the captain.

"There are many guns involved in this case so watch your moves when you hit these places," said Ernie.

"Henry, do you have anything?"

"No, Ernie covered it all."

"Each team leader knows who he is. Come up here, take your paperwork and find your team."

The team leaders did as directed.

"OK, men, make sure that every team member knows exactly where to go and what to do. Those of you that have to travel can leave anytime. The rest, take your time. If there are any questions, see Ernie, Henry or me. Good luck and please be careful, men" said the captain.

The teams slowly left the building to set up on their assigned targets. They would drive past the locations first, set up their plan after looking the place over and move in at exactly six o'clock a.m.

***

Henry's team took Enrique (Ricky) Risotino who lived at #12 Federal Street in Quincy.

They approached the house and Risotino, not knowing that it was a search warrant, acted happy to see Henry. They had met on an earlier date when Risotino was trying to get Ernie and Henry to help in his defense. He had offered them help on the street. He had several people that he wanted to turn in and spoke of this guy from New York who was a dealer. That dealer's name was Eddie Pannoni. Risotino had a very big surprise coming.

Once in the house, Henry placed Risotino under arrest and the search went quietly. They confiscated several pounds of marijuana, three keys of cocaine and a pound of methamphetamine. Hidden in a back room behind a cut-out in a wall was a shoe box filled with cash. They confiscated all of the cash, which added up to seventy five thousand dollars.

***

Ernie joined Paul before the six a.m. hour to hit 'Teeth's house for the guns. Gaining entrance went peacefully. During the search they found so many guns that the ATF would be there most of the day cataloging all of the weapons. This man had more than one hundred weapons of all types in his house.

'Teeth' was placed under arrest and sent back to the station for booking.

Ernie returned to the station to meet his team and start his next search.

***

Detective Jack Wade was assigned to the marijuana field. They went in, cut down all of the plants loaded them onto a flat bed truck that they brought with them and transported the plants back to the station.

Two men were left behind to dig up the roots of the shallow plants and dispose of them.

There were no attests at the plant sight. However, several people were charged with cultivation of marijuana, conspiracy and distribution of the drug.

~*~

Carlos and Jesus, Shortly after six a.m. that morning

Ernie and his team members decided, in advance, to take the Carlos Ruiz and Jesus Riggs warrants because, in their estimation, Carlos Ruiz was the most dangerous person on the list, having already committed several murders.

Ernie had previously obtained the criminal records of Jesus Riggs and Carlos Ruiz, who both lived in Quincy. The plan was that he would supervise the other warrants after picking up and booking Ruiz and Riggs.

Carlos lived in a home at 1924 Vinewood Road in Quincy and Jesus lived at 1922 Vinewood Road directly across the street from Carlos.

Ernie took a double team for these warrants. He didn't expect much trouble, but informed the officers that these men were crazy and dangerous people who had committed more than one murder already; anything could happen.

Because of the location of the homes, they decided to park down the street and slowly approach the houses from both sides of the streets and from the back yards.

Ernie took the Ruiz house while Detective Robinson took the Riggs home.

They approached the front door with two men. The others were spread around the property, covering the escape routes of the house. Ernie knocked on the door and announced that they were the Quincy Police. No answer so he directed the two men with the battering ram to knock down the door. With the first hit on the door something went by Ernie's neck and hit the wall just to the right of the door. It exploded like a bullet hit it.

The three men didn't hear anything because of the noise that the battering ram was making. They saw the bullet hit the door frame and froze for a second, then another bullet hit one of the two men holding the battering ram and he went down.

They pulled him over to an area behind some bushes for protection and realized that the shots were being fired from the house across the street, the home of Jesus Riggs.

Jack and his men saw Ernie and the man on the ground. They realized that shots were being fired from the house that they were hitting.

They gained entrance as fast as possible. Jack worked his way up to the second floor and to the room where the shooter was.

He kicked in the door and saw a man turn away from the window towards him with a gun in his hands. He raised his gun to fire at Jack. One shot was fired and Jesus was dead. Jack had put one shot in the middle of his forehead. Jesus slowly fell to the ground from his crouching position.

The men on the first floor of the house began the search and after that incident the searches went peacefully.

They confiscated four guns from the home of Ruiz and two guns from Jesus Riggs' home. These guns were later checked out in the lab and the firing test tied them into four different bodies that were found murdered over the past three years.

The information and evidence obtained indicated that Carlos and Jesus were a murder-for-hire team, the charges would be murder, four counts.

As soon as the situation was under control, they transported the injured officer to the hospital in Quincy where he was taken care of. After two days he was released from the hospital and treated like a hero by the other men at the police station.

***

After Ernie was finished with his warrants, he returned to the station to face Risotino and to see how the other warrants went.

As it turned out, the only man shot was the man with Ernie and there were no other injuries.

Ernie went over to Henry to discuss Risotino.

"Henry, what do you think we should do about Risotino?"

"I think that I should bring him up to the office and you should be waiting there when I walk in with him."

"Sounds good to me, I'll go up to the office."

Henry went down one level to the cell block where he signed for Risotino. They then took the elevator up two stories to the second floor. Henry unlocked the door to the Narcotics Office. Henry stood back so that Risotino would go through the door first.

Risotino walked in and stopped dead in his tacks as soon as he noticed Detective Ernie Lijoi sitting behind one of the desks.

"Eddie, they got you too?"

"Not the way you mean, Rick."

"What do you mean?"

"You really don't recognize me, do you?"

"What the fuck are you talking about? Did you turn all of us in? Are you a cop? No you can't be a cop. You've proven yourself to everybody. What's going on?"

"Hey, asshole, I'm Detective Ernie Lijoi. You must be in a dream world or something. We sat and discussed your first case right here in this room. I was the arresting officer in that case."

"You know, man, I'm fucked up, I need help. What can I do to straighten this thing out with you guys?"

"You have your preliminary hearing set for tomorrow morning. You should be OK till then," Ernie said.

"Wait a minute, I don't have any money. You guy's took all of my cash. I can't get bail. You gotta get me on the street."

"We don't gotta do nothing," stated Henry.

"I can help you guys, I have a lot of connections."

"Henry and I will not be around for a few weeks. When we get back we'll all sit down and talk. If you can do something,

Rick, we may be able to put a good word in for you, but that's no guarantee that you will not do time."

"I understand. OK, if that's the best you can do. I can put up with a couple of weeks in jail."

***

Henry took the prisoner back to his cell and returned to speak with Ernie.

"Ernie, did you call John Slater?"

"Yes, while you were gone. They took down both Sam Roller of Vermont and Keith Lenard of New Hampshire. They confiscated loads of methamphetamine and over two hundred thousand dollars in cash."

"Ernie, this turned out to be a great day. We took a truck load of drugs off of the street; the estimate of cash is over five hundred thousand dollars. The D.A. will have several houses to use as ammunition in dealing with these people, and thirty-five arrests."

"All except for the dreamer, who can't remember anything. What's next, Henry?"

"I need some rest, Ernie."

"Good idea, we can look at Risotino and the Canadians when we come back from vacation."

"I don't know about this Risotino. I wonder if he can be trusted. He's a real bad speed head. We'll probably have to have him cleaned up."

"Henry, we'll test him. If he doesn't work out we will have plenty of others to talk with. For now, I just want to catch some fish and relax."

The End

Ernest Lijoi Sr a/k/a, Eddie Pannoni

http://www.erniesr.com

EPILOGUE

Ernie and Teresa sat on the deck overlooking the lake sipping on lemonade. The sky was clear and light blue, the sun was shining and the fish were jumping.

"So, Teresa, what would you say if I were to tell you that I have to go back undercover?"

Teresa sat there shaking her head, "I guess there would be nothing that I could say. I would not want you to go, but if you have to, I will support you in every way."

"Thanks, honey, this was a great case and we took a lot of drugs off the street, solved a few murders and arrested major narcotics violators and gun dealers. This case will help save a lot of lives down the road."

Ernie took a sip of his lemonade, sat back and reviewed the case in his mind.

There were several people arrested for various charges. Ernie's team was able to take a few men off of the street that were supplying the narcotics to the New England area.

Although there is no best part of sending someone to jail, there are specific people that Ernie was very happy to have been a part of taking off the street.

Carlos Ruiz was charged with several murders along with conspiracy to commit murder and was expected to receive life in prison.

Johnny ("JZ") Zales was also charged with murder and conspiracy to commit murder with Carlos and Jesus as well as narcotics violations. He was expected to receive at least thirty years in prison

Enrique (Ricky) Risotino was charged with numerous narcotics violations and would most probably receive at least fifteen years in prison. Ernie and Henry stepped in to assist him. His charges were reduced to five to ten years.

The rest of the violators were charged with gun possession and narcotics violations. If the courts were kind they would receive anywhere from three to five years and some may even get suspended sentences.

The writer would like to thank the reader for taking the time to read this book and remind the reader of the other books by this writer which are available, namely, "Street Business", "Shoveling the Tide", "Chasing Snow", "Destructive Obsession" and "Meth or Myth" which may be obtained through your local book store, online or via the authors site:

http://www.erniesr.com.

Made in the USA
Charleston, SC
10 September 2011